STEVEN MOORE

THE SAMURAI CODE

BOOKS

Vinci Books

vinci-books.com

Published by Vinci Books Ltd in 2025

1

Copyright © Steven Moore 2017

The author has asserted their moral right to be identified as the author of this work in accordance with the Copyright, Designs and Patents Act 1988. This work is a work of fiction. Names, characters, places and incidents are the product of the author's imagination or are used fictitiously. Any resemblance to actual persons, living or dead, places and incidents is entirely coincidental.

All rights reserved. No part of this publication may be copied, reproduced, distributed, stored in any retrieval system, or transmitted in any form or by any means, including photocopying, recording, or other electronic or mechanical methods, nor used as a source for any form of machine learning including AI datasets, without the prior written permission of the publisher.

The publisher and the author have made every effort to obtain permissions for any third party material used in this book and to comply with copyright law. Any queries in this respect should be brought to the attention of the publisher and any omissions will be corrected in future editions.

A CIP catalogue record for this book is available from the British Library.

Paperback ISBN: 9781036706791

The EU GPSR authorised representative is Logos Europe, 9 rue Nicolas Poussion, 17000 La Rochelle, France contact@logoseurope.eu

Printed and bound in Great Britain by Clays Ltd, Elcograf S.p.A.

By Steven Moore

The Hiram Kane Archaeological Thriller Series

The Condor Prophecy
The Tiger Temple
The Feathered Serpent
The Samurai Code
Of Curses and Kings
The Shadow of Kailash
The Oak Island Enigma
Killing Koreana

By Steven Moore

The Hiram Kane Archaeological Thriller Series

The Condor Prophecy
The Tiger Temple
The Feathered Serpent
The Samurai Code
Of Curses and Kings
The Shadow of Kailash
The Oak Island Enigma
Killing Koreana

*"The samurai must always prepare for death—
whether his own, or that of others."*

"One cannot escape one's destiny, for existence itself is but a mirage."

Steven Moore

Prologue

A battlefield near Kyoto, Honshu Island, Japan

April 25th 1185

Ravens cawed and stabbed at each other beneath a full moon, fighting over chunks of human flesh.

Ghostly wraiths of mist billowed in the darkness, as if blown by Futen, the Japanese god of the wind, carrying with it the stink of rotting corpses. Shattered, torn bodies lay strewn across the muddy, blood-stained earth. Spilled guts and crushed bones bore grim testimony to the recent battle. After long days of brutality, it was over at last.

The main conflict of Dan-no-ura had raged wildly in the inland sea, not far from Kyoto. The ground skirmishes were just as terrible; thousands had died. And yet, although the fighting was over, the killing was not.

Beyond exhaustion, Katsu Hanzō stumbled. The physical and mental exertions of the arduous battle had edged him to the brink of collapse. Through squinting, bloodshot eyes, Katsu scanned the battlefield. Before him lay acres of churned up muddy ground strewn with fallen samurai, both the dead, and those still dying, most noisily. He was among the few survivors. Today he didn't feel lucky. To die in battle was a great honour, if you died with dignity and courage. His own body had been sliced often, his arms, back and chest crisscrossed with deep, bloody wounds.

Yet destiny had spared him, and he knew why; Katsu had one last duty to fulfil.

He was hurting, agony searing both within and across his body. Though, he would not show it—not here, not in front of his enemy. This same enemy that had slaughtered his father and brother. Their destroyed bodies lay somewhere to the south, where the tide of the bloody battle had finally turned in favour of the Minamoto. It was they, the hated samurai clan from the north, who now encircled his master.

Twenty yards away, Takamochi Taira stood tall, calm and still. He was defeated, and the enemy was closing in around him like a human noose. But he was calm. Takamochi knew what must be done. As his second in command, so did Katsu Hanzō.

The leader of the Taira clan took one last look around. He surveyed the fallen warriors, his own and those of the enemy. A deep, slow sigh escaped his lips, and he wondered inwardly if it had all been worth it. Was it ever? Takamochi's gaze rested on the young warrior waiting in solemn quiet.

He bowed to his second, long and slow. Katsu returned the respect. Then, at last, Takamochi slowly dropped to his knees.

The ravens squabbled, their raucous calls piercing the

silent world as he whispered poetic words heard by no one but himself:

*I'm glad to die
in spring, beneath
Blossoms of cherry,
while a springtime moon
is full.*

Takamochi breathed in slowly, held it, then exhaled even slower. He repeated that process several times. Next, he carefully positioned his white kimono on the filthy ground before him, and readied himself. He closed his eyes and moderated his breaths even further. To an onlooker the breaths would have been imperceptible, such was his calm. Takamochi sensed his trusted *kai-sha-ku-nin*—his assistant, Katsu—move closer and position himself alongside. As the metallic swoosh of Katsu's samurai sword being withdrawn from its sheath announced the moment, Takamochi opened his eyes for the final time.

He pulled out his own short, ceremonial *O'tanto* dagger, its handle bound tight in worn brown leather. Takamochi admired the weapon, feeling its weight as he thought about his next action. His final action.

Narrowing his eyes as his heart rate slowed, the slightest trace of a smile curved his lips. Calmly, slowly, Takamochi turned the blade towards his own stomach and gripped hard.

It was time.

Chapter One

侍

Hiram Kane considered the city of Hiroshima to be a symbol of human endurance. The way it had risen again after its total annihilation in 1945 was awe-inspiring. Yet, he also lamented the fact that humanity still hadn't learned the myriad lessons the devastating atom-bomb attack should have taught.

Instead, he knew the world was more like a vicious cycle, one cruel and violent act followed by another. *What was it Gandhi said?* he mused. *An eye for an eye makes the whole world blind?*

As he explored the city after speaking at a conference, Kane came upon the infamous twisted wreck of the A-Bomb Dome. The former exhibition hall was the only significant structure left standing in Hiroshima after the bombing, and its enigmatic, warped steel frame was left in place, remaining to serve as a tangible reminder of the perils of war and the merits of peace.

After a few restorative Asahi beers at a riverside cafe to

help alleviate his somber mood—and a few coy glances from the youthful male and female staff members who seemed interested in why the tall foreigner was visiting their local hangout—Kane headed back to his hotel as rain began to fall. While he was packing and changing for dinner before his short journey to the island of Miyajima in the morning, something on the television caught his eye. He felt his stomach clench at the scenes playing out on the local news channel, that seemed to be something akin to an ultra-realistic disaster movie. Reporters were battling just to stand upright against the high winds, reporting from beside what looked to be the dangerously bulging banks of an out-of-control river.

Kane didn't need a translator to understand the severity of what was happening. The storm had hit central Japan with frightening speed. It was typhoon season, but no typhoons had been forecast. This one appeared to be a freak storm that had taken everyone by surprise, not least the residents of the city being shown on TV: Hofu, very close to Hiroshima.

Close enough, in fact, that Kane now became aware of the same strong gusts right outside his window. The camera flashed to the river again, and a quick Google search informed Kane it was the Saba River that flowed through central Hofu. His whole body was suddenly firing and alert. The danger of such powerful water was visceral for him. His mind darted back to when he was just eight years old. Playing near a river with his friend Evan back in his home village, he had attempted an unlikely handstand in an attempt to impress his mate. He had over-balanced and fallen backwards into the fast-flowing water and plunged under, his legs quickly tangling in the submerged fronds of stoneworts algae. The more he had struggled against the tidal flow and the weeds, the tighter their clutches became.

He had panicked and was unable to think clearly. If his friend had not dived in and helped dragged him out of the water, he would not have lived to grow up and explore the world as he had.

It was the memory of that terrifying experience, the scariest event of his life at that young age, that prompted his next decision. So, just half an hour later, Kane was on a train bound for Hofu, certain the city would soon need its own rescuers. The swollen, brooding clouds outside the train window painted a dire warning across the darkening sky, but hiding in comfort while people suffered so much nearby was simply not something Kane was prepared to do.

After arriving in the city, he took a short taxi ride and was soon checking into to a small ryokan, a Japanese traditional inn, as close to the Saba River as he could get while ensuring his accommodation was high enough to escape the expected flood waters. The otherwise serious-faced receptionist gave Kane a curious look from beneath raised eyebrows, as if to imply he must be insane to have turned up in Hofu just as the storm of the century was about to hit.

She's probably right, he thought, and caught himself grinning knowingly. The grin soon faded.

Sitting on his futon on the tatami flooring in his stylish yet spartan room, and watching the dated television, Kane knew that the red swirl on the map represented the peak of the approaching, ever-burgeoning storm. He glanced out of the window, but neither destruction nor panic were yet visible. Just twenty minutes later, the evidence on the television was no longer required. The spiteful storm was growing louder outside the thin walls of his accommodation, assaulting the building with a constant roar akin to the pounding of ocean surf.

Traditional wooden ryokan have paper interior walls and sliding paper doors set beneath an ornate tile or carved wooden roof. Kane soon discovered that, even when inside, outside noises could not be escaped.

Before long, Kane could hear objects thudding into the walls. He guessed they were tiles or plant pots, broken branches, and one metallic clash even suggested a bicycle. With his nerves starting to fray and the room seeming to grow darker with every passing minute, he reached out and flicked on the lamp beside the futon. The place was immediately plunged into total darkness as the power went out. Then there was a sudden, violent ripping and crunching noise and Kane momentarily froze as the ryokan's roof was torn clean off like a giant scab, then he dove for cover as rain and jagged splinters of tile and wood cascaded onto Kane's face like bullets finding their target.

The brute force of the wind had escalated tenfold in mere minutes, bringing unprecedented chaos to the city of Hofu and beyond.

Kane sprang into action. He ran to the balcony to see if other buildings had been destroyed and if anyone needed help. He spotted there were people hustling about on the streets who had not made it home in time before the strom hit. Others had seemingly left their properties for fear of being crushed, and they were now under threat from the heavy objects that tumbled down the road like clothes in a dryer. Cars were flipped over like pancakes. Lamp posts, felled like saplings. Road signs zinged through the air like lethal ninja stars hurled by mythical giants.

Kane shrugged into his jacket and pulled on his boots, then quickly made his way out of the swaying, teetering ryokan that seemed on the brink of total collapse, and headed down to the river. What se saw when he arrived made his heart leap into his throat and his guts twist into knots.

Chapter Two

侍

Muddy water raged past with such power and ferocity that the very ground shook, and Kane had to stiffen his limbs and stretch out his strong arms to stop himself falling in and being swept away to a rapid death. It wasn't just the filthy, swollen river that threatened. Clouds roiled above in a black vortex, promising more misery. Across the wild surface, the wind gusted like the breath of vexed, forgotten gods.

Others had not been strong enough to prevent themselves from falling in. Gurgled half-screams reached Kane from all directions. They reverberated off the buildings opposite, some with frightening clarity, others little more than a pitiful wail. The cries for help merged together like a tortured choir, but Kane couldn't make out from which bobbing, floating bodies the sounds came, such was the ferocity of the out of control river.

Kane knew he had to act. And fast. There were plenty more brave volunteers around him, ready to aid the rescuers. But panic had incapacitated many of them, and nowhere near enough was being done. As he glanced around, he understood that people were simply too afraid—or too shocked—to help; too many seemed stunned into inactivity.

He beckoned to a man standing on the bank and clutching a rope. The man was frozen to the spot, his face pale and his eyes wide with obvious fear. Kane's Japanese was limited and hard to recall right now, so with a series of frantic hand gestures he communicated his plan. Kane then grabbed the rope and in seconds he had tied it around himself. He attached the other end to the thick trunk of a massive fallen tree, its exposed gnarly roots clawing at the sky like the fingers of a dying man. After a quick check of the knot's strength, Kane gestured to the other man that he should reel him back in as though he were a fish on a line. The man hesitated, and Kane looked hard into his eyes, trying to impart the strength and confidence needed for the task.

"*Tasukete! Tasukete!*" came a desperate cry from the river. *Help! Help!*

Kane looked upstream and, scanning the surging torrents, he caught the briefest flash of red surging towards him amid the peaks and troughs of churning brown. An instant later, what looked to have been a red jacket suddenly disappeared.

"Dammit!" Kane grunted. He kept searching, his eyes darting across the surface of the maelstrom. After several anxious seconds, the jacket reappeared, a dozen yards closer and nearer to the bank.

That is it. Got to move now!

Kane stepped back, took a few deep breaths and without another thought he launched himself into the deadly river.

His world turned black as he tumbled beneath the

surface. The sheer power and gut-wrenching force of the flow was even greater than he feared. He stretched out a long leg, desperate to brace against something solid below. But the river was at its highest level in half a century, its surface a series of raging whirlpools.

Kane, a strong swimmer and experienced scuba diver, remained calm. With a flurry of powerful, confident strokes, he surfaced several yards upstream, emerging in the path of the helpless little girl in red. He wrapped her in his strong arms, but her flailing limbs dragged them both under the surface. Choking on the filthy river water, he fought the powerful current with all his strength. With exertion burning in every muscle, he pushed up and broke the surface.

He looked down and saw that the girl slumped unconscious in his arms. Water ran over her like a tidal surge, plastering her hair to her face. Keeping both heir heads above water as much as he could manage, Kane kicked hard for the nearest bank. Their bodies jerked and twisted in the rapids, spinning this way and that, first away from the bank and then back again. Then, just as it looked as if they might finally reach the shore, a fierce undercurrent sucked them dangerously away. Kane just managed to keep his eyes above water, but he was battling the full force of the river to try and drag the girl to the surface.

As Kane finally brought the girl up for air, he could see the man on the bank had planted both feet into the earth and was hauling on the rope with all his strength. He was joined by a woman, who had apparently seen what was happening and sprung into action. They pulled again and again until the thirty yards of played-out rope was now twenty. Fifteen. After more heroic effort from all involved, just five yards of heavy saturated rope were left. The woman looked into Kane's eyes, wide and hopeful over the frothing water. The violent river yanked Kane and the girl away once more, almost dragging the two rescuers into the surging water.

With desperation evident on their faces, the man and woman managed to wedge themselves amongst the tangled roots of the ancient tree, scratching and scraping their shins on craggy bark. Finally secure, they pulled on the rope as if it were their own child on the end. It was someone's child, and Kane would not let her go. He could not.

Yard by yard, inch by agonising inch, the pair hauled Kane and the girl closer to the bank. Finally, the river relinquished its death grip. With the last of their ebbing strength, they dragged the sodden people onto the bank.

The little girl flopped pale and unconscious onto the muddy ground. Lying on his back, Kane gasped for air. Even in his exhausted state, he noticed the anguish in the eyes of the man holding the rope, who seemed to be muttering a prayer, imploring some higher power to spare the child's life.

The woman immediately knelt next to the girl and cleared her airways of debris, pulling clear a length of choking, clogging weed. Then she clamped her mouth over the girl's and began to pass life-giving oxygen between their bodies.

Within seconds, the girl's weak lungs blasted water out in a sludgy, brown spray. Her eyes flickered open. She was deeply shocked and clearly confused, but alive.

The woman carried the girl across the stodgy mud to the nearby road, where ambulances and first responders waited to transport the storm's victims to hospital.

The remaining man, who had assisted Kane from the start, held out a hand and smiled weakly, helping Kane to get up off his back. Kane had recovered enough energy to sit up, and the two men shared a silent moment of gratitude and admiration. They hadn't yet spoken a word to each other, but Kane was not surprised when the man looked into his eyes, leaned in a little and with something like hope glinting in his own eyes, said, in English, "Again?"

With a slow nod and the barest hint of a resigned grin, Kane climbed to his feet. The two men shook hands firmly and briefly. After scanning for life amid the troughs and swells of the roaring flash flood, and checking the knots on the rope, Kane turned to face the river then launched himself into its terror once more.

Over the course of the next three hours, Kane and the man took turns risking nature's wrath in order to save the lives of eighteen men, women and children. In a rhythm of diving, grabbing, swimming and pulling, they had saved more people in one day than most would save in a lifetime. They had worked in vital unison but hardly spoken. There was no time for talk or pause.

Only later, after the surging flood waters had abated and the river had calmed to something like its usual placid state, Kane and his new friend slumped down on their backs to rest. Both their minds and bodies were exhausted and battered from the previous harrowing hours. It was only after several minutes that they could exchange a few words.

"Naki," the man said, turning to look at an exhausted Kane, who nodded.

"Hiram. Hiram Kane."

Rescue support workers brought them warm blankets and steaming bowls of miso soup. They slurped in silence, neither possessing the energy to communicate in second languages. What was there to say? Both men had done all they could do. They'd done what they had to do. Kane had not thought twice about putting his own life on the line to help others, and after his initial reticence brought about by shock, Naki had clearly shown his inner courage and strength. That shared bond was far stronger than stuttered words.

After confirming with the rescue team there was nothing further they could do to help, Kane accepted their final nods of gratitude and got to his feet. He and Naki scrambled up the banks of the Saba River, finally edging away from danger.

Naki led Kane to his car, parked a half-mile from the destruction zone, and invited Kane to go with him to his home. Kane gladly accepted the offer, and fifteen minutes later, he found himself standing beneath a hot, revitalising shower. He was safe from nature's fury and, though he didn't fear death, he was grateful to be alive.

But as the clean water pounded his skin and washed away the dirt from the river, it failed to wash away the vivid memories and the haunting sounds of the suffering. Kane was devastated. They had helped save many people. And yet, others had not survived. Tears of sadness and frustration suddenly began to fall, mingling with the running water. Kane took every single lost soul personally.

In that moment, Hiram Kane was sure he would have traded his own life to save just a few more.

Chapter Three

侍

Kyoto

Winter, 1974

"Bring him to me," the Yakuza boss demanded. "I would like to speak with him."

Daiki Okana had heard good things about the young Yakuza enforcer operating in his branch of the Kyoto Prefecture. He was considering promoting the young man to his personal security detail. He just needed to test him first to see if the rumours were true.

Twenty-six-year-old Katashi Goto was ushered wordlessly from the ante room.

His black suit fitted his muscular body like a glove. His long black hair, tied back in a ponytail, shone beneath the room's bright lights. At only five feet nine inches tall, he didn't cut the fearsome figure his reputation suggested. Yet

The Samurai Code

he exuded confidence, and carried an aura of invincibility. The threat of brutality. The promise of violence.

"Thank you for coming, Katashi," Daiki Okana said.

Katashi only nodded, his passive expression unchanged.

"My men have told me many good things about you, Katashi. Very good things. I wonder, are they true?"

Katashi remained silent for several seconds. He was so still it seemed as if he was hardly breathing. "It depends on what those things are, Daiki-san," Katashi finally said, bowing respectfully.

Daiki nodded. He knew they were true. All of them. He had heard from his most trusted men all about the brutality Katashi Goto exerted to keep things in order around the southern reaches of the prefecture. Daiki needed someone like that on his team. Someone feared. As always, there would be a test. But Daiki felt certain the test would not prove a problem for the man he expected to become his latest protégé and number two man.

"Bring out the Kuso-yarō!" Daiko said. "Bring those bastards to me!"

Two men were marched out to stand before Daiki Okana. Their heads were shrouded beneath black hoods.

"Both these men have been found guilty of treachery, Katashi. They conspired with our rivals in order to gain favour with our fiercest competitors. Such blatant treachery is an affront to my sensibilities, and it cannot go unpunished. What do you say, Katashi Goto? Do you agree?"

Katashi nodded, never taking his eyes off his boss's. Daiki held Katashi's glare. He saw the malice in those eyes, the cruelty. He needed this man on his side. He did not want to be against him. Daiki inhaled and looked away, unable to hold the gaze any longer.

The desire Daiki noticed in the young man's eyes spoke of wanting something more than simply gratuitous violence. He seemed to have a destiny, as well as certainty he would achieve it, and Daiki suspected that sycophancy was just part of the journey towards that end game. He feared he was being humoured, rather than truly respected. But he understood that, and his plan for this man did not change. Insincere loyalty, he knew well, was better than no loyalty at all.

Katashi smiled inwardly. This is what he wanted. It wasn't everything. Not yet. Yet, it would be the next step on his rise to the top. He hated sycophancy, but he knew it was an essential part of the game, the only way to scale the ancient hierarchical system within the Japanese mafia. He wasn't above that game. He knew he couldn't afford to be that foolish… that arrogant. For now he would show loyalty.

"I would like you to become head of my personal security detail, Katashi," Daiki told him. "Would you accept this great honour I'd bestow on you?"

Katashi nodded, long and deep. "It would be my honour to accept, Daiki-san. You will not regret your choice." Katashi knew what came next. He would need to prove himself in front of the don. He was prepared. He'd been prepared for a very long time.

"I will leave it to your discretion how you mete out the punishment of these two traitorous ants. Are you ready?"

Katashi nodded once more. "I am ready, Daiki-san."

Katashi inhaled and calmly stepped towards the first man. He leaned in and whispered in the bigger man's ear. "Death and life, they are one and the same. It is merely the immutable law of nature." Katashi reached up and pulled the hood off the man's head, then stepped back. He could smell the fear. The man's wide eyes pleaded for mercy. A bead of sweat trickled down his temple. He would receive no mercy from Katashi Goto. Katashi placed his palm on the man's cheek, distracting him as he reached back and pulled a blade from his waistband.

"It is okay, my brother," he said quietly, his voice soft and his touch gentle. "It is okay." Then, with lightning speed, Katashi raised the blade and thrust it into the big man's throat. Blood spurted from the ragged wound. As the traitor's body pitched forward, Katashi took its weight, lowering him to the ground. Casually, he wiped the blade clean on the man's black jacket. Standing upright, exhaling through his nose, he glanced over at Daiki, who sat, speechless, eyes wide, his expression a mix of awe and respect. And a trace of fear he fought to keep hidden, but failed. Katashi Goto missed nothing.

The second man struggled against the grip of the two mafia thugs holding him. He hadn't seen what had happened from beneath the shroud covering his eyes, but Katashi believed he already knew his colleague was dead. He would also know he was next. It was inevitable.

"Let him go," Katashi told the Yakuza men. They released his arms and stepped aside.

The thug, a huge man with enormous shoulders, dropped to his knees. "Please," he said, fighting to retain some dignity in his voice, "let me go. I... I will make it up to Daiki-san. Anything he wants, I swear, I will do it. I will kill Akihiro. Let me go and I promise I will kill the don. Please. I have a... a family."

Katashi stepped forward. "By collaborating with Akihiro, you have insulted your boss. That was a foolish thing to do. You understand this now. You have insulted his pride, and when a man's pride is injured, death is but a small price to repay that insult."

Katashi pulled the hood from the man's head. Their eyes met. Katashi thrust the knife deep into his left eye socket. The thug's knees crumpled, and he slumped to the floor. Katashi knelt down beside the man to retrieve the knife. It was stuck, embedded in the back of the man's skull. Katashi sighed.

He stood up, placed a black Italian leather shoe on the slain man's face, and gripped the knife with both hands. With a grunt he yanked the blade free, spilling fragments of brain and eye with it. Once again, he wiped the blade clean on the man's jacket.

Katashi stepped forward to Daiki Okana and paused. "I offer you my blade, Daiki-san. It would be my honour if you would accept it." Katashi bowed, both arms held out in front of him, proffering the blade.

Daiki stepped forward. Katashi knew the don would have heard tales of his brutality. What Katashi had just done was likely more brutal than even he had imagined. It was all part of his plan. Daiki reached out and took the blade from Katashi. Katashi stood upright again.

Daiki cleared his throat. "I am impressed, Katashi Goto. Very impressed." Katashi watched as Daiki turned to face the other men. They too looked both impressed and uneasy about what they'd just witnessed.

Good, Katashi thought. That's what he had wanted and why he knew those men would never make it as high as him in the Kyoto Yakuza. "From now on," Daiki told his men, "you will take your orders from my new head of security, Katashi Goto."

Chapter Four

侍

Katashi bowed deeply to his new boss, Daiki Okana. As he rose from the bow and straightened his back, his expression remained impassive, betraying none of the satisfaction his promotion deserved, and ignoring the shiver of adrenalin that surged through his veins. The other men in the room fidgeted where they stood, clearly uneasy, their gazes shifting between Katashi and the corpses on the floor. *Good. They should be afraid of me.*

"Thank you for this honour, Daiki-san." Katashi's words were smooth and measured. "I will not disappoint you." Calculated, too.

Daiki nodded, clearly still wary. "See to it that you do not. Now, Katashi, your first task as my new head of security is to get rid of the bodies of these treacherous bastards and ensure there is no trace of them left behind."

"Yes, Daiki-san. Of course." Katashi swivelled to the other men. "Bring the car around the back. You, go and get cleaning supplies. The strong stuff. Move!"

The men hustled, eager to obey and keen to be away

from Katashi and what he knew was his cold, penetrating gaze. It wasn't an accident. It had been cultured over years in front of mirrors and practiced on anyone that pissed him off. They soon backed down, and he'd learned it was a silent yet powerful tool. As the men left, Katashi kneeled down next to the bodies, checking for any identifying marks or personal items. Finding nothing useful, he stripped them swiftly of their bloodied clothing and effects.

By the time the thugs returned, Katashi had wrapped the corpses in several layers of plastic sheeting. He then watched on as they were loaded into the boot of an unmarked car.

"I'll personally take care of this situation," Katashi told Daiki. "It is better if less people are involved."

Daiki raised a thin eyebrow but nodded his agreement. "Very well. Report back when it is completed."

Katashi bowed his respect again and left Daiki. Moments later he was behind the wheel of the car and navigating the quiet streets of Kyoto. It was a chance to relax and allow the tension of the important last couple of hours to pass, but his mind was already working overtime, pondering his next play. The elevation to head of security had been a solid start. Yet, Katashi knew well it was only the next step in his ambitious plans.

He drove for an hour, cruising along back roads until he reached a deserted area in the surrounding hills beyond the city limits. Katashi knew of an abandoned mine shaft; perfect for his disposal needs. Swiftly and efficiently, Katashi dragged the bodies from the vehicle into the shaft, now working up a sweat. They were big men and literally dead weights. He grunted as he retrieved a can of accelerant from the boot, which he poured over the bodies and, lighting a match and a cigarette, he calmly set them ablaze, watching dispassionately as the flames consumed the evidence. Other than the physical exertion of moving two large dead men, his heart rate hadn't risen at all. This was just work. The corpses, mere objects to get rid of.

As he drove unhurriedly back to the city, Katashi finally allowed himself a brief smile. His reputation for brutality had so far served its purpose. Now he had earned a position of trust in the organisation. Things were progressing well, but it was already time to commence to the next phase.

Back at the base, Katashi provided his boss with a brief, clinical report on the body disposal. Daiki seemed satisfied, yet he seemed to carry a hint of wariness about him. *Good.* Katashi understood that a healthy level of fear and doubt would make the mob leader easier to manipulate.

"I would like to review the current system security protocols," Katashi said. "I want to make sure everything is up to standard."

Daiki seemed to hesitate for a moment, before nodding. "It is a good idea. My assistant Hana will provide you with the necessary files. Hana speaks for me, so you can speak freely with her too."

Over the next month, Katashi set about learning and understanding all aspects of the group's operations. He made a deliberate show of sharpening up security, and also brought in several new protocols that Daiki's thugs mumbled about but dare not disobey. Throughout this period, Katashi gathered knowledge of the organisation and its players, made mental notes of weak points and unreliable members, and perhaps most importantly, he worked out who among them could be useful to his plans in the future, and who would not.

One evening, Katashi was in his office scanning a pile of business documents when a knock at the door startled him. He stood and stretched, and was surprised when he looked at his Rolex and saw how late it was. He opened the door and Hana, Daiki's personal assistant and probably the don's most trusted lieutenant, stood leaning on the frame. Katashi had Hana marked down as a potential ally but knew she was smart and wily, and likely ambitious. Probably dangerous, if crossed.

"You are here late, Katashi-san. Again."

Katashi allowed a hint of a smile. "There is always important work to be done."

Hana entered Katashi's office, pulling the door closed behind her as Katashi went to a cabinet on the wall. "Sake?" he asked. Hana nodded. Katashi poured them each a small measure, handed one to Hana and retook his seat behind his desk.

He watched as she poured the fiery spirit back in one, unflinching, and met his gaze. "I've been watching you," she said bluntly. Neither her words nor the manner in which she'd said them surprised Katashi. He admired her forthright nature, and knew that being so trusted by Daiki afforded her certain privileges most of the men didn't enjoy. He wondered with intrigue what was on her mind. She said, "You are not just here to play guard dog for Daiki, are you?"

He wasn't expecting that, and his hand flinched beneath his desk, automatically moving slowly towards the knife he kept hidden there. His voice was calm as he said, "What makes you say that?"

Hana's gaze remained locked on his. "I recognise ambition when I see it, Katashi Goto, and you stink of it. I see it in your eyes and the way your nostrils flare when you speak with Daiki. I admire a man with such ambitions." She took a step closer to Katashi's desk and leaned forward. "But let me warn you… this sea of ambition you are swimming in is infested with sharks."

The two stared at each other for long moments, testing one another's resolve. If Katashi didn't know better, Hana might even have been flirting with him. He did think she was beautiful, but had decided not to act upon it. Mixing business with pleasure was not something he would allow… and there were always other women to play with for a man in his position.

Katashi thought he understood Hana's little game, and relaxed, leaning back in his chair. He let a small smile creep into his eyes. He might stink of ambition. Katashi had smelled the same on her a month ago. "Well, Hana-san, what do you suggest we do about it?"

A grin spread slowly across Hana's face. "We should work together. Daiki is set in his ways and getting old. This branch needs fresh blood if it is going to continue growing. Everything is stagnant. The boss is too comfortable."

Katashi nodded. He sensed an opportunity, but with opportunity came risk, especially when the one offering it was as clever and cunning as Hana. As ambitious. Katashi needed to be careful. "What would you desire in exchange for your... cooperation?"

"When the moment arrives to act, I want to be there," she stated firmly. "You and I are the future of this organisation."

Katashi inhaled and thought on her words for a moment as he enjoyed her perfume. Slowly, he stood and turned back to the drinks cabinet, recalling her mention of sharks. Turning his back on this shark wasn't wise, however sexy she smelled. He poured two more measures of sake and walked back around the desk. He held out the drink, which she took. He left the hand extended towards her. "I do believe we can come to some kind of agreement, Hana-san."

They shook hands, and Katashi felt that thrill of excitement and anticipation. This was the real game. This was how business took place between the real players. Brute violence proved only that someone was violent. It had gotten him noticed, but Katashi knew it was his words and how they were said—and importantly, how they were received—that would really elevate him. That delicate balance between ambition and intelligence, a dance between emotion and cunning, would propel him to the true power that he craved and knew he was worthy of.

Chapter Five

侍

Over the subsequent months, Katashi and Hana worked closely alongside each other. They used their combination of trust within the organisation, their status over Daiki's other minions and their personal and carefully cultivated relationships with the don himself to slowly and steadily begin undermining Daiki's authority, all while serving him faithfully in all other things regarding the underworld and gangland businesses, and his financial and territorial power base. Katashi also used his elevated position to, one by one, replace strategic personnel with those loyal to him. As this progressed, Hana set about sowing small seeds of doubt into the ears of lower-level members of the organisation, those who currently saw no route of progression and were ready for a change at the top table.

Katashi not only kept up his reign of brutal, loyal enforcer, but raised it to new levels, putting himself into situations only a madman might, and proving through his actions he was willing to do whatever it took to make sure his boss got what he wanted and needed. When rival outfits foolishly stood on their toes and attempted business in their territory, Katashi's reprisals were swift and destructive. So savage was he, in fact, that even Daiki asked Katashi to reign himself in a little. All of this only served to enhance the burgeoning reputation of Daiki's head of security, so much so that the Yakuza boss had come to treat him more like a son than a hired thug.

Then things changed.

A year later, on the anniversary of his promotion, Katashi met with his boss on a routine visit to Daiki's office. Hana was at his right side, almost his equal. Almost. This time, as he stood before the don once again, both knew the balance of power had shifted though Daiki kept up the pretence of a boss, as was his duty.

"What is the meaning of this?" Daiki demanded, his gaze shifting between the faces of those he had once trusted. Daiki had in fact attempted to remove Katashi. He had charged his toughest, still-loyal thugs to kill Katashi, but they had failed on several occasions and had never been seen since. Katashi's influence and the sheer force of his will had bent the organisation's members to his will, and only Hana had enough will of her own to test Katashi, which he admired and used to his advantage.

"The world is changing, Daiki-san," Katashi said, his voice calm yet authoritative. "The old ways... your ways... are not the way forward. I respect you, and am grateful for the way you have treated me, but it is time for new leadership."

Daiki could have protested. He could have demanded Hana take action, or yelled at some of his once-loyal guards to step in and prevent this coup. Yet he knew it was futile. He knew it was over. He stood from his desk and attempted one last show of resilience, eyeballing Katashi, his glare filled with hatred. Yet Katashi knew there was more behind that glare than anger. There was acceptance. There was fear. More importantly, there was respect.

Katashi merely nodded to the old man. He didn't need to kill him. He was no longer a threat.

Daiki Okana's reign of power was over.

The era of Katashi Goto was about to begin.

From the large leather seat behind his new desk—the one Daiki Okana had vacated less than an hour previous—Katashi studied Hana's face, considering her value and appraising her worth to him. He really had admired her over the last few months. She understood the business, perhaps even better than he did, and she commanded respect from the men. Her ambition was endless, and at the very least, mirrored his own and more importantly, probably surpassed it. A very valuable asset when used correctly. For a moment, Katashi even entertained the idea of a true partnership.

He stood from the desk and came around to face her. He breathed in that perfume again and was still tempted to... *No, Katashi. That time has passed.* "I agree completely, Hana-san," he stated, his voice soft and encouraging. "Your vision rests perfectly alongside mine. Like you, I believe that together, we can lift the organisation and carry it forward into a new era."

Usually so cool and in control, Hana's eyes lit up and betrayed her composure, and Katashi smirked inwardly. He knew how she felt, and secretly sympathised. None of that mattered anymore.

"We should continue our discussions..." Katashi said, "but not here. I trust the men... but not that much. Let's go to my place in the hills, away from curious ears and eyes so we can speak in private. Perhaps it is time we… sealed our… union…"

Hana nodded knowingly. "Of course, Katashi-san. When?" He could sense her excitement, and felt it too.

"Tonight," he told her. "Let's seal our union tonight."

Chapter Six

侍

As darkness descended, Katashi collected Hana from her downtown apartment then drove them into the hills surrounding Kyoto and towards his remote cabin. He liked to keep the humble place, which he'd owned for a decade, as somewhere private away from the city. He enjoyed his brand-new penthouse apartment downtown too, but the cabin was where he did his best thinking. The car's full beams sliced through the darkness, casting wild shadows among the gnarly, ancient trees. Beside him, Hana spoke of her plans for the organisation and its future, and how she couldn't wait to prove to Katashi how grateful she was he hadn't discarded her like they had the former don, Daiki.

"We're almost there," Katashi said, gently placing his hand on Hana's long and shapely leather-clad leg. She turned to face him, and Katashi knew what she wanted… what she desired from him. For once, their desires did not align.

Ten minutes later they'd entered Katashi's cabin and he

pretended to fix them a drink while Hana stood in front of the wide bay window, gazing out across the forest canopy.

"It's beautiful," she murmured, as Katashi held back, admiring her silhouette against the dark sky beyond the window.

"It is," he agreed softly. "Look at me."

Hana turned to face him, and in one swift motion, he grabbed the back of her neck in one hand and with his other, he drew a blade across her throat, gripping tight as she thrashed for a few seconds and the glint in her eye faded from excitement to shock to confusion, and then as warm blood flowed down Katashi's fingers and wrist and forearm, she managed to mumble, "Why?"

Katashi lowered her trembling body to the ground and knelt beside her, his gaze fixed on hers as he whispered, "There is only room for one of us at the top, Hana. This, you know."

He watched the light fade from her eyes, until all that was left there was death. He felt nothing. Not triumph. Not remorse. It was a simple business decision. He had long-suspected she would try to eliminate him at some point, claiming top spot for herself. A phone call from a trusted colleague several days ago had confirmed such suspicions, so he had simply acted first. It was just the way of things.

At the edge of the ravine onto which his cabin nestled, Katashi sighed and paused, looking down at Hana's face. She looked less calm now, and her lifeless eyes stared up at him, judging him, warning him, even in death. He closed the lid on the one-foot square box containing her head and turned his attention to the array of body parts in the wheelbarrow beside him, and then one by one, he tossed them into the ravine below, knowing that by morning they would be long gone, scattered across the forest and feeding the foxes, badgers, hawks and owls that dwelled in the darkness of the trees.

"Hana, you were formidable," he muttered into the silent void. "You were a good partner there for a while. But Katashi Goto does not need a partner. I do not need anyone."

Katashi made his way back to the car, the square box under his arm. By the morning, it would be delivered to the office of the organisation's biggest rivals, and photos of his work would be sent to every single one of his own organisation's members so no one could be in any doubt what would happen if they did not display absolute, unflinching loyalty to their new don.

Chapter Seven

侍

Dusk slipped away, and the grounds of the Nakamura estate were silent as a shroud of darkness at last enveloped it. The main living structure's traditional architecture stood in stark contrast to the modern walls of steel, concrete and glass of the Kyoto skyline no longer visible in the distance, its whereabouts only betrayed by millions of twinkling lights. The paper screens of the interior filtered the gentle glow from the lamplights that illuminated the spaces, casting long shadows across the family's ancestral meeting room.

Nori Nakamura, his prematurely weathered face lined with the wisdom of his almost six decades, lowered himself to his knees at the head of the low table, nestling on the tatami floor mats. His eyes, still sharp despite his advanced years, appraised the faces before him. He felt the expectation in the room like a physical weight, pressed down upon his shoulders as heavily as his dark gray kimono.

On his right knelt his son, Naki. His suit, though informal, seemed at odds with the traditional setting. Naki was a humble man and worked a regular job as a high school teacher, though he had always sensed there was more to the family, the Nakamura legacy, than he knew. Maybe today was the day he would learn more, and he shifted his position, unable to get comfortable.

Across from Naki, his eighteen-year-old son Daijiro sat with poise, his chef's whites still clean before his late shift as a trainee chef downtown covered them in grease and all manner of sauces. He had received his grandfather's summons as he always did; with excitement. The old man always had good stories to tell, and Daijiro never left the family estate without new recipe ideas to try out at work.

Beside Daijiro was his sister Mika. Mika had hustled to the estate from her after-school studies club, and, like her brother, always relished her visits here as a dutiful granddaughter who always listened to everything Nori said with a quiet intensity and an insatiable thirst for knowledge.

As was his tradition, Nori poured his family tea with unerring precision. It was the ritual of the slow, deliberate process that gave him a moment to gather his thoughts as he gracefully filled each ceramic cup, each held by generations of Nakamura hands over a dozen decades.

When each of the four in the room had taken their first delicate sips of the fragrant tea, Nori Nakamura began. "Twenty years ago," he said, his voice gentle but exuding the calm authority they all expected, "my own father sat in this very spot. On that day, he shared with me what I am about to share with you." He placed down his cup and inhaled, savouring the jasmine incense that drifted about the space.

Naki tensed. He'd long suspected something like this would come eventually, and had often thought he had sensed the weight of unspoken duties in his father since his own childhood. He glanced at his children, and rather than the concern he felt, in their eyes he saw excitement and intrigue.

"In our own way," Nori continued, "the Nakamura clan has served Japan for over three centuries. Some would call us guardians. The thing that we guard... that we protect, I will not share with you yet. That information will come in due course. But the reason I have gathered you here for this evening is to ask you... are you ready to do your sacred duty for Japan and the Nakamura family, and take the same oath that I took in this very room twenty years ago?"

Nori inhaled again and let is out slowly as he gazed at his beloved family members. He had a good idea of the reactions he would receive, and from what he could see now his assumptions had been accurate. He allowed himself a brief smile as his son spoke first, as was tradition.

Naki leaned forward, his interest piqued. "I have been expecting this meeting for many years, since I was a child myself, yet I can not even beging to guess what it is you're really asking of me... of us," he added, indicating his son and daughter with his hand. "I am comfortable you asking this of me, whatever *this* is. I am not so comfortable you asking it of my children."

"With respect, Father," said Daijiro, "I am not a child. I'm eighteen and I—"

"Please, Daijiro, your father is right. He should not be comfortable with it." Rather than show evidence of the gravity of what he was saying, instead, the patriarch of the Nakamura family smiled and seemed to relax. Nori held up a frail hand, marked with liver spots two decades too soon. His gaze settled on each member of his clan in turn, as if appraising them. The truth was, he didn't need to. He'd been appraising them their whole lives, since they were toddlers. He had absolutely no doubt they were ready. Not only that, he knew they were capable. He was about to place upon all three of them a great burden, one that if they agreed to accept, which he knew they would, would be something they would live with their entire lives. As he had done. And as his parents, and his grandparents had, before him. It was a burden he knew they could handle. After all, they were Nakamura, and they had no choice. It was their destiny.

He inhaled deeply and then exhaled slowly, readying himself and making sure all eyes were on him. "Before I can tell you more," he said, his gaze flitting between the watchful eyes of his family, "you must understand the gravity of what it is I am about to ask of each of you. It is not a responsibility you should accept without much deliberation. Maybe you are wondering why?" None of his family admitted it but he knew they all were thinking it. He told them. "It is because many of your predecessors have died because of it, and you will probably die too."

Chapter Eight

侍

Present Day

Kane endured a night of relentless tossing and turning. Despite his extreme physical fatigue, his reeling mind meant a solid sleep would remain elusive. Images of battered and bloated bodies in the river played on a constant loop, while the desperate cries for help from the storm's victims resonated in his subconscious.

He tried to distract himself from his thoughts. He looked around the room; with its faded tatami floor and hanging scrolls filled with vertical Kanji characters decorating the walls, he imagined it looked just like a home might have done centuries earlier. It brought to mind one of his favourite books, the James Clavell classic, *Shogun*. The epic tale of betrayal and honour in the feudal heyday of the samurai was where Kane had first learned of bushido, or the samurai code, back in his university days.

Kane had enjoyed studying under almost all of his university professors—almost; some of his archaeology lecturers were a little hard with their grades, apparently jealous of his famous ancestor, Patrick Kane, who'd assisted Hiram Bingham in one of the archaeological discoveries of the 20th century—but he adored studying with world-renowned art historian John O'nians. Professor O'nians was considered an expert across many fields of art history, but although he was most famous for his knowledge on the classics of Greek and Roman history, he also curated and taught a popular lecture series on the culture and philosophy of the samurai. Kane had been intrigued ever since he'd taken that module.

There was something about their ideology that deeply appealed. Sure, there was a violent and heroic aspect to their way of life. But underlying all of that, there was honour. It wasn't as if Kane wanted to be an ancient Japanese warrior, a thought that amused him. It was more that he admired what it took to become one. Patience. Skill. Discipline. And above all, selflessness. He knew he lacked patience in most things, especially with himself. He of course possessed some skills and was highly proficient in the Korean martial art of tae-kwon-do. Any patience and discipline he did have had been learned the hard way on the tae-kwon-do mat. Kane wouldn't deny, however, that he sometimes enjoyed being ill-disciplined, especially when no one else could be hurt by it.

Wondering whether he should leave the bedroom or not, he was glad when at last he heard a respectful knock on his door. He eased his tired legs off the futon bed, stood up and pulled open the door. He was greeted by a grinning Naki holding a steaming cup of coffee in one hand and a newspaper in the other.

Naki handed Kane the newspaper, who glanced at the headline and smiled ruefully. "I can't read that."

"It says, 'Unnamed Englishman the Hero of Hofu.' I believe it is accurate, no?"

Kane shook his head. "We were only helping, as were many others. It must have been another Englishman," he added with another smile.

Naki simply nodded and turned, motioning for Kane to follow. Kane followed him into the lounge area of the apartment, where the two sat wordlessly across from each other at the simple wooden dining table for a few moments. Finally, Naki broke the silence.

"Thank you," he said. "Thank you for helping us."

Kane was a little surprised by Naki's proficiency in English, but he didn't embarrass the man by saying so. "You have no reason to thank me, Naki," he said instead. "It's what anyone would have done. I just… I wish we could have done more."

Naki nodded, a sadness in his eyes despite the smile. "We did what we could. It was very dangerous."

They sat a while longer in silence, and Kane was sure Naki was fighting a mental battle, just as he was, trying to come to terms with the traumatic events of the previous day. After a few moments, Naki spoke again.

"Why are you here in Japan, Mr. Kane?"

"Please, call me Hiram. There's no need for the honorific."

"For the *what*?"

"Oh! I'm sorry. It means adding a polite part to someone's name, like 'sir' or 'Mr.' I guess in Japan, it would be '*san*.'

"It would. But there is no need to use it with my name."

"Thank you. Though I will be sure to use it when I address older people. I know respect for elders is still a very important tradition in Japan."

"That's true, but you don't need to use it if you meet my grandfather, which I hope you will. He believes that kindness is more important than blind tradition. He also believes that thinking is more important than following. His mind works differently to most."

"He sounds very interesting."

"He is. He is a man who has dedicated his life to research and museums."

"Even more interesting," Kane added. "His work sounds similar to my own."

"Really? You didn't seem like an academic out on the river, if you don't mind me saying so. You seemed more... I have learned this English word... outdoorsy."

Kane smiled. "My research can get *very* outdoorsy."

"I would love to know more Mr... Hiram. No longer the unnamed hero! So, please tell me—why are you here in our country? For research?"

"I'm here for work, really. Well, work and pleasure."

It was mostly true. The pleasure part was entirely accurate, but the mention of work was an oversimplification. It was more about fulfilling what Kane saw as his accepted duty. Long ago, he graduated from the University of East Anglia in the UK as an archaeologist. Yet, after finding more fulfilment searching for things than in the act of digging them up, he had changed his focus and had quit his master's degree just months from finishing, and with absolutely zero seconds of regret. Now, he was known around the world for being both an explorer and a brilliant expedition leader after setting up a successful expedition company —Hike of the Condor—in his adopted hometown of Cuzco, Peru.

Because of his outstanding reputation, and the reputation of the Kane family name known for philanthropy and exploration—the Kane name is as synonymous with Machu Picchu as the name Bingham—he was often invited to speak at adventure seminars around the world. Although he often declined the offers, preferring to lead expeditions rather than talk about them, this year's event in Hiroshima had appealed more than others.

Having told Naki about the event, he went on to explain, "I agreed to speak at the summit, though I'm the first to admit I'm not very good at it. Anyway, that's the main reason I've come to Japan. But it definitely won't be all work and no play, and I intend to explore the region."

"Will you visit Miyajima?" Naki asked. "As I'm sure you know, the island is a must for many visitors because of the famous shrine."

"Of course. I remember seeing photos of the famous red gate when I was a child."

"When you go, you must meet my grandfather, Nori Nakamura. He is the curator of the Itsukushima Shrine Museum. My family has strong ties to the island. Many of our ancestors were born there. My brother actually has a restaurant along the seafront. It's quite expensive because it is the most renowned restaurant on the island, but I will ask him to provide you with a free saké or two."

Kane smiled. "Ari-gatou gozai-mas, Naki." *Thank you.*

Naki chuckled. "You are welcome, and your Japanese is…" He paused.

"I know, it's terrible, even though I have studied it at points during my life," Kane confirmed. "But I mean it. Thank you. And thanks for everything."

Chapter Nine

侍

Now in his mid-sixties, Yakuza boss Katashi Goto was a supremely healthy man, though it hadn't always been the case. Several years earlier, Katashi had needed a life-saving liver operation.

The diagnosis had come suddenly—advanced cirrhosis brought on by historical heavy drinking and the hepatitis C he'd contracted as a young man from a poorly sterilized tattooist's needle. His physician—a doctor who had worked for the don for decades and whose gentle warnings had always gone unheeded—had delivered the news with a knot in his gut. Bearers of bad news often suffered in Katashi's world. The prognosis was grim: without a transplant within months, he would die.

For a man who held indomitable power over hundreds of men, and with a reach of hundreds of thousands more, and who had expanded his empire through cunning and brutal violence, that betrayal by his own body felt like an unforgivable personal insult.

Katashi had called in every favour. He had threatened hospital administrators. He had tried everything, but Japanese politics conspired against him, and he was unable to find any surgeon in Japan willing to perform the procedure.

Thus, in exchange for a few whispered mafia secrets to the FBI via the Yakuza's US-based cohort, however, he was given permission to enter the States for the urgent operation, to be performed by a leading surgeon in Los Angeles.

Recovery had been arduous. For six months, Katashi had retreated to his estate in the hills outside Kyoto. Daily injections of immunosuppressants, careful monitoring of his enzyme levels and a rigorously vetted diet had all tested the man's legendary patience.

Katashi had emerged transformed, however. He'd abandoned alcohol, more or less, and had developed an almost spiritual reverence for his body's resilience. Now, almost a decade on, Katashi was as fit as a man half his age, yet despite the new lease of life—or rather because of it—after the drama within the Yakuza's Yamaguchi branch and his health issues, the once-feared crime lord now seemed set on an unlikely transition into Buddhism.

Yet there was something about Katashi Goto that not many people knew—including even his closest and most trusted henchmen in the Yakuza:

Katashi's family were descendants of the mighty samurai!

While it was true that many Japanese families could claim such storied ancestry, there could in fact also be an element of shame attached to that heritage. This was especially true if their ancestors were not famous samurai or rōnin.

The result was that nowadays, in super-modern Japan,

few families ever publicly claimed or admitted their samurai lineage.

In Katashi's case, he had always known who his illustrious forebears were. And, although he had always kept this knowledge largely to himself, it was something of which he was extremely mindful. Yet he was also angry. The Japanese government had never recognised his connection to such a revered family, and over the years that same government had constantly denied him the right to claim what was one of the nation's most valuable cultural treasures: the suit of samurai armour now ensconced in Miyajima's famous museum.

Katashi had tried and failed on numerous occasions to have the national treasure attributed to his family's name. But—it was obviously because of his Yakuza association—he had always been rejected. He had even promised to donate the armour directly back to the museum, so it didn't even have to leave the building. It hadn't helped one bit. The disrespect shown to him by successive governments, organisations that were quick to accept bribes and backhanded payments for a multitude of other sins, had burned like fire in Katashi for three decades. Quietly, he had for a long time considered ways in which to rectify the situation.

In truth, that near-death experience years before had clarified something deep within his soul—a determination to complete unfinished family business before his time truly came.

That's why the armor mattered so much. It wasn't just a priceless artifact; it represented his family's honor, stolen generations ago. And Katashi Goto had not cheated death merely to leave such debts unpaid.

Thus, now, on the eve of his unlikely transformation

from Yakuza don to Buddhist priest, the time had come to claim justice and finally lay his hands on that sacred object.

Katashi Goto was stealing the samurai suit. His suit.

And no one was going to stop him.

Chapter Ten

侍

The Kane Estate

Two Months Earlier

No one did it better.

Ridley had organised a party, and it was to be a celebration of several things.

First and foremost, it was to celebrate the fact Kane's brother Danny was alive and well, and reintegrating seamlessly back into the family fold after close to three decades of absence. The party was also a way to celebrate their friends and to commemorate those who'd lost their lives. Many people had made the journey out to the Kane estate, including Professor John O'nians, Kane's friend, former professor and beloved mentor.

The most important guest of all, of course, was Danny himself.

Kane was just eleven when he had led his younger

brother Danny into an ancient abandoned rectory just a few miles away from the Kane estate. Like all curious kids, he and Danny had been wanting to explore the Old' Rectory in Oulton Broad for years, and one day they just couldn't resist. They had bunked off school and, riding their bicycles as fast as their legs would take them, they went to the crumbling old building with adventure in their hearts and mischief on their minds.

Two young boys entered the building that late afternoon, but only one of them was ever seen again. That was, until the anonymous letter arrived from Mexico and changed everything.

The Kane family was known for its generosity, and their humanitarian deeds and their philanthropic efforts. But that didn't only apply to those who needed it most. Funded by Kane's grandparents, Ridley had organised a magnificent party. Several local bands played throughout the evening, including Kane's friend Ben's band, *Crumbs for Comfort*, and rock band *The Darkness*, whose singer Justin had been a teammate of Kane's in their youth football days. Internationally known for their glam rock songs, Justin and the guys toned down their amps for a more appropriate acoustic set.

During an evening in which the drinks flowed freely and all the guests caught up with old friends and new, Kane called on them for a moment of quiet. Standing on a chair, somewhat wobbly if you were looking closely, he tapped a spoon against a pint glass filled with his local favourite, Adnams Ale.

"My friends," he said. "On behalf of myself, Danny and all the Kane family, I want to thank you all for coming."

The crowd cheered and whistled. Kane waited for silence before continuing. "We would just like to say a big thanks to you all for being here and celebrating with us. We also want to take a moment to reflect on those that aren't here today. Our mum, Melanie, of course, my best friend Evan, and all those other good people we've known and loved but who are sadly no longer with us. I hope you'll all join me in offering a hearty round of applause to celebrate their lives."

With that, everyone erupted in joyous clapping. It was a poignant moment no one would ever forget.

Danny stepped forward and took his brother's place on the chair. "Thanks everyone. I'd just like to say a special thank you to my buddy Kenny. I met Kenny in San Miguel, and it was his friendship that kept me going through some of my darkest moments. Of course, it was his foresight to send that letter to my family. If he hadn't have done that, well…"

Danny didn't need to say anything more. Those gathered clapped and cheered again. Kenny, who'd flown over especially, was never one to shy away from the limelight. He waved his one remaining arm—he lost the other going up against the crazed professor beneath the pyramid in Mexico—in a royal wave, which may or may not have been mocking the Queen of England.

The elder Kane brother continued. "Finally, let's not forget all those around the world who are not as lucky as we are here today. I'm talking about all people, children and adults alike, who suffer on a daily basis. Hunger. Disease. Oppression. Religious persecution. I don't need to mention any of these unfortunate groups individually. My heart goes out to all of them. There are just a few of us here today, perhaps forty, and we alone cannot change the world. What we can do is to try and make it better. If we all continue to do just a little bit, then we can help. Like one of my heroes, Gandhi, once said, *If you can't help someone, then don't hurt them.*

It's simple, isn't it? I believe with my whole heart it's something all humans are capable of."

There followed a few seconds' of silent appreciation for Gandhi's famous words before Kane added, "Now all the sombre and serious stuff is over, let's party."

And they did. They drank, ate and danced long into the night to the tunes of *The Darkness* and *Crumbs for Comfort*, celebrating their friendships, their love, and their shared hope for humanity. When at last the final guests had made their way home or to their guest rooms, Ridley, Kane and Danny sat together under a full moon. The summer air was still warm as they gazed up at the starry ceiling above, sipping quietly on their drinks as they each thought of how things might have been and how things might still be moving forward.

For the first time in far too long, Kane's hopes for humanity were as bright as the moon above.

Just then, however, a cloud drifted across the moon, pitching them all into near darkness.

For a fleeting moment Kane wondered if that were to be a harbinger of things to come.

Chapter Eleven

侍

Kane and Naki chatted for the rest of the morning as they continued to relax and recover. Naki poured endless cups of tea, as he continued to insist on hearing more about Kane's unbelievable life and crazy adventures... almost as endless as the supply of tea.

Kane had visited Japan several times over the years, and he had always enjoyed the depth and beauty within Japanese culture and history, both ancient and modern. He'd spent a lot of time in the capital, Tokyo, and many other cities for pleasure, but he had also been there in a working capacity, having led more than one hiking party to the summit of Mount Fuji and beyond.

He was yet to explore farther west than Kyoto, however, which was the main reason he had jumped at the chance to be a guest speaker at the annual Adventure Tourism Expo.

The conference had been held over two long but rewarding days. It wasn't that Kane didn't like to share his vast knowledge and stories of adventure. He did. But he preferred more intimate settings, and was more comfortable and at his happiest chatting about his adventures over beers in a mountain campsite or under the desert stars—or one-to-one in a new friend's house, like now with Naki, who insisted on hearing Kane's account of the conference.

"Taking the stage in front of hundreds of listeners is not an ideal situation for me," Kane explained. "But after a few shots of saké, and knowing that after a couple of question-and-answer sessions I'd be free to leave, I did my best to entertain. People were smiling, so I guess I succeeded."

"And what exactly did you talk to them about?"

Kane was glad to be mentally transported back to the convivial seminar a few days earlier, which was much easier on the mind than the events at the river.

"... and that's how I got this pretty little scar," Kane had informed his attentive audience. With his trademark wry smile, he had leant over to his side and raised his shirt above his ribs, revealing a dreadful eight-inch scar across his right flank that drew gasps from those close enough to see it.

"Did you need many stitches?" someone in the front row had called out.

"Twenty-seven. But, I have to say, it was worth every single one."

He had obtained the scar during one of his overnight expeditions in the Peruvian Andes a few years back. The group had set out and headed on a bearing just east of Cuzco. All had been going well when, as they often did in such unpredictable landscapes, things suddenly took an unfortunate turn.

Kane had reacted first when a trekker had succumbed to the dreaded altitude sickness. In her dizzy and confused state—the altitude can be crushing above 5000m—she had tripped and stumbled off the trail, suddenly out of control and sliding down the steep bank. Without a moment's pause, Kane had flung himself over the side after the woman, deliberately sliding down after her and letting his speed build. He had managed to draw level with her and arrest her momentum, bringing them both to a halt on the hard slope. She had escaped more or less unharmed. Kane, however, had not. In moving so instinctively, he hadn't noticed the vicious shard of ancient Inca stone that had ripped through his abdomen, tearing a big chunk of flesh away in the process and leaving a wide open wound.

It was a nasty injury, but as Kane would later say, "A man without scars is a man without memories." Always a quick healer, and after just a couple of days sat recuperating at his favourite bar in Cuzco's Plaza de Armas, sipping plenty of Cusqueña beers—purely medicinal, of course—Kane was back doing what he did best: leading expeditions in the Andes.

"Who was the lucky woman?" Naki asked, eyes wide in awe of Kane's bravery.

"Alexandria Ridley. Alex... my girlfriend." Kane explained how Ridley had been his on/off love interest for most of the last two decades. He would have preferred it more on than off, but he'd yet to convince her to agree. Kane added that he would have reacted the same for anyone who needed his help. But in that case, it just so happened she was someone he cared deeply for. He wasn't going to mention that to the audience, or to Naki in that moment, but in protecting Alex Ridley, back then Kane hoped he had been protecting the future mother of his children.

"Did the audience ask you any interesting questions?" Naki enquired. "Sometimes, we Japanese are too afraid to speak English!"

"A young girl said to me, 'People who trek with you

claim you are like a goat? Is it true?' Her English was impeccable, and the question was met with smiles all round."

"And what was your reply?"

"I told her that goats smell bad, and most of them have scruffy beards, so yes, it's true."

Gripping the cylindrical, ceramic *yunomi* teacup that Naki had once again refilled, Kane was now envisioning himself in the mountains he so loved. "It's strange," he told Naki. "I mean, when I'm in the mountains, especially the Andes, it's almost as if I belong there, as if I'm meant to be there. Like that goat the little girl mentioned. I have a good friend, Sonco, an Andean native from just outside Cuzco in The Sacred Valley. He feels just the same as I do. It's as though we're somehow a part of those mountains, and in turn, they are a part of us."

"I'm sure the people in Hiroshima enjoyed your talk, Hiram. Maybe you don't realise how interesting these kinds of adventures are to people, especially in big Japanese cities where life can become quite... repetitive, I think is the word."

"Well, some even asked for autographs and... photographs with me... so I think they must have liked it. That was a bit of a surprise!"

Naki drummed his fingers on the table, apparently deep in thought.

"Would... would you mind doing one more meet-and-greet? Actually, you have met this person before, but not in ideal circumstances."

Kane raised an eyebrow. "Of course. Who is this mystery person?"

"The girl we saved at the river. The girl in red. She is actually my niece."

Kane now raised both eyebrows as intrigue turned to shock. "Really? Wow."

"We had work to do, so I didn't say anything. But I think she would love to meet you. I have been told she is sitting up in bed at the hospital. Could we visit her briefly?"

"Certainly," Kane confirmed, already standing.

Thirty minutes later, the two men stood by the girl's bedside in the immaculately clean hospital. Standing at the other side of the bed was the woman who had given the little girl the kiss of life. Kane now realised that this woman was the girl's mother, which made her composure at the river even more impressive.

"I'm Sayaka, Mr. Hiram-san," the girl said with a slight croak in her voice. "Thank you for saving my life."

"Your mother saved your life, Sayaka. I just did a bit of swimming."

The woman laughed, and Sayaka turned to smile fondly at her.

"I heard you are an explorer, Mr. Hiram. Is that true?"

"It is true. And please, call me Hiram. Your English is perfect, but there's no need for the 'Mr.' part!"

"Thank you, Hiram. I am also interested in history and geography. I know a lot about both subjects."

"Do you? That's wonderful."

"Ask me any question, and I will answer it."

Everyone in the room laughed except for Sayaka, who seemed confused as to why.

"Okay, give me a moment. What is the name of the famous Inca citadel found in the mountains of Peru?"

"Oh! I know this. It sounds a bit like Pikachu." Sayaka turned to her mother for help. Instead, she was told:

"I think you should be resting, Sayaka, not working your brain. And I'm sure that Mr. Hiram is very busy."

"No, I can get it. It's… um, it is Machu Picchu!"

Laughter and applause echoed off the walls.

"Well done, Sayaka," Kane said. "I'm sure you could be a great explorer one day."

"Actually, I want to run a museum, just like my grandfather on Miyajima. He is like a hero to me. Some people are action heroes, but he is a hero of thinking. He is strong in the brain."

"I like how you put that, Sayaka," Kane said. "And I am sure you can follow in his footsteps. But for now, I think you should do as your mother says and give your strong little brain some rest!"

Chapter Twelve
侍

Kane's shoulders and arms ached... and his legs, as he thought of it... *Jesus, I'm totally exhausted.* Yet, despite his extreme physical and mental exertions in the Hofu rescue operation, his mind raced and he couldn't sleep. And, sitting on the train towards the Miyajima ferry terminal made him feel as if he were on another planet. The quiet efficiency of Japan's Shinkansen bullet train was a far cry from the noise and chaos of the last few days. The storm had fully passed, and the countryside that blurred silently past his window seemed barely touched by nature's fury. The well-maintained train tracks were among the few things to have survived unscathed, and not a single train accident had been reported.

As the world sped by, Kane's thoughts returned to Hofu.

He had done everything he could. And yet, he had always known that humanity could never compete with the power of nature. Too many people had died. He also knew that in times of adversity, the true human spirit often shone through. And, much like in bushido, the ancient code of the samurai, there was much honour in selflessness. Naki was as selfless as anyone he had ever met, reminding Kane of his old friend and guide on his Andean expeditions, Sonco Amaru. With a smile, Kane pondered the notion that, had Sonco been Japanese and from a previous era, he would definitely have been samurai—and so too would Naki.

After stepping off the train at JR Miyajima-guchi Station, and snagging his ferry ticket and a takeaway coffee, Kane made the short walk to the ferry terminal. Just outside the terminal, his keen eyes spotted something tumble from a woman's handbag.

"Sumi-masen," he called out. *Excuse me.* He trotted over and bent over to scoop up the purse he'd seen fall. The lady turned, and he handed it to her, smiling.

"Arigatō," she replied, and then in English added, "Thank you." The woman appraised Kane's face, clearly alarmed at the series of angry cuts and bruises. "What happened to your face? Are you okay?"

"Oh, it's nothing. I was in Hofu—in the storm. But I'm okay, thanks. I'm on my way to Miyajima—"

"Miyajima? Really?" she said, obviously concerned. "Be careful," she added, "the typhoon—"

Kane could barely catch the woman's last words, as at that moment the sound of the ferry's horn drowned out everything else. Before he could ask her to repeat what she had said, she was gone.

What was she was trying to tell me? he wondered. *Typhoon? Was she warning me about the weather?*

Kane seriously hoped not. He'd witnessed enough bad weather in recent days to last a lifetime.

Out on the serene, glistening water, it was as if the awful storm had never happened. It was a clear and sunny autumnal day in Hiroshima Prefecture. Kane always thought autumn was the prettiest season in Japan, another reason he'd agreed to attend the conference. Through the ferry window, he could see the island across the water, some of its trees the deepest reds, some a range of regal bronzes, oranges and golds.

Kane had wanted to visit the island for years, and he couldn't wait to lose himself on the forested hiking trails and explore the many temples and pagodas, remnants of a classical era in Japan's long history. He felt sure he would get an even greater sense of the world portrayed by Clavell in *Shogun*. After admiring the island from afar, he picked up an English language newspaper that had been discarded on the empty seat beside him. He absentmindedly flicked through the pages while simultaneously admiring the view.

Kane skipped past any articles related to the storm—he didn't need to read about it to know what had happened. Living through it was quite enough. Then, ignoring the tedious entries about celebrities, business and politics, he scanned until something snagged his attention; the words 'Yakuza' and 'priest' in the same headline.

Kane knew the Yakuza was the Japanese mafia. His knowledge extended little further than that. A connection with someone religious, however, came as a surprise. Intrigued, he read the article. He learned that a notorious Yakuza boss was allegedly going to be giving up his successful, not to mention fruitful, life as a crime lord in order to retrain as a Buddhist priest. Mildly entertained, Kane thought the change in career was as striking as the colours of land and sea beyond his window.

He read that the Yakuza man in question, a Katashi Goto, was apparently one of Japan's most notorious underworld bosses. Over the course of the three previous decades,

Katashi had amassed a fortune from a range of illicit endeavours, including the running of protection rackets, prostitution rings and money laundering. Throughout this time, the man had acquired a well-deserved reputation for extreme violence. Gossip about why the mafia boss was set to enter the Buddhist priesthood was rife. The most popular theory, however, was that after his volatile behaviour had begun to cause fractures within the tightly-run Yamaguchi crime syndicate—one of the country's biggest and most powerful—Katashi was being forced to step aside. Whether being forced to leave by his superiors or departing of his own volition, it was to be a startling transition for such an eminent figure of the crime world.

Katashi, now in his sixties, was a high-ranking member of that criminal enterprise. And yet he had allegedly upset his bosses after media reports of him mingling with a range of celebrities, most notably young female models and pop stars. His actions, those of a man past his best, were giving the mafia a bad name. Not only that, but he was also under suspicion from within the Yamaguchi gang following revelations he had acted as an informer to the FBI about some of the organisation's frontal companies and even their nefarious links with North Korea.

Kane thought it was a bizarre story, but nothing more, and he closed the paper just as one of Japan's most iconic structures came into view. All thoughts of priestly mafia dons were instantly forgotten.

Standing high out of the water a couple of hundred yards ahead of the ferry was the noble O-Torii Gate. Its sheer size and its striking vermillion red paint made it impossible to miss, especially against the welcome blue skies. The massive gateway was impressive. It had been designed to appear as if it were floating on the surface of the ocean, and the effect worked. Historically, a *torii*, such as this one built in the 12th century, represented the metaphorical gateway between the human and the spirit worlds, illustrating a liminal state between the sacred and the profane. As in many cultures, the colour red was significant; it was believed to ward away evil spirits.

The remarkable O-Torii Gate was associated with the Itsukushima Shrine, the magnificent temple on the rocky shores of the island several hundred yards away. The huge temple was just one of the many important, historically significant structures on Miyajima. As the ferry began to slow, and approached the modest terminal, Kane mused that if first impressions were anything to go by, he was in for a fabulous time exploring the island's monuments and its rugged, natural beauty.

Stepping onto the small but busy dock, Kane glanced skyward. A high sun suggested noon. With no specific plan in mind, and several days to explore, Kane did what he always tried to do when arriving somewhere new: he sought out the nearest bar. Being a tourist is thirsty work, he often said. He also felt he'd earned a beer or three after the dramas of Hofu.

Kane always felt more alive with the sun on his face, and he set off on a leisurely twenty-minute stroll towards the island's main town—really nothing more than a couple of quaint streets lined with the usual gift shops and craft stalls, and a range of eating options. He had soon snagged a chair at the first place he found that had a neon beer logo hanging outside, and just as soon found himself supping an icy Asahi while glancing at a tourist map of the island.

At just over ten square miles, Miyajima was small. After studying the map for a few moments, Kane believed two or three days would be sufficient to wander the entire island on foot. He was in no rush, though, and when he threw in a visit to a few temples plus a museum or two, Kane believed that a relaxed week settling into 'island time' would suit him just fine. Besides, he could certainly do with the solitude.

Kane thought he was in just the right place.

Chapter Thirteen

侍

With several beers quenching his thirst and a lunch of soup, rice and steamed vegetable dumplings satisfying his stomach, Kane found his hotel and checked in. This one was another ryokan, set in the woods up a hill, and just a few hundred yards beyond the tourist village.

At least this one has a roof, he thought, allowing himself a rueful smile.

Relieved that the frightening, lethal storm was now a thing of the past, Kane quickly headed out and took a trail looping east across the island. It seemed to be the path less frequented by tourists, which suited him just fine. He loved to be in the wilderness leading his expeditions in a working capacity. However, given a choice, when he could, Kane strode out alone.

Just fifteen minutes after leaving the ryokan, powering on in long and rhythmic strides, Kane was soon breathing in the fresh air on the rising slopes of Mount Misen. At a little over fifteen hundred feet in altitude, he thought that whomever had named it a mountain was being a touch generous. There wasn't another person anywhere in sight, and the peace and serenity he found in the primeval forests was just what he needed. It afforded him time to think and to clear his head, and to start considering his plans for the coming year.

Kane had recently been invited to apply for a very culturally and politically important role for the following year, and though he hadn't privately decided whether or not he would take the position if offered it, he believed in the as yet top secret project and knew it would not only be a fun challenge, but a very rewarding one. Thus, today was a good time to start mulling over the meticulous planning involved. He would probably try and rope in his business partner in Peru, Sonco. He had come to depend on the stout Quechuan, and they'd become like brothers over their years of trekking and working together. Kane was even a proud godfather to Sonco's two young children, though the word god was one Kane felt uncomfortable using—he preferred a more earthly name, such as Uncle Hiram.

Kane let his mind wander as his lengthy strides ate up the ground, and he felt himself start to relax as he passed remote, out-of-the way shrines and a series of weathered stone statues of the various deities of the island. He knew the Japanese had a name for what he was doing right then; *shinrin-yoku, or* forest bathing. Kane understood *shinrin* translated as forest and that *yoku* meant bath. In essence, it is the practice of absorbing the forest through one's senses. It isn't supposed to be exercise. Rather, it is the simple act of being in nature and connecting with it through the senses of sight, sound, touch, smell and even taste. The Japanese consider *shinrin-yoku* as a kind of bridge. By utilising one's senses in nature, Kane understood, forest bathing can act as a bridge between ourselves and the natural world we occupy.

The forest right now was a haven of quiet, peaceful solitude, and other than the gentle rustling of trees and the occasional twittering of birds, the only sounds were those of his own footfalls. It felt as if it were the very antithesis of the recent chaos he'd experienced, and Kane revelled in the solitude of his 'natural bath.'

The island sanctuary of Miyajima had long been known for its large population of tame deer, though Kane had yet to see any since he'd left the dock. The deer, considered sacred in the Shinto religion, had become so comfortable around humans that they would often eat directly from the hands of tourists as they posed for their obligatory 'selfies.' But being surrounded by gaggles of humans is not how Kane preferred to see animals. He hoped that up in the hills, away from the madding crowds, he might get lucky.

Kane had read that the name Miyajima translated to Shrine Island, and it was easy for him to see why from his modestly lofty position on Mount Misen. Aside from the most famous shrine of Itsukushima, which he had seen from the arriving ferry, there was the Daishoin, the main temple of the Shingon Buddhism school of Omuro. There was also the stunning Daiganji Temple, whose roof he could just about see off in the distance to the west. They were the two most well-known religious structures on the island, but from up here he could see there were many more. With such a proliferation of religious buildings and monuments, it wasn't difficult to understand why Miyajima was regarded locally as the Island of Gods.

Why does everything have to be about gods? mused Kane, striding on with a sardonic grin crinkling his face.

By mid-afternoon, Kane had descended the mountain's grassy eastern slopes and found himself on the east tip of the island. With a panoramic view of the bay's other islands spread out before him, like a series of emerging turtle shells, Kane found a dry patch of grass beneath a tree and slumped back against its wide trunk. Pulling a luke-warm bottle of Asahi from his pack, he closed his eyes, letting his ears pick out the gentle lapping of waves and the sound of tuneful birdsong.

With such tranquility all around, and the warmth of rare sunlight on his face, Kane soon nodded off, and started to doze like a man who'd felt a great weight slip from his shoulders. In his half-sleep, he smiled, the beautiful face of his on/off girlfriend Ridley prominent amid his protracted dreams. He saw Sonco and his family, cheerful and happy with their lot in the world. He imagined his grandfather Hiram Snr was alongside him. He also saw a faltering image of his younger brother Danny, with whom he'd only recently reconnected after believing he was missing, or worse, for close to three decades.

A glorious hour had passed when Kane was startled awake by the sudden snap of a nearby twig. When he looked up, he gasped. Just twenty yards to his left was a small herd of deer, comprising of a few adults and several fawn. They hadn't seen him. More importantly, he was downwind, so his scent wouldn't be carried to alert them to his presence. He exhaled slowly, keeping as still and quiet as possible. This was nature at its finest, and in that moment he fell in love with it all over again.

Then everything changed.

A sudden flash of lightning lit the entire sky, followed by another, and then a third as the loudest clap of thunder Kane had ever heard shook the very ground he was slouched upon. Instinctively, the deer shot into the undergrowth en masse, clearly as surprised as Kane. He jumped up, his spot beneath the tree precarious during a lightning storm. A quick glance around showed him how the recently blue sky had faded into an ominous and familiar swathe of bruised grey.

Then the wind hit, rushing him with shocking force from out across the bay. Kane peered out into the rapidly descending darkness, certain an immense downfall was imminent. He didn't mind the rain—in fact he enjoyed it. However, today was not a day to be caught in yet another ugly storm. Without a moment's hesitation, he hoofed it back up the trail, hoping his reputation as a 'goat' wouldn't fail him.

Back on the town's main street, he quickly headed for the one establishment that surely wouldn't kick him back out into the rain at closing time: the restaurant owned by Naki's brother, Daijiro. He found the place and ducked through the *noren* fabric that almost always hangs over older Japanese doorways.

Now ensconced at the bar at the front of the restaurant, a line from *Shogun* came to him unbidden. "It's good for a man to get drunk once in a while," he muttered. "It releases all the evil spirits."

Then he promptly ordered a beer and the first of many shots of saké, its warm aroma mixing with the scent of the bar's century-old wood furnishings. Outside, the deluge picked up power.

Chapter Fourteen

侍

Daijiro shifted uncomfortably, thinking about the aged, well-dressed man and his three sullen companions who had taken up residence at the rear of his restaurant. As requested, a long, wide curtain hid their table from the rest of the customers, mostly tourists, who had huddled inside to shelter from the sudden downpour. He knew the men had arrived on the island the day before—word travelled fast in the small island community—and they were now settling in to what appeared to be a formal business meeting over lunch at his establishment, a favourite of wealthy visitors to the island due to its well-earned critical acclaim. Daijiro was also the head chef, and he had gained somewhat of a reputation in the Hiroshima region over recent years. He wasn't quite Michelin starred, not yet, but he was working on it.

Daijiro had his suspicions that the men were, if not exactly criminals, perhaps more than a little unsavoury. Nonetheless, he accommodated them for their long lunch and did his best to keep them happy. Earlier that morning, one of the men had handed him a hefty cash advance to reserve the private table for the entire afternoon. Since the envelope contained more money than the restaurant would usually make in a whole day, Daijiro asked no questions. Despite his subtle disquiet about the men, whom he suspected might even have mafia affiliations, Daijiro was just about comfortable enough with the arrangement to turn a blind eye and indulge them, however edgy they made him feel. Tempted as he was to listen through the curtain, he did not. Anyway, he had work to do. The tall foreigner at the bar wanted another saké.

"The bad weather is good news for us, Katashi-san," said Taichi, one of the Yakuza boss's massive henchmen. "There are fewer tourists when the weather is bad."

Katashi Goto grunted. He knew it was true. It didn't mean what they had planned would be straightforward. Despite the inconvenience, Katashi knew that in the bigger scheme of things, the weather would ultimately prove insignificant. However easy or difficult it turned out to be, it did not matter. He had a plan, and he would not leave the island until that plan had been executed and he was fulfilled.

It was his destiny. Katashi Goto would have his success.

"The storm will continue," the big man persisted.

"You must enjoy hearing the sound of your own voice," one of the other thugs said.

"Sadly, nobody else does," replied the third of Katashi's men, chuckling.

"It might even get worse," Taichi continued, apparently unphased by the comment. "If it does worsen, I suggest we wait two more days. That will be Wednesday, and

Wednesday is the slowest day for tourists on the island. With the weather as unprecedented—"

"Enough!" barked Katashi as he stared at the man. He then glanced at the other two lieutenants and nodded subtly, hinting at shared knowledge unknown by the younger man. "Listen to me," Katashi demanded, his voice now quieter yet laced with authority. "You know why we are here, Taichi. I have chosen you for this assignment because I trust you. You may not yet understand the importance of this mission—perhaps you are not smart enough?" His eyebrows raised questioningly, and Taichi looked down at his lap. "Regardless, you will be rewarded for your loyalty. As you already know, our plan is to take something away from here that has always belonged to me. It matters little that there will be fewer people the next day, or the day after that. It is inconsequential. We will succeed in our task tomorrow, and then I will have what is rightfully mine. I am not afraid." Katashi's brow furrowed now, as he leaned forward in his chair and locked narrowed eyes with his minion. "Are you afraid, Taichi?"

There followed the briefest of pauses before Taichi sat up a little straighter in his seat and replied, "No, Katashi-san. I am not afraid. You are correct, of course. I will do as you command." With a subtle bow from the neck, he ceded to the powerful mob boss. Katashi noticed as Taichi slowly, and unconsciously most likely, curled in his fingers and pulled his hands towards himself across the table. Many Yakuza had lost fingers through careless comments.

Katashi nodded. Satisfied, he leaned back again, his chest deflating with a long exhale. "So. It is just as it was. We visit the shrine museum in the morning for the final checks. Tomorrow afternoon, we shall proceed with our endeavour. We will follow the plan to the smallest detail, and when we are finished, we will transport the item to the dock. My helicopter will take us away from the island before anyone even knows what has happened. If someone—anyone—interrupts my plan…" He paused, eyeballing the men slowly, one by one. "Anyone at all, then I trust you all know what you must do?"

All three Yakuza men nodded.

Katashi knew that he especially had Taichi's attention. Taichi clearly wanted to prove himself to his boss and to the older Yakuza men beside him. Katashi's concern was whether overenthusiasm would lead to error. But there was no room for regret over his decision to appoint Taichi as a henchman. The man was more vital to his operation than either of the other two, even though Katashi liked him the least.

Chapter Fifteen

侍

The restaurant owner, Daijiro, apparently also acted as its main waiter and host. He was just delivering a bowl of spicy noodles to Kane's table when a curtain Kane hadn't noticed before was swept aside and four well-dressed men emerged, three of them very large men indeed. Their solemn faces and sharp suits immediately nudged at something in Kane's subconscious. On their way out of the restaurant, they paused to speak with Daijiro. Almost without looking, the owner placed the noodles down a little too heavily and accidentally splashed the bubbling broth across Kane's hand.

Clearly these men make this guy nervous, Kane reflected.

In small, artisanal restaurants like this, attention to detail was what built a favourable reputation. But Kane didn't mind the mess, and he didn't comment. There was enough tension already. Instead, he turned his attention to the noodles and his saké. Out of the corner of his eye, he watched as the eldest of the men quietly spoke to the owner. The others stood tall and alert, in total silence. If they meant to come across as intimidating, Kane thought they were doing a solid job.

The hushed conversation lasted just a few seconds, after which the older man handed Daijiro an envelope. The restaurant owner took it in both hands and bowed deeply. He offered a tip of his head to the others. Without another word, the four men turned and seconds later, they were gone.

Daijiro then swivelled back to Kane and began fussing with a cloth. With a wide-eyed, nervous expression, he uttered, "So sorry," before disappearing behind the curtain.

A frown carved a furrow across Kane's forehead as he found himself wondering about the men. They were big, at least three of them were, and one was certainly older than the others. The older guy was a distinguished looking man, Kane thought. His long hair, grey and tied-back in a pony tail, only added to his presence. Kane thought the man had an air of confidence about him, as if he were in complete control of everything and had not a fear or concern in the world. To Kane, it appeared as if the younger, bigger men were his entourage, probably even minders. There was definitely a hierarchy among the group, and without doubt the old man sat at its zenith.

And then it hit him. *Could the old guy be the mafia boss whose picture I saw in the newspaper on the ferry this morning?* It was the Yakuza don, who was about to become a Buddhist priest. Now he was sure of it.

Well, what do you know? Of all the bars in all the world, you had to walk into mine. Kane felt a smile curl his lips. It was probably wry.

Kane knew from what Naki had told him, Daijiro's restaurant was known all across the region and frequently attended by the wealthiest members of society, not to mention visiting celebrities. However, Kane decided that was surely not enough of a reason for these four men to be in the area. They must have business on the island.

Yakuza boss? The man didn't look like much. Perhaps five-ten, medium build. Then again, bosses became bosses for a reason. Strong willed, intimidating. Ruthless. And that's what the thugs were for, to carry out the will of the powerful men looking down from above them. Thinking back to the newspaper article he'd scanned, Kane recalled some of the details of the man's intention to become a priest. But wasn't it Buddhism? There were many shrines on the island, but Kane believed most of them were Shinto or other, older religions, not Buddhist. He would have to check that out. Nonetheless, now Kane was intrigued.

One thing was certain—the four men did not look like jolly tourists. Far from it. He smiled again as he imagined them posing with the native deer for their obligatory Miyajima 'selfies', just like normal tourists. Kane also assumed the envelope he'd seen them give to the owner was stuffed full of cash.

Maybe this relaxing getaway will be a little more exciting than I thought? Kane mused, his eyebrows raising in anticipation.

Chapter Sixteen

侍

Two men, cousins, sat cross-legged on the tatami floor of their ryokan. Their boss Katashi had retired to his room. Taichi was standing guard outside. As Katashi's room was just down the corridor, the two men spoke in whispers, their faces inches apart.

"Are you ready, cousin?" Yosuke asked.

"Yes. I am," Yoshi replied. "We have waited. Perhaps too long. Now the time is almost here."

They remained sure Katashi couldn't have known about it—they'd taken all requisite precautions—but a few weeks before their visit to Miyajima Island, the cousins had met for a chat. Yosuke had called Yoshi to a secret meeting in a dive bar away from any known Yakuza hangouts in Kyoto.

"It is good to see you, cousin," Yosuke had said. He embraced his younger family member. Yosuke had long suspected how Yoshi felt, but he needed to find out for sure.

"It is good to see you too. Always. Especially away from all those idiots." Yoshi grinned, nodding in the direction of the city their branch of the Yakuza controlled. "Away from Goto." He held Yosuke's gaze for a moment, then chuckled.

Okay then, Yosuke mused. *A good start.*

"Listen, cousin," Yosuke said. "I have been thinking about something. Thinking about it for a long time. I need to know something, and though I do not like to ask, I have to... It is simple. Can I trust you?" Yosuke knew it was risky for him to talk shit about their boss, just in case he was wrong about how Yoshi felt.

Yoshi appeared hurt. They had been close for thirty years, since they were young kids growing up in Kyoto. The glint in Yoshi's eyes confirmed his true feelings. "For real?" He shook his head. "Of course you can trust me, cousin. What is it? What is on your mind?"

"Good. Of course, I knew I could trust you with anything. Well," he said and leaned in, "I was thinking of a plan. If the plan works, we will no longer need to be ants for Katashi Goto to tread on. We will no longer need to be donkeys to carry his load. No longer need to be skivvies to carry out his every whim."

"What are you saying, cousin?" Yoshi asked, though Yosuke was pretty sure he knew full well.

"It is our time to step out of the shadows, Yoshi."

"You mean..." He raised his right hand and shaped it into a blade, then ran it across his neck.

Yosuke just nodded, then said, "Yes, cousin. Exactly. I am tired of being a slave to a failing master. Katashi has us running around on stupid, mindless errands. I want more action. I want to be involved higher up. For example, in a few weeks, do you know what we are going to be doing for him?"

Now Yoshi nodded. "You mean, the stupid thing on Miyajima? That muddy island, with that old relic in the museum? Oh yes, I remember. Fucking kids' stuff. He should have some new younger saps doing that kind of thing, right?"

"Right. Exactly. It is kids' stuff. We are not kids. We are men, Yoshi. We should be doing men's work. Are you with me?"

The two huge, powerful men rose from the tatami mats. Yoshi stepped forward and embraced his older cousin. In his ear, he whispered, "I am with you. I will do whatever it is you need me to do."

"Then I am happy." Yosuke pulled Yoshi in tighter. "It is our turn to take control. We will take a course of action that will see our fortunes rise. Think about it. The samurai armour will be worth several hundred million yen, several million dollars to the right collector abroad. We both know the rotting thing is wasted on the old man anyway."

Yoshi eased out of the hug and looked with anticipation at his cousin.

"I will take the lead, Yoshi," Yosuke said, "but do not fear, you will be my equal in all things. You know how it works. The other men will need guidance. It must appear that one of us is in charge."

"It should be you, of course. You are older, and you have earned greater respect among the men. I will be happy to follow you."

"As I said, in all matters you will be my equal. Let us get it right, though. No mistakes. Once we remove Goto, everything from that moment will be equal between us. All the financial rewards. All the power. In all things, we will be equal, I swear."

Both men confirmed they were content to split whatever spoils came from the selling of the suit of samurai armour. They also agreed to use that money to finally emerge from

Katashi's shadow and emancipate themselves from the outdated confines of the Yamaguchi Yakuza. That moment was coming soon. First, there was work to do.

"You must not speak of it to anyone, Yoshi," Yosuke implored, gripping the man's shoulders tighter than he planned.

Yoshi held his gaze a little longer than Yosuke felt comfortable with, but that was okay. *It is the way of things.* "I understand. It is important," Yoshi stated. "You can never know whom to trust in the Yakuza. You can trust me, as I trust you."

"Yes, cousin. I trust you," Yosuke had told his cousin in the ryokan's musty room, now just weeks from putting his plan into place.

Looking at him now, on the eve of their plans, with their boss just a dozen yards away, Yosuke's eyes narrowed and he inhaled deeply, letting it go as he said, almost in a hiss, "It is soon to be our time."

"Yes, Yosuke. And I am happy that the time has arrived. I remember our chat back in Kyoto all those years ago. It seemed impossible back then, but I trusted you. Now, I am ready." He nodded, then added, "Okay, cousin, I am going to speak with Taichi now, to ensure he is still a dumb fuck and none the wiser to any of this."

Yosuke grinned too and took a seat back down on the tatami mat, leaning back against the wooden wall. Breathing deeply, he let his mind drift back to what seemed like an altogether different era. In essence, it was. The new era—Yosuke's era—was upon them.

Chapter Seventeen

侍

The garish yet familiar neon glow of Kyoto's entertainment district lit up the night in a rainbow of sickly colors, yet Yosuke's world was shaded in gray. Barely in his twenties, the huge man already comported himself with the confident attitude of a predator. His dark eyes were permanently scanning his surrounding area for both threat and opportunity.

Yosuke spotted Yoshi approaching before his cousin saw him. At nineteen, Yoshi weaved his way through the crowd with the swagger of someone who seemed to think he owned the place. Yosuke shook his head. He sometimes still thought of Yoshi as a snot-nosed kid tagging along on his heels.

"Yo, Yosuke!" Yoshi yelled too loudly and from too far away, his grin wide and carefree. "What's with the hush-hush routine? You look like you're about to mug someone," he stated as he arrived in front of his cousin.

Yosuke grabbed him by the scruff of his leather jacket and dragged him back into a shop doorway. "Keep your voice down, idiot. You want the whole street to know our business?"

Yoshi just laughed, straightening his jacket. "Relax, man. You're wound tighter than a geisha's kimono. Why are you so worried?"

Yosuke appraised the younger man for a moment, choosing his words carefully. Yoshi was always quick with a joke, yet there was a sharpness to his tone that informed Yosuke he wasn't as dumb as he made sometimes out. It was time to put him to the test.

"You and I need to talk about our future," Yosuke said quietly. "About our standing in the… the organisation."

Yoshi's smile remained, but something flickered in his eyes. "Our future? I thought that was pretty much laid out. Do what the old man says, bust a few bones, and maybe operate some pachinko rooms when we're wrinkled and too old for the fun stuff."

Yosuke grunted. "That's too narrow-minded, cousin. I'm better than that. You could be too. We should be running this whole damn city. We just need to play our cards right."

"Whoa, easy there, big fella," Yoshi said, raising his hands. "Are you suggesting moving up the ranks? Or something more… ambitious?"

Yosuke flashed that predatory grin he knew had unsettled even the most hardened Yakuza men. "Well? What do you think?"

Yoshi whistled. "I think you have lost your mind. Or you're a genius. Perhaps both." He leaned in closer, and whispered, "You know what happens to guys like us who get too ambitious, right? We tend to take a long swim with the fishes… wearing steel shoes."

Yosuke chuckled, but remained serious. "Only if one is

stupid about it," he countered. "I've been learning. I watch them carefully, those in the upper echelons of the syndicate. Whatever they do, I keep mental notes. I miss nothing. They are nothing special, cousin. I am better than them. You too, Yoshi. Believe me, the old guard is getting complacent. They take everything for granted. Their position. Their wealth. Their lifestyle. Most of those idiots are so busy counting the money they can't see the future that is coming."

"Oh yeah? And what changes would those be, oh wise one?" Yoshi's tone was mocking but his eyes remained alert.

Yosuke didn't like to be mocked, and pulled Yoshi deeper into the doorway. "Be careful who you make fun of, little one," he growled, though Yoshi was very far from little. He exhaled. "Technology, for one. The internet, cryptocurrency, the way money is laundered... mark my words, it is going to change everything. Soon, the old protection rackets and vice dens won't be able to handle it anymore. We need to stay ahead of the curve."

Yoshi nodded, the usual smirk fading into something more thoughtful. "Okay. You have my attention. But... I have to ask, why are you telling *me* this? Why not go direct to the boss with these... big ideas?"

Yosuke met Yoshi's eyes with his own flinty gaze. "I need someone I can trust," he stated, his firm grip on Yoshi's shoulder tightening further, leaving the younger man in no doubt how serious he was. "Someone with the brains to see the big picture. Someone with the balls to do what needs to be done. Whatever that might be. That is me. It is you. I want you alongside me. So... are you in, cousin?"

Yoshi remained quiet for long moments. Over his shoulder, Yosuke noticed the night revellers thronging the paths and spilling into the streets, oblivious to the men in the dark doorway. These were his people. His future business interests. Some would be friends. Others, potential foes. When Yoshi finally spoke, his tone had lost its playful edge. "This is serious, Yosuke. What you are talking about goes against everything we have ever been taught, against the code that we have always lived by. Are you sure about this? It's some serious shit you're saying. Dangerous!"

Yosuke set his jaw with determination, and nodded. "Dead sure. Make no mistake about that, cousin. But I need to know. Are you with me? And I mean, with me all the way."

Yoshi laughed, and to Yosuke it sounded sharp-edged and without joy. "You asking, or telling?"

"Both," Yosuke stated matter-of-factly. "We are family, Yoshi. We share blood. But blood and family only goes so far, in this world above all others. I need to know… are you ready and willing to step up? Ready to become more than just another foot soldier taking orders from tired old men, even with the risks it will bring?"

"And if I am not?" Yoshi kept his tone carefully neutral.

Yosuke nodded, and let their silence hang for a moment as the hum of the city filled the void beyond. When at last he spoke, his words were heavy, each a stone marker in his vision of their future. "If not, you will stay right where you are. A minion. A glorified bully. An errand runner for lazy, cowardly bastards who see you as little else but a tool at their disposal. A nobody." He released his grip on Yoshi's shoulders and stepped past him onto the bustling path, then turned to face his cousin, his face now in shadow. "But know this—I am moving onwards and upwards, with or without you. I can not promise I'll be able to protect you when things kick off."

Yoshi's eyes narrowed. "Is that a threat?" he asked, though he stayed in position.

"No, not a threat. It's a reality check. We are not kids anymore. The choices you and I make here and now will set in place the path into the rest of our lives. This is a chance to be part of something much bigger. Rather than serve an empire, let us build one. Together!"

As he sat there now, on the eve of what was to be nothing short of a coup, Yosuke understood that the last twenty years hadn't gone as smoothly for he and Yoshi as he'd expected. The boss, Katashi, was nothing if not resourceful, and had managed to hold onto his position within the Yakuza far longer than anyone had expected, perhaps even himself. Nevertheless, the cousins had risen, and it had been Katashi himself who had enabled that rise. Yosuke also remembered telling Yoshi back at that meeting that loyalty only got men like them... men like Katashi Goto... so far.

Better late than never, Yosuke mused, *better late than never.*

Chapter Eighteen

侍

Rain hammered against the wooden walls of the restaurant like ballbearings as Kane swirled the cooling saké in its ceramic cup. Glancing towards an exterior wall where the rain pounded loudest, he sat more upright as a knot of anxiety formed in his gut. *Not you again,* he thought dismally.

"Can I get you another drink, sir?" the owner asked, bringing Kane back to the cosy interior. There was noticeable reluctance in the man's voice.

"You must be tired," Kane replied. "It's late, and I've watched you hustling about for hours now. How about taking a seat and letting me buy you one?"

"So sorry, but I couldn't do that, sir."

"I understand. But I don't want to make you have to work any longer, so I guess the alternative is for me to head out. Everyone loves a walk in a storm."

The owner smiled. Seeing that he had understood the joke, Kane realised that English proficiency must run in the erudite family.

"Well, thank you. This might shock you, but I do enjoy a saké or two after my shift." Daijiro rummaged behind the bar and pulled out a bottle with a gold label. "The best I have," he said, pouring two shots. "And it's on the house."

"I know it is," Kane replied. Seeing Daijiro's expression suddenly turn to one of concern, he worried that the restaurateur might fear he had another thug on his hands. He quickly added, "Your father Naki told me you would shout me a few drinks."

"Hiram Kane!" Daijiro exclaimed, the first of the rice wine already running through his veins. "I mean, Mister…"

"Hiram is fine. And of course, I will pay for my drinks. Yours too."

"You will *not*. My father told me about how heroically you helped at the river. Your meal is free also. Everything."

"We'll talk about that later! First, let me tell you that your father is a hero. He was there by my side for hours. He saved many lives."

Daijiro's head fell forward as he looked down into his cup. "I should have been there," he said quietly.

"The storm came too quickly. Leaving this island by boat would have been dangerous. And who was to know this area would be spared the worst of the damage? You might just have easily been needed here."

"You're right," Daijiro conceded, though clearly with some reluctance. "Miyajima is our home as much as Hofu is. It is our family's ancestral home. Only some of us moved to the mainland. But, please, tell me: what was it like? How did you save so many people?"

"If you don't mind, I'd rather talk about something else," Kane replied, having enough life experience to know that honesty was almost always the best policy.

"Of course. I understand."

"Actually, there is something I would like to ask you. Though I realise it may also be an awkward subject."

"After a cup of saké, for me there is no such thing as an awkward subject!" Daijiro said through a wry smile Kane recognised as one he'd often been accused of.

"Great to know. So, the four big men who were here earlier. The guys in the serious suits. Who are they? Do you know them?"

"Unfortunately, I think I do. They are..."

Daijiro was interrupted by a hefty knocking at the door. It sounded like someone was hitting it with a mallet, though it may have been a heavy hand. The owner's brow scrunched up, the glow of saké and conversation disappearing from his eyes.

After briefly half standing, he leaned back on his barstool once more. The movement suggested he was considering not answering the door at all.

"Do men like that really knock and wait?" Kane asked, knowing that the owner would guess which men he was referring to.

"That's true," Daijiro replied as he stood slowly, then he seemed to rally and moved quickly towards the sliding door. He drew it open, and a figure bundled into the room. The person was around half the size of the goons who had mercifully left the restaurant already, reassuring Kane before he even saw her up close.

The young woman was drenched, her black hair clinging to her heart-shaped face. Behind her fashionable round spectacles, even her long eyelashes seemed to be soaked.

"Mika! Are you okay?" Daijiro said loudly, doing Kane the favour of continuing to speak in English. He sounded half excited and half annoyed as he addressed the younger woman. "What were you doing out there? It's raining so hard!"

"I know it is!" she said, glancing at Kane and rolling her eyes.

Kane laughed. He liked this young lady already. Mika turned to face him. "Mr. Kane?" she said, much to his surprise, though it didn't sound like a question.

"Er, yes, I'm Hiram Kane. How... how did you know?"

"I have been expecting you. You recently met my father Naki Nakamura. He told me all about you. My name is Mika." She smiled and held out her hand.

"I know it is!"

Mika's lips curled into a smile. "And now I see you have met Daijiro, too. I guess I am late to the party."

"Ah, yes," replied Kane, shaking her dainty hand. "Naki told me about you both. It is my pleasure to meet you."

"You still haven't answered my question," Daijiro chimed in, interrupting the pleasant greetings in very un-Japanese fashion. "Why are you out in this horrific weather at night?!"

"I was working late at the museum... as usual," she added, though not with any obvious regret, "and I saw the clouds gathering, but I wanted to finish the filing."

"The filing? That was really so important it couldn't wait until tomorrow?"

"If it waited until tomorrow, then something else would have to wait until the next day."

Now it was her brother's turn to roll his eyes. Kane grinned. "Anyway, we have a guest, and I am sure he doesn't want to hear us bickering. Saké?"

"Yes, please," Mika replied.

"Not you!" Daijiro admonished his sister.

"Why not? I'm old enough."

"Because I said..."

"How about one drink, to toast new friends?" Kane suggested. Daijiro smiled, like being mad with his sister had all been an act anyway. Mika pulled up a bar stool between Kane and her brother.

"So, Mika," Kane said as Daijiro poured, "I guess you're interested in history and museums just like the rest of your family?"

"I am. Ancient ancestors left us with some terrible things. Resentment, grudges and glorification of war. Recent ancestors even left us with the climate change that in part causes these storms. But they also left us with so many amazing artefacts I admire and which fascinate me, and I can't take my eyes off them. Things that transport me to the past, like the most adventurous travel I can imagine."

"Very well put," Kane said. "A wise head on young shoulders."

"Wise, and old enough for another drink," Mika said, sliding her already empty receptacle in the direction of her brother.

"Her love of history comes from her grandfather," Daijiro told Kane, "and I guess her love of drinking comes from me. Even though I try and disapprove."

"It's not that I love drinking," Mika advised, winking in Kane's direction. "It's that I love doing something you just told me not to."

Daijiro frowned but could not prevent the smile that appeared once the saké cup left his lips. Kane liked everyone he had met in this family so far, and he was keen to meet the much-loved and evidently revered grandfather. The thought of the four men who had recently darkened the restaurant with their looming, threatening presence concerned him, but he was reluctant to bring it up in front of Mika. He hoped the men would depart from the island with the storm clouds.

He also knew that preparedness was much more important than hope.

Chapter Nineteen

侍

With their clearly expensive and tailored black suits, combined with their surly countenance, the four men stood out a mile. They could not have looked more different from the garish rain-jacketed sightseers holding soggy maps and wafting smartphone cameras in all directions.

The men strode with intent, businesslike, and not only because of the threat of more rain. The brief late morning sun was quickly losing its battle with the ominous clouds that still hung over Miyajima like a bad omen. Katashi and his men hurried forth under a sky that looked likely to unleash its fury on them at any moment.

To any of the tourists who bothered to look—it wasn't many; most were absorbed with their phones and maps—it would have been obvious that three of the men had spent more time in the gym than admiring world heritage sites.

The fourth man, the eldest by some distance, radiated a distinct aura, setting him apart even from his associates. Though shorter and leaner, and well into his sixties—the others were in their twenties and early thirties—he oozed authority. The man's eyes shone with a glint of excitement and a clear appreciation of the wealth of history and cultural importance all around him. It was almost as if he himself were a part of that rich history, as if he somehow belonged to it. In his heart, he did. He had explained to his men during the preparation for the mission that, at the end of the 12th century, one of his ancient ancestors had built the Itsukushima Shrine.

Minutes later, Katashi Goto and his cohort silently entered the shrine built by Taira no Kiyomori more than eight centuries earlier. The henchmen were at least aware enough of the significance Katashi placed on the shrine to act with reverence and respect. They also knew what would happen to them if they didn't behave in an appropriate manner. At best, they'd be relegated to running errands back in the shadows of the city. At worst...

They understood the assignment well. They had each been thoroughly briefed about their respective roles and responsibilities. Yet, despite that knowledge, only two of them understood the true significance of the object they would be stealing tomorrow. As far as the youngest of the Yakuza men, Taichi, was concerned, mafia bosses did whatever they wanted, whenever they wanted. So, if Katashi-san wanted to steal a dusty old relic like a samurai suit from a long-forgotten time in history, then who was he to question that?

It would also be the easiest job he had ever done for the man, considering the lack of any real security on the island. It seemed simple to Taichi. They could move about the shrine with freedom and secure the building from within—though exactly what they were securing it against he really had no idea. Then they would grab the suit, let the old man play dress-up, watch as he performed his ridiculous ceremony, then escort him to his waiting chopper.

How difficult can it be? Taichi wondered.

Today's visit to the shrine was merely a trial run to make sure each man knew his position, what he needed to do and, more importantly, where he needed to be at all times. The structure of Itsukushima Shrine was vast; a sprawling maze of enchanting corridors with ornate carvings, paintings and sculptures situated tastefully throughout the atmospheric space. It was perhaps most famous for being built out over the sea where, at high tide, the water level rose with the tide, giving the appearance of the shrine literally floating on the surface. The effect, in good weather, was magical. It was far from magical this morning.

"What is it with old men and their toys, anyway?" whispered Taichi, a gorilla of a man with a name to match. Taichi's parents couldn't have known the cruelty they had inflicted on their only son in his formative school years. The rotund kid had been more than a match for his name, which meant 'large one' in Japanese. Only years later, when he learned to fight back, did he finally earn some respect. It was to become a recurring theme. With a taste for violence and a talent for brutality honed with practice, Taichi fought his way all the way up through the various ascending ranks of the Yamaguchi mafia gang. Finally, he had become entrusted to Katashi Goto's private security team.

In the end, his parents' worst infliction had been to lead their son down a path of violence and crime that lasted for many years beyond the school bullying.

"Why do you care?" replied Yoshi, rare words from a man whose name was equally applicable to his manner. His parents had also chosen accurately. Yoshi: the 'quiet one.'

"I mean, think about it... why does the old man want a

fucking samurai suit, anyway? Is he not a little old for playing fancy dress?" Taichi chuckled under his breath.

Yoshi just looked away. Taichi did not like it. He persisted:

"What is it with you? And what is so special about this particular suit? Can he not just go to the costume shop and buy one?"

Now, Yoshi turned and glared hard at the younger but bigger man. "Katashi-san does whatever he wants. The speaker may well be a fool, Taichi, but the listener is wise—you would do well to remember that. Anyway, it is not stealing. That samurai suit belongs in the Goto family. He is only taking what is rightly his."

Taichi's eyebrows raised, a feeling of genuine respective for Katashi briefly replacing the usual resentment. But it lasted no more than an instant. "Why did I not know that? How is it that you know, but I do not?"

Yoshi sneered, his lips curling into a dismissive grin. Taichi felt his fists clenching tight. Jealousy was a long held weakness, and he wanted to know why he was not aware of the full backstory.

"I suppose it means Katashi-san does not trust you. But that is not important. Focus on your task," Yoshi said, and once again he turned his back on Taichi.

The big man didn't respond this time, but in his mind, he seethed.

No one talks down to me like that. No one.

Chapter Twenty

侍

Kane maintained his distance, but he couldn't help himself; he had to follow.

He had just finished his breakfast at Daijiro's restaurant and paid his bill, and was just leaving when he spotted who he now believed were mafia men, probably Yakuza, based on what he'd read in the paper and what Daijiro had told him, not to mention what he had witnessed with his own eyes. He discreetly set out on the tail of the three thugs and their boss, who were a hundred yards ahead of him and seemed to be veering towards the island's most important landmark, the Itsukushima Shrine. Kane recalled that's where Naki's father Nori worked as the museum curator. Kane hadn't met with Nori yet, as he'd arrived while the curator was enjoying a few days off. But after calling Naki, he'd been told Nori Nakamura would be back on the island sometime late tomorrow, and he would search him out then.

Kane thought the men were probably just going to pay respects of some kind at the shrine, based on the little he'd read in the newspaper about Katashi's new religious calling.

On a whim, he kept following regardless, his interest more than a little piqued. *Curiosity killed the cat*, he warned himself, as usual, his grin wry. He kept tailing the men anyway.

As the vibrant red of the famous shrine came into view, the streets became more crowded with visitors, holding up their phones and sodden maps, evidently unperturbed by the downfall. As Kane walked past a group of young women, one word from among the idle chatter jumped out at him. "Yakuza."

The women were talking in low voices and looking in the direction of the shrine while talking with excitement and urgency, like they had just seen a wild animal that was rare but also dangerous. Being careful to avoid appearing too obvious about listening in, Kane glanced at the women then followed their eyeline towards the shrine.

He watched from afar as the Yakuza men entered the shrine at its main northern entrance and disappear inside. Kane had always intended to visit the famous shrine and its adjoining museum anyway. It was the most famous of many famous landmarks on the island, and one of the most culturally important in all Japan. With a hard-earned degree in archaeology and an innate love of culture and architecture, visiting here was a no brainer. With the weather deteriorating rapidly and any chance of an afternoon hike seemingly off the cards, now seemed as good a time as any.

Kane hung back a few minutes, knowing he would come across them inside later should he want to. Once he felt they were far enough ahead, however, he stepped out from beneath the huge maple tree under which he had been loitering and hustled inside. Then he approached the ticket desk, took the 500 yen entry fee from his wallet, and handed it to...

"Mika? I thought you worked in the museum offices? Um, good morning…"

"Good morning, Hiram. Ha, well yes, I do. I also do other jobs from time to time to help pay for my studies. This is one of them." She held out her hand. "It's good to see yo again. I hope you're, you know, feeling okay after all those sakés?"

Kane chuckled. "It wasn't that many," he said sheepishly, neglecting to tell her he had taken Daijiro's generously donated bottle back to his ryokan hotel room for a nightcap or several. Kane was just lucky he didn't really get hangovers. *Too much practice*, he thought, though also kept that to himself. He and Mika chatted amicably for a few minutes as Kane kept a subtle eye on the corridor. The mob men were out of sight inside, so he said goodbye to the youngest of the Nakamura clan and casually made his way into the famous shrine.

Mika waited until both Kane, and the men in suits, had filed deeper into the museum before she let her thoughts turn to the Englishman. She had heard about his exploits in Hofu from her father Naki, and she had been impressed by her dad's tales of Kane's bravery. He had told her how Hiram had put his own life on the line, time after time, in order to help save many people from the flash floods.

From what she had seen and heard herself during their time at the restaurant, he seemed normal enough. Handsome, in that weird Western way, and pleasant to speak with. He also seemed to lack any kind of ego, and was humble and even embarrassed when they'd labelled him a hero. Otherwise, normal. Not really a hero but, then again, there wasn't much to challenge him in a cosy restaurant bar while knocking back rice wine. She had noticed a certain glint in his eye, as if despite the passive exterior, something else resided within... something tougher. Maybe even a hint of darkness...

Mika had a choice now. She knew who the men were that had passed through moments ago. Her brother, Daijiro, had informed her the previous evening when the Englishman was out of earshot. It had only been a matter of time anyway.

Regardless of how her brother wanted to approach the situation, Mika felt duty bound to warn Kane, to tell him he should not go inside. But how could she? He was unaware of the danger and would probably think she was crazy. And anyway, if she did that for Kane, she would have to do it for all visitors. She had not yet figured out a way to do that subtly.

She, however, knew exactly what was going on. Her family had known this day would come. That it would happen was an inevitability. They had only been wrong about when. Their informant had suggested the event might take place later in the year. That was the rumour on the street, too. But Mika and her family knew never to trust anyone. Their man on the inside of the Yakuza was not immune to the lure of the yen. He would sell out his own mother if the price was right. Sadly, he was all they had inside, and he had been right as many times as he had been wrong.

Mika's instincts told her Hiram Kane would somehow be an ally before the event was through. Thus, she decided to hold her tongue. She had watched on as he walked away and into the museum, seemingly oblivious to those men who were also inside. She was left wondering if she had done the right thing. It was too late, at least for now. Now, it was time to make the phone call she hoped she would never have to make. For security reasons she ignored the landline on the desk and grabbed her mobile from her purse beneath it. Inhaling, and glancing about to ensure no one was listening, she found the number and hit call.

When it was answered on the second ring, she said, "Grandfather, it is not wise to come to the island."

Nori Nakamura chuckled softly down the line. "Ah, Mika. You are wise to tell me. But you know very well I cannot heed your advice. We have our duty. You have yours. I have mine. It is no more our choice to accept and respond to that duty than it is to choose to enjoy the cherry blossom in spring. It is in our blood, and it is in our nature. We will respond accordingly. You know, my girl, as do I, that I will come to the island. I admit, I had not expected this day to arrive so soon. It is my understanding it will be tomorrow that matters. Not today. That it is so soon, either day is a surprise. So be it. My dearest Mika, will you promise me something."

"Yes, grandfather?"

"Promise me you will not do anything foolish."

Now it was Mika's turn to feel like laughing, though she held it in.

"Foolish? I promise," she said honestly. "Dangerous? Maybe."

"Dear Mika, tell me you will not do anything foolish *or* dangerous!"

"So sorry, grandfather. You know I cannot promise that. Not to you. Not least today. If you wanted me to stay out of danger, why did you always insist that I keep up with my *bujutsu* practice in the gym?"

"That is for self-defence, granddaughter, not attack."

"Sometimes, they are one and the same." She could

almost hear her exasperated grandfather shaking his head, and she smiled.

"Just as I thought. You are too strong-willed to stay safe. Then I must tell you this. Whatever happens, I will be proud of you. I know it is not luck you need. You only need to be you."

"To wait for luck is the same as waiting for death," Mika replied. "You taught me that. You also taught me that karma and shadows follow us everywhere. I will not wait in the shadows, grandfather."

"Thus, neither will karma ignore you, my dearest granddaughter."

"Nor you, grandfather."

Mika ended the call. She was not afraid. Not of anything. Just knowing her grandfather would be there later filled her with steel forged many centuries earlier, in an altogether different era of Japanese history. An era when men were noble, and everyone lived by a different code. Bushido. As her grandfather had said… it was in her blood.

Chapter Twenty-One

侍

Kane was just entering the main corridor beyond the entrance lobby where he'd just left Mika when a large group of what he believed to be Korean tourists came into view, bringing with them a cacophony of noise and a riot of colour. The sudden eruption of chatter echoed off the ancient wooden beams, their excited voices rising and falling like waves. Sun rays from a rare break in the clouds filtered through the paper screens, catching on the buttons of a woman's garish yellow jacket and the lens of her camera. A child's shrill laughter pierced the air. Kane's nostrils flared at the heady scents of perfume and the slightly musty, woody aroma of the structure itself. He took himself towards a side corridor and avoid the crowds.

Too many people, he thought, feeling his shoulders tense. *I don't like it!* The highly polished wooden boards creaked softly beneath his boots as he angled left, glad the sounds of the tourists was fading as he moved away.

If the shrine's exterior was a remarkably spectacular and beautiful piece of architectural engineering, then its interior was no less stunning to Kane. In 1996, Itsukushima Shrine had been declared a UNESCO Cultural World Heritage Site, due to its unique architecture, the thousands of culturally important national treasures it contained and its intrinsic place in Japanese history. Kane had studied archaeology at university, almost completing a Masters, and as part of his course he had also taken many related units on art and architecture. He remembered devouring textbooks over dozens of mugs of tea and the satisfaction of connecting historical dots. Since then, he had always been fascinated by the multitude of ways the world's differing cultures and religions revered their gods and deities and how they represented them in artistic ways.

A shaft of golden light fell across Kane's path, illuminating motes of dust that danced in the air like tiny spirits. He stood still for a moment, brushing his fingertips against a red-painted wooden column, enjoying the feel of the wood grain beneath multiple centuries of varnish. The wood felt warm, as if it retained the intangible memory of countless hands before his.

So much history, Kane thought, a familiar sense of literally being amidst antiquity running through him. *Peace. War. Emperors and peasants—treading these very same creaking boards.*

The shrine was truly magnificent. Kane had read that its structure had benefitted from nearly constant maintenance and refurbishment, due to its cultural and historical importance. Thus, it was believed to still look exactly as it had when it was first built in the 12th century. *'With its vermillion painted columns and intricate carvings, beneath its series of beautifully tiled roofs, it remains an architectural wonder that leaves any visitor in awe,'* Kane had read in one particularly gushing travelogue before he'd left the UK on this trip.

He inhaled deeply, detecting the faint scent of the sea

mingling with aged wood and paint. The red columns gleamed in the hazy light, their color so vibrant it seemed almost wet. Kane came to an open-air section of wall and gazed out, admiring how the curved tiles of the roofs created striking silhouettes. Every inch of the ancient structure told a story—dragons whose scales caught the light, demons with seemingly shifting expressions at different angles, wood-carved phoenixes spreading their wings in eternal flight.

Kane moved deeper into the shrine and made his way along its wide hallways in relative silence now he'd left the Korean contingent behind. The only sound he heard now was the soft padding of his own boots on the archaic wooden decking. The boards exhaled gentle creaks beneath his weight as he walked as many countless thousands of pilgrims once had in bygone eras. A distant bell sounded with resonance. The tension in Kane's neck muscles eased as the tranquility wrapped around him. He inhaled the salty air wafting in from the bay.

Kane was in his absolute element when outdoors, usually hiking in the mountains, but exploring ancient cultural monuments came a very close second. Cool air from outside drifted through the open sections of the shrine. Goosebumps appeared on his skin. Kane would have been happy spending hours soaking up the peaceful atmosphere while admiring the view of Hiroshima Bay and the mysterious O-torii Gate, visible a few hundred yards off shore. The gate stood out as a dark mass against the darkening sky, though the occasional burst of sunlight set the red afire. The gate's reflection wavered in what for now remained the placid water that surrounded it, though Kane sensed the weather could only deteriorate as the day wore on, whipping up the sea.

I could stay here all day, he thought, feeling at one with the peaceful surroundings. *Just me and a thousand years of history.*

Yet, there was just something about the four men that remained front and centre in his mind and jostled for his attention, and he couldn't resist trying to find out what it was. The memory of their purposeful movements. The image of their hard faces. How they clearly stood out as not being tourists. Kane recalled spotting hints of tattoos peeking from beneath suit sleeves. The slight bulges that potentially suggested concealed weapons. His mouth went dry as he considered what he was about to do.

Am I really going to follow Yakuza? In a sacred shrine? His rational mind screamed caution, but something deeper—a familiar tug of curiosity—pulled him forward.

After stopping briefly to study the mesmerising details of a Shinto dragon wood carving, its scales seeming to ripple in the shifting light, Kane turned a corner and abruptly stopped. Just twenty yards ahead were two of the Yakuza men. They were standing outside a wide entrance Kane believed led into the main Treasure Hall, if his memory of the map he'd seen served him well. The men's dark suits absorbed the dim light around them, creating sharp silhouettes against the shrine's warm wooden tones. Kane caught a whiff of cigarette smoke mixing unpleasantly with aftershave. It was obvious to Kane the two men were guarding those doors. Equally apparent was the fact they didn't want anyone to enter.

Kane's pulse quickened, blood rushing in his ears like far-off surf. His lips felt parched, and he tasted salt—whether from nervous sweat or coastal air, he wasn't sure.

Kane wanted to go inside. He somehow needed to know what the Yakuza boss was doing. Every instinct for self-preservation told him to walk away, to return to the safety of the tourist areas, but his feet remained rooted to the spot. Since he was a boy, Kane had harboured an almost insatiable curiosity about life and a thirst for knowledge. It is what had spawned his now inbuilt wanderlust and willingness to explore the world.

His fingertips buzzed with adrenaline as he pressed himself against the cool wooden wall. *I should leave*, he thought, even as his mind raced through possible ways to get beyond the guards. *Dude, this isn't some fun archaeological exploration—these men are likely dangerous.* Yet Kane found the pull undeniable, like gravity itself.

Unlike the fabled cat, however, Kane thought abstractedly as he remained against the wall and appraised the two henchmen, that curiosity was yet to kill him. He tasted metal on his tongue, the familiar brassy flavor of anticipation and... *and danger?*

Chapter Twenty-Two

侍

Until curiosity did eventually kill him, Kane knew he'd always be the same.

Right now, and with the gaggle of Korean tourists nowhere to be seen, it was going to be difficult to remain inconspicuous to those men guarding the Treasure Hall.

He was starting to wonder what the hell he was doing there, when a growing clamour came echoing his way. Kane had studied the Korean martial art of tae-kwon-do whilst at university and still participated in the sport to this day, though not as much as he'd like. It was during those long, hard sessions on the mat that he'd also learned to speak the Korean language, hanguk—and those were definitely Korean voices he heard. Many Korean voices.

This was his chance. Knowing Koreans as he did, Kane knew they wouldn't pay much attention to the burly men at the doors to the Treasure Hall. If they wanted to enter that room, they simply would. And, unless the guards wanted to cause a scene, there would be little they could do about it. Most potential visitors might have been put off proceeding inside with a simple stare. Not the Koreans. He admired that trait in his Korean friends. Today would not be the time for it.

Kane's hunch was right. A minute later, two dozen neon-clad Koreans of all ages swarmed around the corner, led by a middle-aged woman holding a small Korean flag on a tall stick, yelling, "Il-li oh-se-yo. Ga-ja." *Come here. Let's go.*

The guide led the large group to the doors of the Treasure Hall, and almost as if the two massive surly sentries weren't there, they streamed inside as one organic swirl of humanity before the men could so much as react. Kane made his move and with a few swift strides, he'd joined the group and slipped into the melee unnoticed at the rear of the pack.

Once inside the central hall, the energetic Koreans dispersed in all directions, leaving Kane to look around in relative anonymity. In the far corner of the main Treasure Hall he found a separate room. Above that door he spotted a sign that declared 'Armour Room' in a number of languages. Kane casually made his way towards it, almost certain who he would find within.

Standing just inside the door was the solid figure of the third henchman. The man was at least six feet tall, with broad shoulders to match. Though the man stood with his back to the entrance, it was clear he was on guard. However, he was paying close attention to something inside and not focused on what or who was behind him. Kane edged nearer, treading lightly in an effort to stay silent. When he was close enough, he was able to take a peek beyond the man's wide frame.

What he saw was completely unexpected. Crouched on his knees and gazing up with obvious reverence at a magnificent suit of samurai armour was the main man, Katashi Goto. The mafia don had both hands clutched to his chest, and although Kane couldn't see his face clearly, he sensed the man was emotional, maybe even crying.

A muted echo of shouts broke Kane's thoughts, and the guard's head twitched in response to the sound. Kane was sure the man would turn and spot him. He didn't wait to find out. Turning on his heels, he ducked away around a corner, just in time to evade the roving eyes of the guard. Not far enough away, however, that he couldn't hear the guard mumble something like, *Noisy fucking Koreans.*

As Kane had frustratedly watched many tourists do during his travels, the Koreans didn't take any time to admire the sculptures or paintings on display around them. Instead, they cast largely uninterested glances towards them and stopped for 'selfies' with the object filling the background behind them, almost as if it were evidence they had made the effort to visit. Thus, after no more than three minutes, the group of 'tourists' had swarmed out of the main hall of the Treasure Room.

It meant Kane now found himself alone between guards at either end. He wasn't afraid. He hoped that as far as the guards were concerned, he was just another dumb tourist. And yet, a small knot of trepidation began to tighten in his guts. He had a choice of two routes: one out of the shrine and away from the situation, and one that took him deep into the underworld. He had no clear evidence that the Yakuza members were planning anything criminal at this location, and from what he had just witnessed, it appeared Katashi Goto had come to visit something that was seemingly of great importance to him.

Yet he knew Mika was sitting in the ticket booth near the entrance, probably feeling some greater responsibility towards a place that meant so much to her family. Naki's grandfather, Nori, was curator of the museum. If something abhorrent was going down in his museum, Nori himself would be devastated, even if he was away from the island and not in immediate danger. Kane was yet to meet Nori himself, though he knew from Naki's testament that Nori was a good and humble man, respected in his role as curator of one of the most important cultural museums in Japan. With so much at stake, Kane was not willing to simply hope for the best.

He raised his eyes upwards, searching his brain or the ether for inspiration. His gaze landed upon a striking scene of two samurai warriors in battle. It was a large, dramatic oil painting with a brooding dark sky that was the perfect backdrop for the enigmatic warriors fighting in the foreground, their swords flashing and clashing under a bright full moon. Kane could almost feel the movement of the steel and feel the rush of air as they swung towards each other. He swore he could feel the beating of their hearts. He stood, mesmerised... until he realised it was his own heartbeat he could feel, responding to the sound of conspiratorial voices, the rushed Japanese words echoing off the ancient walls.

"It does not matter what you think, Taichi. Understand this. Tomorrow afternoon, we will be away from this muddy rock, and Katashi-san will have his treasure." It was the slightly smaller guy—still large—who had spoken. He sounded pissed off.

"Well," replied the younger man, "I suppose you are right. And the sooner the fucking better." He chuckled, and despite his size Kane was reminded of a child's laugh. Then his voice hardened. "Samurai warrior my arse," he said, and Kane sensed the obvious disdain in his tone of voice. "Suit or no suit, the old man is finished."

"Be very careful what you say, Taichi," came the hissed response. "That big mouth of yours might get you killed."

Kane understood little of what was being said, but the hostility between the men was clear. He had no choice but to acknowledge there was always danger around people like this. Yet, somehow, walking away did not seem like an option to Hiram Kane.

Chapter Twenty-Three

侍

From where he stood twenty yards away, and though he couldn't be certain, Kane believed he'd understood at least some of what the mafia men had said, if not the exact words. He had picked up the word 'samurai' and assumed it must be a reference to what he had witnessed shortly earlier, when the older man was on his knees in front the armour display, paying some kind of emotional homage.

Could they be planning to steal it?

Kane saw no possible way it could be done without getting caught.

Even as he thought it, he remembered who these guys were. He was now in no doubt whatsoever they were members of the notorious Yakuza crime syndicate, and men like that paid little attention to rules. In fact, they probably made the rules. Thus, if they wanted it, they would take it.

In that moment, a rather obvious question came to him again.

Even if I wanted to do something about it, what the hell could I do?

He assumed the men were armed. If they were armed, they were dangerous. For now, all that meant for Kane was that he would have to watch and witness while staying out of sight. If that was even possible.

He crouched and pinned himself to a wall. After a few minutes of waiting, the sound of voices rose behind him, and he peered around the corner to see the mafia boss and his minder exiting the Armour Room. He turned back the other way to face the location where the two other thugs were standing, guarding his only exit. Between the approaching Yakuza boss and his men, Kane understood he was trapped. He had to hope the boss would keep walking, putting all the men in one location with the potential to be followed. Katashi kept walking. Then he slowed, and stopped. He extended his index finger and gestured towards the corridor where Kane was crouching, clearly signalling to his man that the area should be checked.

Shit!

Kane held still. He had done nothing to offend the men, and he hadn't allowed them to notice that he'd been hanging around. He could still be just another tourist. Exhaling, he stood, took a deep breath, then forced a passive smile onto his face and strode nonchalantly towards the exit. Hopes of a quick exit soon died an ignoble death. The two big men closed ranks, their huge shoulders inches apart and blocking the way through. Their cold eyes bore into Kane's. Violence was written in the scars on their faces as they eyeballed Kane, no shrinking violet himself at a shade under six foot. The stares were like the drawing of blades before battle. Kane was not afraid of a fight—in truth he wasn't really afraid of anything—but he had the basic fight-flight instincts of any sentient creature. Now was a time for the latter; he would figure out the rest later.

He stopped and widened the passive smile into his friendliest. "Excuse me, gentlemen."

The men glared, impassive and unmoved. It was time for Kane to try out some of his limited Japanese skills.

"Su-mi-masen," he said. "On-e-gaishi-masu." Luckily, *excuse* me and *please* were among the words he had learned.

The younger one of the pair didn't flinch. The other, however, smirked in amusement a little, seemingly surprised the foreigner knew some Japanese. They still didn't move an inch. The first addressed his boss.

"Katashi-san. Perhaps this man was listening. Maybe he heard something."

Katashi Goto approached Kane. The ageing don smiled, but his hard eyes locked on Kane's. "You are American?" he asked calmly and in near perfect English.

"No, sir," Kane said. "I'm from England. Just visiting. If your men would let me pass, I'll be on my way. Have a nice day, chaps," he said and took only two steps before the big gorilla on the left of the pair put a firm palm on his chest. Kane thought he heard the man growl, though his lips hadn't moved.

Turning to look at the Yakuza boss, Kane remained calm as their eyes met. Both men fixed their smiles in place. Katashi held Kane's gaze. The mob boss stood perfectly still and unruffled, and evidently patient. Kane sensed just a hint of respect in the old man's eyes. He might have even been enjoying the moment.

After a beat, he spoke to his minions. "Let this man past, Taichi."

The man Kane now knew as Taichi's jowls clenched, then he inhaled, his face appearing as if he'd smelled something rotten. Finally, he nodded and relaxed his tense shoulders. Kane turned from Katashi Goto and stepped towards the thugs who, after a few seconds, moved aside, albeit with obvious reluctance. Kane had taken just a couple of strides when Katashi called after him, the smile gone and his tone laced with unmistakable authority.

"I do not want to see you here again. Understand? This is a private viewing of a family heirloom." Katashi stretched out his arm and pointed in the direction of the main exit, making clear the most important part of his instruction.

Kane did not reply. The translation was irrelevant. The tone mattered now. He stared back, willing himself to remain calm and fighting back his old, innate instincts as they began to swell. Picking a fight with four hardened mafia men was foolish to say the least. But Hiram Kane did not appreciate being told where he could and could not go, and those inbuilt tendencies threatened to lash out, even if he knew it would be a terrible idea.

He finally exhaled and swallowed down the urge to at least say something to Katashi. His own demons had risen, but this time he had managed to quell their rage. It wasn't always so.

The instruction to leave had at least proved to Kane something shady was going on here. These last moments had forced him to focus and had instilled in him further determination to do the right thing. But it would have to be the smart thing, too. As yet, he still wasn't sure what either of those things was.

He turned and brushed past the mafia goons with more than a trace of nonchalance in his step, ideas of hierarchy and blind respect left back with the exhibits in the Treasure Hall.

Chapter Twenty-Four

侍

"He is nothing," said Taichi, with obvious derision and his shoulders out. "That tiny man is completely harmless. Even if he did hear something, what could he possibly do?" Taichi huffed, but it came out more like a snort. His shoulders lowered a fraction.

Katashi nodded. "You are probably right," Katashi replied quietly. "But, young Taichi, my question is this: what might he have heard? What were you talking about that would matter if he heard it or not?"

"Well, Katashi-san, I... I was just saying to—"

"Shut up! You are not paid to talk." Katashi cut him off with undisguised scorn. His voice remained calm, but it exuded dangerous contempt. "I pay you for only two things. The first is to be big and ugly. The second is to act as my escort. That is all. A condition of the payment is that I expect you to say nothing, unless I ask you a direct question. That is all. Is that clear?"

Taichi nodded, the adrenaline surge reddening the skin

on his thick neck. He somehow managed to keep his mouth shut.

Yoshi caught Taichi's eye and smirked, as if to say *I told you so*. The younger man hung his head a little, both in shame and embarrassment at being chastised in front of the others. But inwardly, that emotion had shifted to something else very quickly. He was more than embarrassed. Now, Taichi was angry. He did not let it show. At least, he believed he hadn't. One day, he knew, they would all learn just how powerful he was.

"However, I think you are right," Katashi said quietly as he walked along the corridor in slow, measured steps, his men following closely behind. "He is most likely harmless. But... There was something about him... something in his eyes." He glanced back at Yosuke as he walked. "He did not seem afraid to me. Did he seem afraid to you?"

Yosuke shook his head. "No, Katashi-san. He did not."

"No... not afraid. I do not like it when people are not afraid of me." He stopped and turned to face his men, who stopped too. He looked all three in the eye and said, "Maybe it is time I got a new security detail. Men who people are afraid of." He held first Yoshi's gaze, then Yosuke's, challenging both. Taichi had noticed and was pleased not to be the one who was being condescended to. Yosuke simply nodded. Yoshi looked away. Katashi strode onward. "Keep your eyes on him."

Over Katashi's shoulder, Yosuke's dark eyes fixed on Yoshi's, apparently sending a silent message. Taichi frowned when he spotted it.

The Yakuza men left the shrine and stepped out into the miserable late afternoon. The dark clouds were swollen with the promise of imminent rain, and the wind gusted with a newfound tenacity. The thickness of the roiling clouds brought forth an early dusk, and the multitude of lamps fought to cast their ethereal glow around the village as the last scattering of tourists waited for their return ferry back to the mainland. Taichi knew they were the lucky ones. If any of them happened to be in the way tomorrow, he would have some points to prove to the arrogant pricks who continued to look down upon him.

Tomorrow, Taichi would show them who he really was.

Taichi and Yoshi returned to their respective hotel rooms. With Yosuke stationed outside his door, Katashi ruminated about tomorrow's long-awaited event.

He sat crossed legged on the tatami floor mat in the centre of his humble room. He could have afforded the most luxurious of suites on the island—probably in all Japan—but Katashi had changed. He retained his power, but his taste for the flamboyant had shifted, and it was tranquility he yearned for now. Peace and quiet.

And justice…

Katashi closed his eyes. Surrounded by a series of paper lanterns, and with jasmine incense permeating from small burners all around the room, he inhaled deeply through his nose. He held the breath in for a few seconds then exhaled slowly, stilling his thoughts and relaxing his body. Katashi felt content with his plan. It had been long in the making, and he knew everything else was ready. He had to make sure he was ready too, both emotionally and physically.

What he was about to do had been on his mind for a long time—many, many years. Timing was everything, and being this patient did not come naturally to a mafia boss more accustomed to getting what he wanted, whenever he wanted.

This was different. It had to be. This was special. He was about to retire from the Yakuza, so taking the samurai

The Samurai Code

suit—or stealing it, which is what the authorities would call it—would be much easier while he still had the power of the mafia behind him. The police could be controlled... he'd been controlling them in Kyoto for decades. The local superintendent was not averse to being persuaded, with benefits, that a non-violent crime could be overlooked. Technically, the suit itself was worth a lot of money, but to whom? Sitting behind a glass case being gawped at by tourists, it was effectively worth nothing. The only real victim would be the bookish history-lover who polished the glass case. In other words, a nobody.

However, retrieving the suit of armour was just one element of his plan. The other part, the element that caused his heart to race, was to be the main event. Nobody would be able to overlook it, and that was the whole point. Yet enough money, paid into the correct greasy palms, would still make it possible for the Japanese authorities to find a legal loophole and fail to prosecute. All legal systems have loopholes, Katashi knew well, if you just know where to look.

With everything in place, and with his men ready and willing to do whatever it took to succeed, Katashi's flagging patience would at last be rewarded. By nightfall tomorrow, the don would be back at his family mansion on the outskirts of the city of Kyoto. And once there, the samurai suit worn by his ancestor many centuries ago would at last be where it belonged, on display and taking pride of place in his home, and not rotting away in that dingy museum on that shit-hole island.

Yet, despite his imminent glory, something deeply troubled Katashi Goto and gnawed away at this calmness like a rat gnawing through a cable. Now, as he meditated, he understood what it was. Katashi was not a superstitious man. Throughout his life, instead of superstition, he'd always relied on his shrewd intelligence and astute instincts to guide him. The combination of both had rarely, if ever, let him down, and were in fact what had powered his rise to the pinnacle of the crime world. Since coming across the Englishman at the shrine today, however, an unusual niggle of apprehension had settled over him like a fog over Hiroshima Bay. He just could not seem to shake it off.

The mob boss couldn't exactly pinpoint what his concerns about the unknown man were. After all, he had three hardened, dedicated men of his own alongside him who would deal with the stranger at the mere nod of his head. Though tall and well built, the Englishman was no physical match for his thugs. They were, of course, also carrying guns. So what the hell was it?

There was just something about the stranger that bothered Katashi. He had appeared from out of nowhere, and at first glance he looked like any other stupid tourist. At least he wasn't Korean. But why hadn't he appeared more alarmed when faced with four huge, tough men? Not only was there no trace of fear on the man's face, but there was, if anything, a challenging look in his eyes. Why would a mere tourist think he could interfere with the plans? Surely he wasn't undercover police? Interpol? Katashi knew that was impossible. Only three other men alive knew of his plan. They were sworn to secrecy under pain of death, and he trusted them. Taichi was new to the detail, but he wasn't smart enough to have his own ideas. Yoshi and Yosuke had been with Katashi a decade and had never once stepped out of line. *No... it's something else...*

Katashi raised himself slowly to his knees, ignoring the tension in his ageing joints and stiff tendons. The rest of his body, though, remained as supple and strong as a man of thirty something. He knew he was a warrior. He knew samurai blood coursed through his veins. Katashi let his mind drift, transporting him onto a blood-soaked battlefield of the past, where man fought man in mortal combat, and where there was only ever one result.

Death.

Give a man a gun, he is just another hired killer. Train him as a samurai, and his skill transcends all else.

Katashi Goto was samurai, and he would have his victory.

The legend of the betrayal by Minamoto on his ancestor Takamochi Taira was well known in Japan. School children were told the story as a reminder about how to respect one another and how to respect their teachers and their elders. Despite the fact that the aura surrounding the samurai had been allowed to fade over recent decades, that was one story deliberately kept in the psyche of the population. The lesson was important, and it should not be forgotten. Katashi Goto was determined to make sure it remained that way.

Beyond the walls of his room and across the island, the storm continued to grow in power with every passing minute. Within the walls, it was matched only by the surge of power Katashi Goto felt in his heart. The time was coming.

His destiny was close.

Chapter Twenty-Five

侍

"What a wreck," Kane muttered. He winced as his grim reflection stared back at him from the mirror, his puffy eyes a reminder of what an awful night's sleep, or lack thereof, he'd endured.

Probably just early middle-age.

Another wry grin appeared, the rueful expression almost a permanent fixture since he'd arrived in Japan a couple of weeks earlier.

With some reluctance, he glanced back at the mirror. *Early old age? Jesus!*

Middle-age was something Kane hadn't given much thought to. He hadn't yet turned forty, though a life of sport and strenuous outdoor activities had put his body through an unusual amount of stresses and strains. Though his hair was thick and his hairline was still only a forehead—and not a *five-head* like a few of his old friends possessed—it was turning a little grey earlier than he'd like. Some people said it made him look distinguished, as if he were growing old gracefully. That always made him chuckle. Kane knew there was nothing graceful about him these days. He was gallivanting about the world, getting himself into unwanted scrapes and adding new scars to his impressive collection like stamps in his passport. Graceful was an exaggerated adjective at best. Disgraceful? That was looking more and more appropriate with every passing year as he crept towards the big 4-0. Sometimes, he wondered if he'd even make that modest milestone.

Punctuated by a combination of the wind's relentless rattling, stark dreams of the recent horrors in Hofu City and his absolute certainty the Yakuza were going to steal a priceless artefact from the museum, Kane reckoned he'd snagged three hours of fitful sleep at best.

He knew he would get over the events of Hofu. Kane would always feel for those who'd died and the pain felt by their loved ones, and he felt great empathy for all the people displaced by the horrendous storm. And yet, it didn't affect him directly, and he would eventually put it behind him. That's just what he did, what he had to do. With all that had happened in the last few years, he'd have gone mad if he couldn't.

As for the storm? Well, that was just nature at her best, and at her very worst. He took one last look at the unfortunate creature looking back at him without sympathy from the mirror, offered a weak salute, and went out into the living area. Grabbing his coffee from the table, he moved over to the window and pulled open the curtains. Black clouds skudded west to east across the bay below. Rain fell in drifting swathes and thrummed on his roof, leaving rippling pools on the small terrace before him and all along the path that led around the detached ryokans of the hotel. He sighed. It could be worse, he knew that, and although the weather had deteriorated significantly over the last twenty-four hours, it was still far from dangerous.

The weather he could manage.

It was the imminent theft and the dangerous Yakuza men that had really ruined his sleep.

The problem was trying to figure out what on earth he could do about it. Thinking it was none of his business was no longer an option. Not to a man like Hiram Kane. For two decades, he had been an aficionado of art and history. It was his grandfather Hiram Snr who had first introduced the young and wide-eyed Hiram to the wonders of the world, and it was he who had taken him on his first adventure, all the way to Peru, when he was a teenager. Ever since that maiden trip to the Andes, during which he was shown art and architecture, and even examples of how the Incas had created art within the very landscape in which they lived and worked, he'd held a great respect and fascination for what humans were capable of creating. "The artistic mind knows no bounds or borders; it is free and brings freedom." That's what his grandfather used to tell him, and Kane knew it was true.

The magnificent suit of samurai armour that the mobster Katashi Goto was intent on stealing, and which was listed as a Japanese National Treasure, was another such item. If he turned his back and did nothing, Kane knew he would feel in some way complicit. But it was more than that. Kane had always abhorred injustices of any kind. Whether it was bullies in school, sexist bosses, racial aggravation—any situation where one individual or group abused their power over another—Kane felt compelled to fight back. He always took the side of the underdog, always. And in this case, the underdog appeared to be Nori Nakamura.

On the other hand, it was a dangerous game to go

against a gang of organised criminals. Especially those with such a notorious reputation for violence as the Yakuza. Kane also knew it wasn't just as simple as informing Nakamura and the authorities. He almost laughed. *What authorities?* He hadn't seen any on the island. He didn't want to call Naki and worry him. He also didn't want to trouble Mika with knowledge he couldn't be entirely certain about.

Who would believe me anyway?

Kane smiled when he thought of the reaction he might get. He would probably be arrested for ranting about premonitions of the future.

- *Excuse me, officer?*

- *Yes. And you are?*

- *Well, you don't know me because I am no one important.*

- *A tourist?*

- *Yes, I am. Anyway, I wanted to let you know that the Yakuza are going to steal a priceless samurai suit.*

- *And the Yakuza told you this?*

- *No. I saw them looking at it.*

His smile soon faded.

Reporting a future crime was out of the question, but he had no idea what he *could* do. He decided to stop thinking and act instead.

He snatched up the hotel phone and dialled reception.

"Yes, hello. Could you please put me through to the Miyajima Tourist Office? Thank you."

He waited for a few moments before the receptionist said, "Your call is connected."

"This is the Miyajima Tourist Office. How may I help you?"

"Ah, yes, hello. I would like to speak with Nori Nakamura. I am sure you know is the curator at the Itsukushima museum. Is he available?"

"Sir, I am sorry to inform you the curator will not be arriving back until later. The storm has disrupted his travel plans."

"Ah, okay. Then, may I have his mobile phone number? It is very important."

"So sorry, sir. Mr. Nakamura does not have a mobile phone."

Shit!

Kane considered telling the tourist office lady what he believed might be happening, but thought better of it. On a whim, he asked for the number of the local police station. At least he could retain the option.

"Is everything okay, sir?"

"Yes… Sorry, I mean, yes, everything's fine, thank you."

"If you are sure?"

"I am sure."

"Okay then, sir, I will connect you now."

"Wait! I just wanted the number, not…"

Kane waited as the phone rang for a full minute, during which time his mind raced through newspaper articles he had read about Japanese police. They apparently had a worrying third-world element to their policing, including extracting forced confessions. Corruption and bribery couldn't be ruled out. He cut the call. "Well, this is great," he muttered. "Me against the mob."

Then, he had an idea…

Chapter Twenty-Six

侍

The rain fell in cold torrents, though it didn't fall vertically. It assaulted them horizontally, like a swathe of samurai arrows, such was the strength of the wind. Taichi and Yoshi huddled under a tree, caught in the deluge while walking through the village.

"Great," Taichi said. "Just great."

"Why are you always moaning? You sound like a little girl. Is that what you are, Gorilla, a little girl?" There was no humour in Yoshi's words, only disdain.

Taichi flinched at the insult, but again, he knew it was best to bide his time. "I just don't know why we have to wait," he growled. "We could just go right in there, grab that dusty fucking suit and get out of this shit hole. Who can stop us? Katashi-san and the Yakuza control almost all of Yamaguchi Prefecture. Fuck, they even own half the police force. There is nothing to worry about."

"You are as stupid as you look. Do you not understand anything? It is not only a question of stealing the suit. The samurai were respectful, dignified people." He paused, and

Taichi knew the man was studying his reaction. He did not offer one, so Yoshi continued. "Katashi-san is samurai. The man has honour." Yoshi paused again, eyes as hard as flint. "Something you know little about."

Taichi turned to Yoshi, ready to show him who the man among them really was. *Honour? Of what real value does honour have?* Taichi mused.

He was younger than Yoshi, but nevertheless he knew power was the only important currency in the Yakuza. He didn't feel much like being reverent right now, and he opened his mouth to speak about how honour among men was dead. However, just at that moment, he thought he spotted the Englishman away in the distance. He blinked, wiping the rain from his eyes. Now, he saw nothing, no sign of the bastard, so he chose to keep it to himself. He didn't want to be labelled a nervous coward. In fact, he decided to say nothing more to Yoshi. He had come to understand that Yoshi and Yosuke were tighter with Katashi than he was— perhaps tighter than he'd ever be. This prick would probably report his insolence to the boss.

Kiss arse... I will deal with you later, he mused, and watched on with what was at first surprise and then renewed interest as the Englishman trotted past their position without so much as glancing his way.

Kane left the hotel and angled through the village, for once using the horrific weather to his advantage, and he wasn't surprised to learn he was the only person daft enough to venture out in what was now a maelstrom of swirling, driving rain. Hunkered deep into his jacket, Kane moved at a steady trot as he angled straight for the Itsukushima Shrine. As he ran, he kept trying to convince himself it was a good idea.

He asked himself again whether a single historical artefact was worth risking his life for. Yet he also knew there was more to it than that. He supposed it was because of his admiration for Naki and his family, and the bravery and selflessness the man had demonstrated when faced with such inherent danger at the river. Kane guessed Naki's father, Nori, must have been cut from the same cloth a generation earlier. Likewise, his grown children, Daijiro and Mika. Good people. Good, honest people who deserved for someone to stand up for them, just as Naki had stood up for the storm victims at the river.

Kane had formulated a simple plan in his mind, though it hardly filled him with confidence. At best, it was crap. At worst? Well, it was probably a suicide mission, and he knew it. He had an ill-defined notion of somehow concealing himself in the shadows of the Armour Room, somewhere he could at least record the theft on his mobile phone camera. He would later show the incriminating evidence against Katashi to the authorities—perhaps even go international with the story and involve the wider media if the Japanese police couldn't be trusted. That was, if he ever made it out of there again.

Kane believed that with such priceless and important cultural artefacts on display at the museum, there had to be a security system in place throughout the building. He figured Katashi and his men would have already considered that too, and that they had possibly disabled it already, around the time he had first spotted them near the suit of armour.

With no obvious alternative, and no sign of any authority to turn to, Kane accepted that he was probably on his own. Being alone was something he usually enjoyed. Not today.

Ten minutes later, after hustling in and out of the trees

and dodging between stalls at the abandoned market, Kane arrived, dripping wet, at the ethereal shrine. Its ambient lighting had served as a beacon in the bleak afternoon, luring him inside. Feeling confident he hadn't been seen by anyone, certainly not any Yakuza men, he entered the shrine. He stopped in his tracks and raised an eyebrow when he saw the ticket office was open. And there was Mika. He hadn't expected to see her again that day.

Damn it! What should I do? Should I warn her?

Kane was torn. Warning her against something he had no real proof of was risky. She would probably close up the museum. That would potentially force the Yakuza to apply more aggressive tactics and put Mika and any unlucky tourists in added danger. He was certain the mafia men would not be denied in their mission—not at any cost.

Kane bought himself a moment to think by rummaging in his bag while contemplating his choices. There were only two options as he saw it. Tell Mika what he believed to be true; that the Yakuza were planning to steal the samurai suit. In turn, this would risk their wrath when they turned up at a potentially locked down museum. Or, he could say nothing, act normally and hope to record it on video and present the evidence to the relevant people later? Neither option filled Kane with anything resembling confidence.

There appeared to be zero tourists anywhere to be seen. Kane figured, much to his chagrin, that it was probably safer to sit back and let the theft go ahead unhindered. With any luck, the mafia men would be in and out of the shrine in minutes, and no one would get hurt. The professionals could then set about retrieving the artefact with due process.

Mika smiled widely as he approached, her positivity still evident despite the distinct lack of tourists and shrine-goes there today.

"I thought you would have closed the place up," he said, returning her smile, then motioning with his head back outside. "The storm would have been a good excuse!"

"Why would I need an excuse?" Mika asked. "I don't want to close the museum!"

"But there are no tourists today, and it's not likely any will come later, not in this shi— in this weather."

Mika chuckled. "Yes, it's shitty weather. Look, I like to be close to the shrine. It's like... it's kind of part of our family."

Kane thought he understood the reasons, but the reality was, no tourists were going to show up any time soon. At least he'd tried to get Mika away from there. "Okay, but do me a favour, would you? Could you stay here in reception for a while until I come back? If the storm hits hard, I might need your help!"

"Sure. I'm not going anywhere."

"Okay, *arigatō*, Mika," Kane said as he paid his entry fee.

Kane sensed a questioning in Mika's eyes, as if she were wondering why he was back at the shrine museum again so soon. She was aware he wanted to meet her grandfather, who wasn't due back until later in the day at the earliest. Yet she didn't say anything and accepted his money with another smile. With a quick scan of the area around the entrance, Kane felt certain no one else was coming. He said goodbye, and entered the Itsukushima Shrine once again, taking time to carefully wipe his shoes on the thick doormat.

It was eerily dark inside, despite the proliferation of traditional lanterns that cast flickering shadows about the ornate carvings and the complex architecture. Other than the dull drumming of the rain, he had entered a sanctuary of near silence, the only sounds the ghostly echoes of an abandoned building and the Shinto spirits of a distant past.

Chapter Twenty-Seven
侍

What am I actually doing here? he questioned as he stalked along the empty corridors. *What the hell sort of ego would make me do this?*

Kane walked on anyway, determined to at least get to the Armour Room. If there was any realistic place to hide and film the event without getting caught, he wanted to find it. With each step deeper into the complex, he became more edgy. He felt sure of one thing: if the Yakuza men did discover him, there would be only one outcome for him here today; his inglorious death. With no one around to witness what was going on deep inside the shrine, they would extinguish his life and deal with his body as efficiently as they had no doubt dealt with others throughout their glittering mafia careers.

Kane's pounding heart was like heavy knocking at a door, as if someone was trying to warn him of danger. He reached the now familiar doors to the museum's central hall, the exact place where he'd been warned directly by Katashi Goto to stay away from. And yet, here he was, cold, wet and probably about to put his life in grave danger. *Not for the first time*, he mused inwardly.

Leave now… take the sensible choice for once, he thought briefly. *Go while there's still time.*

Then he remembered the self-assured look on Katashi's face as he gave out his instructions to stay away. The man was clearly used to being obeyed.

It's good for people to experience new things once in a while, Kane thought. He almost smiled.

A minute later, he slipped into the Armour Room. Once inside, he soon realised it was more of a grand hall than just a mere side room. He quickly scanned the walls and exhibits for somewhere he could stay concealed with some semblance of confidence. There were no security cameras, at least none he could see. He knew that Japan on the whole was a nation of respectful people, with Confucianism deeply entrenched in their collective and cultural psyches. He figured the result of that was low crime levels, especially compared with so-called Western nations. Thus, the need for heavy security here was little or none.

But the Yakuza? They were an exception. It wouldn't have mattered what kind of security was installed at the Itsukushima Shrine museum. The mafia did whatever the hell they wanted to do, consequences be damned.

Allowing all of his senses to guide him, Kane moved swiftly towards the far end of the gallery, cringing as every footstep echoed throughout the hall. He stopped suddenly when his eyes settled on the samurai suit. Now he could see it clearly for the first time, and he was stunned by its commanding presence. It wasn't 'seeing', really. It was witnessing. Experiencing.

The ancient suit of armour truly was a thing of beauty.

It was a tool of war, and yet if war could be won by art or creativity, it surely would have seen many victories.

Power and history oozed from every finely crafted detail. Stepping closer to it now, Kane could easily imagine how intimidated an enemy would feel if confronted by such a sight. He felt daunted himself by the inanimate object, yet he looked upon it with admiration.

Protecting the warrior's head was an impressive multi-plated *kabuto*—the helmet—complete with a wide neck guard known as a *shikoro*, at least according to Kane's quick glance at the information plaque at the feet of the exhibit. Kane presumed its large turned-back wings were as much a decorative feature as they were functional. Completing the headwear was the gruesome *mempo*—the mask. Embellished with a fearsome expression, the mix of bronze, gold and leather combined to forge refined beauty from what was its necessary strength.

Beneath that was the *dõ*—the armour. It wrapped around the body from back to front and was intricate yet clearly sturdy, as were the wooden and leather-covered guards that shielded the arms from the lethal swing of deadly swords. Below the waist hung the *haidate*, an armoured smock that protected the thighs. Kane cracked a childish and untimely grin as he considered the other important anatomical parts it might save.

Each section of the incredible armour was fabricated from varying sized plates of iron or wood. They were arranged in overlapping horizontal rows—much like the scales of an armadillo—and the entire suit was woven together with a combination of what looked to Kane like fine silk and thick threads of some kind of hemp-like material.

Despite its graceful beauty, in totality it comprised a

hefty object, and with some admiration Kane knew it would take a strong man to wear it. Appraising it, however, he doubted it could withstand a bullet from a modern-day gun. However, when facing the arrows and swords of the distant past, it appeared to be almost impenetrable. Momentarily distracted, Kane imagined the magnificent figure before him wielding a lethal sword, the flickering lamplight all around animating the suit and twisting the grisly features of the mask into a fearsome gargoyle. In battle it would have been a frightening proposition.

The armour was a masterpiece. Kane wasn't surprised at all why Katashi might want it for his private collection. Of course, something so old and of such exceptional quality was no doubt priceless to the right collector, which could only have added to its allure.

Before this latest visit to Japan, Kane had re-watched *The Last Samurai*, a movie he knew to be very loosely based upon Clavell's classic book, *Shogun*. He'd admired the superbly choreographed fight scenes in the film, but until seeing that movie, Kane would never have believed such violence could be graceful. And yet, grace was indeed evident in the balance, discipline and poise of the warriors. It was the same grace he'd seen and admired in the oil painting yesterday. Standing now in front of a suit of armour, he found it easy to envisage those scenes in real life; fearless soldiers in battle, the clashing of swords, the stench of blood and the horrific screams of the fallen. And death. The glorious deaths befitting all great warriors known as samurai. The past suddenly did not seem so distant, and his situation was certainly no movie.

A sudden sound shook him. He froze, instantly alert. Kane strained to hear but heard nothing beyond the eerie whining of wind rushing through the empty, deserted corridors. His imagination threatened to get the better of him, but he forced himself to remain calm. He turned to scan the darkened hall for any movement in the shadows. Nothing. Not even a hint of anyone nearby.

Then, tightening his face into a grimace, Kane saw a patch of wet footprints he'd left, the moisture having made its way down from his sodden clothing and onto the footwear he thought he had dried. He almost wanted to laugh at the challenges nature kept throwing at him.

Almost.

Then he heard their voices.

Chapter Twenty-Eight

侍

Twenty Years Ago

Katashi Goto stood at the floor-to-ceiling window of his lake view apartment, a glass of 30-year-old Hibiki whiskey in his hand, as yet untouched. Far to the east, Kyoto's neon heartbeat glowed through the rain-blurred skies. He slid a finger down the scar that ran from his left ear to his jaw—Hana's farewell gift from that night a little over twenty years ago.

Beautiful, lethal Hana. He could still see her face in perfect detail: dark eyes that could make a man quiver with excitement or quake with fear, the gentle curve of her elegant neck. The way her breast rose and fell as she breathed... It wasn't just her beauty. Katashi had witnessed her speed up close and personal when her hand drew a blade; the movement was like liquid lightning. He'd witnessed the same result on others, and was always impressed. Truly, it was such a waste. Then again, that was the nature of power... you either had it or you didn't, and though Hana had plenty, Katashi had more, and used it to remove the threat of hers forever. It had been swift and decisive. Yet, Hana had left her mark... a good reminder to Katashi to stay on his toes and ahead of the game.

He finally took a sip, savoring the aromatic sweetness as the ice clinked in the glass. He felt the same way he had that night two decades ago—electricity zinged in the air with the promise of violence ahead. He could almost taste it. He was in his twenties then, hungry and ambitious... a dangerous combination. Hunger and ambition could be costly, Katashi knew that. Hana was the perfect example... except her greed and impatience had tricked her into backing the wrong horse.

Before he had dealt with Hana, they had visited their boss Daiki together.

Daiki had looked up from his desk with weary eyes. "Our world is changing," he had said in a tired voice. "We must change with it." The old don was right; change was inevitable and required. He was only wrong about the direction it would take. Daiki spoke of legitimacy, realigning their business ventures onto the right side of the law, into corporate boardrooms... more or less going straight, or as straight as the mob world allowed. In Katashi's eyes this was a terrible mistake he had seen coming for years. The real future would look different; digital corruption, the dark web, cryptocurrency... new technologies in bed with the old mafia ways.

Hana had understood that, as Katashi had. It is exactly what had made her so dangerous. She had stood alongside Katashi in Daiki's office, her mind as sharp as her designer dress. He sighed... such a waste. Yet, that was twenty years ago... she wouldn't be so beautiful now... her mind not as sharp.

Then again… nor is mine. Katashi smiled, flexing his fingers, recalling the weight of the knife and the way she'd struggled against him, her shapely arse pushing back against him… She hadn't gone quietly… somehow managing to extract her own knife from somewhere on her person and slicing his face before she succumbed. He could so easily have lost an eye. It would have been fair enough.

He hadn't enjoyed it. At least, he told himself that. Hana had been more than worthy of his respect. He had killed her himself as a sign of that respect. The sounds of that night stayed with him; the surprise in Hana's breaths as she struggled. The whisper of the blade as he wiped it on her dress. The sound of her body parts crashing through the foliage as he dumped them into the gorge… No, he hadn't enjoyed it. Not really.

Yet Katashi knew power wasn't about enjoyment. It was about necessity.

Just like it was now.

He knew he had to stay focused. He knew he could show no signs of weakness, or of slowing down. Just as he had watched for it with Daiki decades earlier, the young pups were watching for it, waiting for those little signs of fragility; like sharks scenting blood in the ocean.

He noticed conversations occasionally faltered when he entered a room. A slight hint of a delay when following his orders. His favourite was hearing the whispers about modernisation, exactly as he had whispered it with Hana when Daiki wasn't around all those years back. *Everything changes, and yet everything is the same*, he mused.

He understood the game perfectly. He noticed the hungry eyes of two of his most trusted lieutenants; the cousins, Yosuke and Yoshi. One day he was certain they would challenge him for his throne. It was the way of it, and he didn't blame them. Yet he knew the game, and even if they knew it too, Katashi knew it better. *I am their master now. I will be their master in ten years… twenty. Until they kill me!*

He set down the now empty glass and returned to his desk, pressing his palm against the single folder that sat there. Inside, he knew, was his master plan, written by his own hand on old-fashioned paper; some things should never leave a digital trail. Two decades of preparation, of plotting, of careful manipulation. It was a game of chess, yet Katashi moved his pieces so smoothly and with such delicate precision, only he could understand them.

The young ones probably though of him as past it, as he had with Daiki. He was a little younger than his old boss was then… not yet fifty. They were mid-twenties. But they would underestimate him, of that he was sure. They likely had ambitions to take his throne and probably his life within the next couple of years. The difference was, Katashi expected it. He didn't possess the same ego Daiki had, who had realised what was coming all too late.

That moment was coming. A coup. An attempt to usurp him. Katashi could feel it. Yet it mattered little. He was ready, and he would show Yosuke and Yoshi how to lead… and if they ddn't fall in line and play their roles, it would be their blood on his expensive carpets before their bodies underwent the same dismantling as Hana's had years before.

Katashi poured himself another glass of whiskey and he welcomed the burn of it on his throat as he went back to the huge window and wished for only three things… that the icy rain would cease, that winter would finally pass and that the next two decades would pass much like the last two… with Katashi the master of his ever-expanding domain.

Chapter Twenty-Nine

侍

Present Day

For a few brief moments the rain eased up long enough so Taichi and Yoshi could continue their journey to the shrine without getting drenched. Taichi still moaned.

"Fucking cold and fucking wet," he mumbled as they hustled up the wooden steps and ducked into the entrance, arriving at the shrine's ticket office, where the girl behind the counter watched them intently. Taichi tried his best to disguise the fact that hardened mafia men could shiver with cold. Members of the Yakuza never paid for tickets—most people were simply too intimidated to ask. Nevertheless, the girl remained calm and gamely asked each man for their five hundred yen entry fee. Taichi merely smirked, although he was impressed she didn't cower at their arrival. It was obvious they weren't regular tourists. Neither man spoke as they ignored her and walked right past into the labyrinth of darkened corridors towards the Armour Room.

As they got closer, they diligently scanned the route for

anything that might cause problems. In other words, anything that could piss off their boss. Neither man saw any potential trouble. Despite Katashi's uncharacteristic concerns about the Englishman, the thugs were not at all worried. If that dumb tourist had any sense about him, he would be long gone from the island by now. As it was, there was no sign of him, nor anyone else for that matter. By the time they got to the Armour Room, both men felt confident that everything was all set and ready to go, and that there would be no further distractions.

It was a straightforward plan. Taichi and Yoshi were to secure the entrances to the central hall. One of them would be stationed at either end. Unlike yesterday, when they had allowed the group of noisy Koreans and a handful of other tourists into the room, no one was permitted to enter, under any circumstances. It mattered little. There was nobody around. They both believed that, by now, the remaining tourists would be shacked up in their hotel rooms. Better still, the sensible ones would have already left for the mainland. Either way, they did not expect to be called into action.

Later, once the area had been secured, Yosuke would accompany Katashi to the Armour Room… and the samurai suit. Then, the three-strong security team would stand guard while the Yakuza boss went through his ritual. They thought it was arduous. Though they would never admit, even to each other, and even though for the most part they respected their country's samurai traditions, all of them thought it was stupid. But he was their boss, and if you no longer respected the boss's wishes, you either had a death wish or a strong dislike of your appendages. It was that simple. As was the plan.

Finally, once the ritual was completed, they would escort

their boss to the shrine's dock, and once there they would board his waiting helicopter and be flown from Miyajima to his home on the outskirts of Kyoto. If anybody interfered with any single part of their plan, whether they meant to or not, that person was to be eliminated, with no questions asked.

The citizens of Japan, at least those who operated on the right side of the law, knew very well not to get in the way of Yakuza business. If any were stupid enough to do such a thing, then whatever fate they had coming was entirely their own fault. Sensitivity was not a common or respected trait among Yakuza members. And, although most were traditional men who lived by a strict code, compassion was not to be found anywhere in the rule book. Death would come swiftly to anyone that stood in their way, and their body would disappear like blood down a drain.

Mika watched as the two thugs disappeared down the corridor. She knew better than to protest about the non-paid entry fees. That was irrelevant now. This wasn't about the job anymore. It was about their family history. About culture and tradition. About upholding the Nakamura legacy and safeguarding the samurai suit and their secret. Keeping those things safe had cost Mika's mother her life. She wondered now if it would cost her own.

Her thoughts turned to Hiram Kane. He was already in the shrine... the only other person other than the thugs. She had thought there was something a little different about him the first time they'd met, and hadn't changed her mind when she'd seen him here at the shrine yesterday. But what was it?

Does he know about those mafia guys? Was he somehow using

the Nakamura family for his own agendas? That didn't seem at all likely, not considering what she knew of his history and his heroic actions at the river in Hofu. So what the hell was it? One thing was certain; he seemed as if he could handle himself if it came to any trouble. Was he deliberately putting himself in harm's way in order to help Mika and her family out?

What the hell should I do?

Chapter Thirty

侍

In his hotel room, Katashi Goto waited to hear from his lieutenant, Yoshi. Patience was not among the don's strongest virtues—though he knew that in his new life he would have to improve in that area. But he was starting to feel a little agitated because Yoshi should have called Yosuke ten minutes ago. He had meditated long enough. Now, the mob boss paced around the room like a caged wolf, his fists clenching and unclenching, his small, bare feet treading the wooden boards in short, almost silent strides.

Finally, Yosuke's mobile phone rang. He snatched it up before the second ring and listened for several seconds before nodding and looking towards his boss.

"Katashi-san," he said. "It is the pilot."

Katashi glanced at Yosuke. He had expected Yoshi and did not want to hear from the pilot. He took the phone wordlessly from Yosuke and stared at it in his hands for a few seconds. Finally he spoke. "*Hai?*"

"Katashi-san, the storm is so bad, and it is getting worse every hour. So sorry, but I cannot land on Miyajima."

Katashi did not speak for several beats. The pilot's nervous throat clearing and short breaths could be heard down the line.

"Katashi-san?" the pilot said. "Are you still there?"

"I am here, Kuru," the mafia don answered quietly before he fell silent again.

"Katashi-san?"

Another few beats, then he said, "Your son... his name is Kai, is it not?"

"What? Yes, it is... Why?"

"And your daughter... is her name Komaki? Pretty little Komaki?"

"Yes... why are you talking about my children?"

"And your wife, Himari. Is she not pregnant with your third child. Kuru?"

"Katashi-san, please. The weather... it is too dangerous. I cannot—"

"Do not say those words to me, Kuru. Do not."

"The winds are so strong. I just cannot land on the jetty as planned. I might... Maybe tomorrow it will be better."

Katashi's voice remained calm and quiet. "Kuru, do you remember the new apartment complex I am building in Kyoto? Not far from your home, if I recall correctly? Tomorrow, we will begin pouring the concrete for the foundations..."

"Please Katashi-san. Please do not—"

"If you do not arrive here at the jetty at the exact time I have told you, then that concrete will be strengthened by the flesh and bones of your wife and your children. Is that clear?"

On the other end of the line, Katashi heard only silence. He continued: "Then I am pleased. I will see you at the time we have arranged. I know you will not let me down."

The Samurai Code

Katashi ended the call and took a deep breath, handing the phone to Yosuke, who grinned. Katashi did not. He knew Kuru would be there.

Kuru stared at the mobile phone long after Katashi Goto had disconnected. He found his body tensing, and his throat was suddenly dry. Landing the small helicopter in those conditions was almost suicide. He knew that. However, not going there to try would bear consequences he could not even comprehend. Kuru knew Katashi Goto did not make idle threats. He knew the don would uphold his promise, and as Kuru thought of his pregnant wife and two children being thrown alive into the foundations of his boss's new construction project, heavy tears streamed down his burning cheeks.

Yosuke's phone rang again five minutes later. Again, Yosuke listened silently for several seconds, then finally, and with a quick nod towards the don, he said the words Katashi had been waiting to hear for far too long.

"Katashi-san," he said with quiet respect. "It is time."

The notorious boss of the Yamaguchi Yakuza crime syndicate nodded in return. After a couple of deep breaths, he walked slowly across the room to the tall mirror, stopping in front of it. He stood tall, pulling his shoulders back a little and straightening his back. The don closed his eyes, then rose to his full height, even extending onto his toes. Finally, he settled onto the soles of his feet. Another series of deep breaths followed. Only then did he appraise his reflection.

This was it. This was the moment he had been anticipating, the moment in which he would claim back what rightly belonged to his family but had been denied them for generations stretching back centuries. Katashi knew if his more recent forebears had been blessed with any balls, he would not need to do this today. Yet, they had been cowards, all of them. Thus, it had fallen to him to right those wrongs. He was the first in too many weak, failed generations to have amounted to anything. Not just anything. *I am everything!* Finally, one among them would put things right.

Not just anything. Looking himself over for the final time, Katashi saw staring back at him a feared and revered member of his country's most powerful criminal gang.

He was a Yakuza boss. That came with rewards. Today, he would claim his biggest.

Katashi knew that this was to be his last act as an active boss of the Yakuza. In just a few short weeks, he would remove himself from this way of life and begin his training as a Buddhist priest. His long life in the mafia had been a calling, something he could no more resist than the sight of a beautiful woman to a young man. But destiny only called upon some such men. From a young age, Katashi knew his calling had been the Yakuza. Through a potent mix of intelligence, ambition, courage and ruthlessness, he had battled his way from the very bottom rung of the Japanese mafia ladder all the way to its pinnacle. Almost.

Bad luck and a series of sloppy actions had seen the path to the very top blocked. It had angered him for many years. And yet, he was content, and he had enjoyed the many spoils that this unique life had given him.

Katashi knew that if the mafia had been a calling to his younger self, so was becoming a priest to his older self. It was a decision few people who knew him could understand. Equally, it was something none of them would ever question. He had earned his peaceful retirement, and if he wanted to spend it locked away in some dull old monastery, with no saké, no fighting... no women... then that was the don's choice.

Few mafia men would make that same choice, nor even consider it. But each man followed his own calling, and Katashi Goto would soon follow his.

Besides, destiny didn't allow for choices. Everything was in place. All was ordained.

His time had come.

Katashi looked into his own grey eyes in the mirror, his gaze unwavering. He nodded, and then turning to make sure Yosuke could hear, he stated:

"Nothing can stop me now."

Chapter Thirty-One

侍

Kane wasn't a man used to the feeling of panic. It was a new and uncomfortable sensation.

And yet, with no time to exit the treasure hall in either direction, he had to think on his feet. He hustled back towards the impressive samurai suit… and skidded on the wet floor, crashing to his knees just in front of the display. His chin also hit the unforgiving surface and for a moment he saw stars. "Mother fu—" he muttered, cutting himself short and gathering his wits.

Dammit!

He inhaled, silently cursed his stupidity. What Kane saw from that lower viewpoint, however, provided him with a glimmer of hope.

The weighty suit or armour, held upright by a cleverly hidden, almost invisible mannequin, was actually situated upon a raised stage, similar to an Egyptian dais. Set into the front of that stage was an air vent, perhaps a foot long and six inches high. On a hunch, Kane scrambled to his feet and hustled around to the back of the display, where he found that edge of the platform open for access. He nodded and inhaled, realising with satisfaction that the open side of the dais afforded him just enough room to crawl beneath. He glanced back over the top of the dais, his eyes settling for a few seconds on the back side of the samurai suit, glimmering under the display lights.

Just as impressive from behind, he thought. *Nice arse.*

It was a critical moment, and Kane was torn over what to do. Hide under the stage, potentially becoming trapped, and at risk of discovery by the Yakuza men? Or try to leave his phone behind, positioned and set to pick up some kind of recording?

He glanced beneath the stage again at the air vent. The spaces between each of the metal slats of the vent were wide enough that he could squeeze himself in and position his phone and record the events through one of those gaps. Kane closed his eyes for a few seconds, then made his decision. He would slide in beneath the stage, start the phone's video and, at the first possible chance, he would get the hell out of there.

He checked his phone was on silent. It was still fully charged, which meant in theory it could record a couple of hours' video before its battery died. With such damning video evidence, visual proof he could later show the police, Katashi Goto would surely be brought to justice. There was a risk the recording would for some reason not be completed if he left the phone alone, but the plan also gave Kane the opportunity to be closer to Mika in case she was somehow drawn into the situation. Human life came first. Including his own.

He was about to check the front of the stage one more time when the combination of voices and footsteps just beyond the entrance froze him in his tracks. "Bollocks!" he muttered. He threw himself beneath the stage just as two of the thugs strode with purpose into the room.

Kane crawled what he hoped was in near silence on his belly towards the front of the stage. In the darkness, however, he misjudged the height and banged his head hard against the wood. He gritted his teeth, cursing inwardly as he peered through the small grate. The mafia goon he knew as Yoshi had paused, as if he'd heard something—like a hunter on a game trail. Then Yoshi shook his head, and Kane hoped the man was dismissing the sound as one of the many bangs and creaks in the building caused by its age and the wind. Kane was sure he couldn't be seen, but the inevitable anxiousness caused him to hold his breath. *Is this what panic feels like?* After a few seconds, the first huge goon advanced into the room, followed by his brutish companion.

Kane watched as their dark eyes scanned the shadowy exhibits for anything untoward. They moved from object to object, looking behind display cases and around statues holding weapons, moving into the corners, and apparently searching for anything that looked out of place. Once they appeared to be satisfied after a full sweep of the room, they came together in front of the stage.

One pulled out his mobile phone and made a call. A few seconds later, he stated, "All clear." He slid his phone away and took another step closer to the dais, as did the other guy. Kane held his breath as their heads and bodies moved out of view but their expensive yet dirty black shoes came to rest just two feet from his face.

Chapter Thirty-Two

侍

"I admit it, it is a beautiful thing close up," Taichi grumbled, admiring the samurai armour.

Yoshi ignored him. He had spotted water on the floor. He stared at it for many seconds. Something wasn't right. He squatted down to analyse the footprints.

Taichi continued, oblivious. "You know, if I had lived in an earlier time period, there is no doubt I would have been a samurai warrior—deadly with a sword and a legend of the day." He looked down coldly at Yoshi. "People would have feared me."

If it was a veiled threat, it was wasted. Yoshi actually looked up and smiled. Not because he agreed with the *aho*— the idiot—but because the very idea that Taichi would have been samurai was genuinely funny. That son-of-a-hog had learned nothing of honour and weaponry, and Yoshi knew Taichi would not last more than five seconds in a fight with him. Despite Taichi's superior size, man-to-man Yoshi knew he could take the guy down with embarrassing ease. It was all about patience, timing and intuition, and these were skills Yoshi had in abundance. That lump, Taichi, Yoshi knew, possessed none of them.

Smiling to himself, Yoshi forgot about the watery footsteps and stood up, glaring at Taichi. Then he turned and set about doing a second sweep of the room. Taichi followed suit, and Yoshi heard him still rambling on about how he was a more worthy samurai than their boss, Katashi.

For the next ten minutes, they covered every square inch of the entire Armour Room. Then they did it a third time. They searched everywhere. That is, except one place.

Kane lay there silently, unable to believe his luck that they had failed to realise there were any gaps in and around the stage he was jammed beneath. For him to have found it, it had taken a fortuitous slip, for which Kane thanked his occasional clumsiness. One of the men had stopped and listened one more time, but it seemed to Kane that all the thug could hear was the rain.

Right now, however, Kane did not feel fortuitous. The stage's low wooden structure was squeezing him like a clamp, though he was distracted from his discomfort when he heard one of the men make another call. He was on the phone for mere seconds, and though Kane didn't understand exactly what was said, he sensed it spelled bad news for him. Yakuza boss Katashi Goto was probably on his way to the Armour Room right now, which meant the henchmen would not be leaving anytime soon.

His fears were proven right as the call ended and he watched the two men move off in different directions and take up their positions, one at each exit. He knew there would be no escaping now. All he could do was wait it out in silence and hope no one spotted him.

He hated to admit it, but the fact was Kane had no control over his situation. He didn't subscribe to luck, fate, or whatever the hell people called it these days. To Kane, organised religion had perished a century and a half earlier, when the likes of Darwin and Wallace had forever put a spanner in the perceived workings of God. However, in his mind he offered a silent petition to whatever Shinto or Buddhist deity protected people within the Itsukushima Shrine. Even in his dire predicament, Kane felt foolish for even contemplating what essentially amounted to a kind of prayer. Yet, right then, he needed some external assistance, from someone, or something... anything... or he might never leave the island alive.

Kane still believed that even if for some reason the men looked directly at the stage, they wouldn't be able to see him. But what if he coughed? Or sneezed? He glanced at the floor inches beneath his nose and grimaced. It looked as if it hadn't been swept in years, and a dusty sneeze was not only possible, but likely.

Any sound from him and the game would be up. There was no doubt. They would drag him out of there, likely at gunpoint, and kill him on the spot. Kane knew no tourists would be coming that day. He also had more than just a hunch that the small police force allegedly on the island— he'd seen no evidence they existed—were already on the Yakuza payroll.

Kane thought about Katashi and his thugs. He had been warned. He wondered briefly if he should have heeded that warning. Yet, it was only briefly. Kane was invested now. Though he had grave feelings about it all, he was glad to be there attempting to do the right thing.

He had in the past been accused—usually from behind a smile—of having something akin to a death wish. It was true that he had no wife or children to care for, and he had spent half his life on high-risk adventures that might have stolen him from anyone who did happen to care about him. He did have a huge place in his heart reserved for Alexandria Ridley. He knew she would understand his actions here today. She would be doing the same thing; he felt sure.

But a death wish? No chance. Yes, he had a family who loved him, and he was worshipped by his grandparents. His father didn't often speak to him, but that was made up for by his recent reconnection with his brother Danny.

He understood what those good-natured accusers meant. His job entailed leading groups of unqualified people on treks and expeditions they were often ill-prepared to undertake. Mountain trekking in the Himalayas, for example, and hikes across Mongolia. Kane also had a natural ability to inspire people, to ease them out of their comfort zone and help them excel. *Carpe diem*, he would tell them. Seize the day. They usually did… with both hands. True, there had been some incidents in recent years, where a couple of people had lost their lives. Though he carried the guilt of their deaths, he wasn't at fault. The fault had been at the hands of others and of nature itself.

Despite it all, Kane had decided to seize this day. The situation in which he now found himself was not his usual type of adventure, yet there was great value in it; good people needed help, and that was all the inspiration he needed. If the worst came to the worst, and he wound up being injured or killed, then so be it.

Just don't let me be killed by a sneeze, he implored his newfound yet undefined gods.

On the floor in the darkness, Kane grimaced again, not even close to appreciating the revelation that perhaps he did have a death wish after all.

It mattered little now. He was trapped, which meant he was committed, whether he liked it or not.

Chapter Thirty-Three

侍

Kane had been lying motionless, pressed against the floor beneath the dais for close to twenty minutes, though it already felt like hours. His bones ached from the unforgiving hardwood floorboards. His chin and head were sore from cracking them against the ground and stage ceiling respectively. It wasn't his finest afternoon. Yet Kane had no choice. He simply had to endure it.

Then, he heard the gentle thud of more footsteps. New ones, not the heavy strides of the two thugs from before.

He somehow knew they were the steady footfalls of the mafia boss walking calmly into the hall, though he couldn't make out the old man's face. There was something in the careful, equal pacing of the footsteps. Something in the measured stride and the unhurried placement of the expensive Italian shoes. Catching a glimpse, Kane could see that Katashi's shoes had remained clean, despite the mud and deluge outside. It all indicated the man was in complete and utter control of what was soon to come. Kane couldn't see his face, but he didn't have to. Katashi Goto's grand plan was about to take place, whatever the hell that entailed.

And to Kane, that was the question; what exactly was about to happen? If they were only going to steal the samurai suit, then it would probably all be over inside two minutes. There were no tourists about. Nor were there any staff, other than Mika, who may or may not still be on the premises. There appeared to be no cameras, and there were definitely no security guards or police officers anywhere on the island. So why weren't they just grabbing the artefact from the mannequin and getting the hell out of there?

Kane somehow understood it wouldn't be over that quickly. There was more to it, he sensed. The timing seemed important, and not just because of the convenient lack of tourists. Kane believed the Yakuza boss needed time, though for what he didn't yet know. His lips curved into yet another grimace as he decided to look upon it all as a dark theatrical performance for his own entertainment.

Katashi Goto's eyes settled on Taichi as he entered the Armour Room. He kept them fixed on the young thug as he approached, but then offered the barest hint of a nod. The big man nodded solemnly in return. With Yosuke at his side, Katashi approached the stage that held above it the venerable samurai suit. When Katashi was within just a few feet of the dais, he stopped. His heart raced, and the first spikes of adrenaline prickled his fingertips. It heightened his senses and helped him tune out everything else around him. Deep inhales. Long, slow exhales. Composure. That was the key.

He looked at the suit. But Katashi's eyes saw more than just an inanimate object before him. They saw past it, beyond that room, and beyond that island onto a distant, ancient battlefield, where his Taira ancestors were once defeated in the Genpei War by their hated rivals, the clan of men known as the Minamoto.

It was during that battle Katashi's most revered family member was slain. Though it happened more than eight centuries earlier, stories of Takamochi Taira's legendary valiance and heroism—and of his ultimate betrayal—had been passed down through the generations.

Takamochi had been brutally murdered by Fujiwara Minamoto. It was a heinous, cold-blooded act that went against the very essence of what it meant to be samurai—against the samurai code of bushido. A defeated warrior was always permitted to take his own life through the ritual act of seppuku. Not only permitted. Compelled. Expected to.

It was the indignity of the defeat that held importance. There was no ignominy in dying, no fear of death. But to be defeated brought shame onto the individual, so it was not only his right to take his own life, but it became his duty. The act itself was barbaric. A man took to his knees, and with his own ritualised dagger he would slowly slice the blade across his stomach, spilling his guts onto the floor for all to witness. His seppuku assistant—the kaishakunin—would then decapitate him with the single swing of a sword, putting an end to the unimaginable pain.

After the act of seppuku, the shame of the defeated man was immediately erased. His death became honourable. His lost dignity, restored. That is not what happened to Katashi Goto's famous ancestor.

Takamochi Taira's demise was a shameful death, though not through his own actions, but through the actions of another. Defeated in battle, Takamochi took to his knees, as was the ancient custom. Before he could erase his shame by committing seppuku, however, he was coldly and callously beheaded by Fujiwara Minamoto, who had been hiding himself shamelessly nearby.

That one act brought immediate dishonour onto the Minamoto clan. At the same time, it had bestowed a kind of immortality upon Katashi's ancestor. They had lost the battle. But the moral victory was to be theirs for all time.

Revenge against the Minamoto clan had been sworn for almost nine centuries, but one generation of the Taira clan after another had let that vengeance slip by unclaimed. Over time, the cult of the samurai had slowly faded, the once timeless culture allowed to become a system from another era. Progressive Japanese governments had eventually made that romantic way of life obsolete, slowly relegating it to myth and folklore to all but those who were themselves samurai—to those who still chose to claim that honour.

Now the day of reckoning had at last arrived. The Taira clan of noble samurai descent were just minutes from reclaiming their honour in the form of the revered samurai suit of their famous ancestor.

Yet something far more important than that was at stake. On a stormy afternoon on Miyajima Island, at the venerated shrine of Itsukushima, the Taira clan would at last have their revenge.

The blood of the despised enemy would once again be spilled.

Chapter Thirty-Four

侍

Kane was pressed so tight to the ground he felt his pounding heart vibrating against the floorboards. It sounded so loud to him in such a confined space he felt sure Katashi would hear it. He was in serious trouble, he knew that, and if he made the slightest sound, they would find him. If they found him, they would kill him.

Kane was a tough man, rugged, and not afraid of any other human. Neither was he scared of dying, but that didn't mean he would serve his life up on a plate.

Kane sashimi anyone?

He realised that wasn't funny as he focused on the old man's feet. Kane relaxed his breathing the best he could and fought off the urge to sneeze caused by the dust an inch from his nose.

Jesus, how long since anyone swept here? A century?

He tried to ignore his predicament and instead focused on making sure his phone was at least picking up audio of whatever it was that was about to happen. If he could somehow get out of the situation alive, he would need proof beyond just his own account, especially against a man with the influence Katashi almost certainly wielded. And if Kane was going to go international, hoping that media outlets would pick up on the crime at one of the world's most beloved heritage sites, he would need to offer them more than just his own rambling recollections. Once the theft became a global story, the Japanese authorities would be compelled to act. Positioning his modern device carefully on the ancient wood floor, he once again focused on his breathing.

Katashi Goto struggled to control his breathing. The time had come for him to fulfil his destiny, yet he was more excited than he had expected. Almost feverish. He felt as alive as he had in years, maybe decades. It wasn't that he was unhappy to finally claim the suit of armour, although it would give him great satisfaction. And it wasn't down to the sense of power and justice it would bring to himself and his family, though again, that was something to be proud of. No, it was none of those things.

It was something else entirely that exhilarated Katashi Goto and had his pulse racing like a tidal surge across Hiroshima Bay. He was not a violent man by nature—far from it. At least that's what he had always told himself and others. Few ever believed him. He didn't really believe it himself... he just did what needed doing, and that was sometimes violence. However, after rising through the ranks of the Yakuza, from teenage errand boy to security for the two previous dons, right up to his position as a top boss of the Yamaguchi Prefecture, violence had become part and parcel of his mafia life, and he had seen his fair share of death—often at his own hands.

The ceremony he would soon act out was something he had been thinking about incessantly for years. Yet, there had always been one important piece of the jigsaw missing. Following a lengthy period of research and diligence, that missing piece had finally slotted into place. Everything had become clear. The timing was right. Now, the logistics were perfect.

Just a few months earlier, when he had made his decision to retire from the Yakuza, his own boss had thought it best to assign him extra security. If a rival faction wanted to make a serious statement of intent, then taking out one of their competitor's high-level leaders was always a good tactic. Once Katashi was outside the protective circle of the Yakuza, however, his death would become unimportant. With word out on the streets of Kyoto and beyond that Katashi Goto was soon to be out of the game, an organised hit had not only become a genuine possibility, but a near certainty. Hence the extra security.

As he always did when new men were promoted to his detail, he had asked his trusted cronies to carry out background checks on potential candidates and their families. Even their family histories. That was when the brilliant idea had occurred to him.

One of the men recently assigned to him had been Taichi, a man Katashi had personally selected after reading the files on his connections, his family and his personal history. Taichi's family history marked him out as an enemy and a traitor, unbeknown to the man himself. He was perfect. Katashi signed him up immediately.

Once Taichi had reported for duty, Katashi had taken an instant dislike to the jumped up, disrespectful Neanderthal. Not that his feelings towards the man were important. The plan would be carried out either way. Taichi just happened to be that vital missing piece in the ancient puzzle.

Taichi was Minamoto.

Katashi glanced at Yosuke, then bowed. The don now felt alive with anticipation. Yosuke bowed back, the model of respect, and Katashi knew he was as loyal a man as had ever served him. Alongside Yoshi, Yosuke was his most trusted sidekick, and they would do anything for their boss. They would prove it now.

It was time.

When Yosuke walked steadily and purposefully to the entrance guarded by Taichi, the big younger man heard him approach. He turned and looked Yosuke directly in the eye. He had never liked them, neither Yosuke nor Yoshi—he thought them far too familiar with their boss. Kuso-yarō! *Bastards!*

They were a generation older than him, so of course they were more trusted. However, he had also served Katashi well, albeit for a shorter time, and he expected to be shown more respect than he was getting. A lot more. One day, he would teach them all a lesson.

"Taichi," said Yosuke with zero respect at all, "Katashi-san wants to speak with you. Go to him. Move, now!"

Taichi was surprised by Yosuke's orders. He didn't like receiving them from this son-of-a-whore, and he held Yosuke's steely glare. Yet he was glad the order had come. He thought it might be a good thing, an opportunity to at last advance his position, of course, long-overdue. He strode through the hall and made his way to the don with a spring in his step. Upon seeing Katashi standing solemnly in front of the samurai suit, however, he stopped. After a deep breath, he straightened his suit jacket and moved to stand quietly by his boss's side.

"Katashi-san. You sent for me?"

The don remained silent for a moment, seemingly focused on and consumed by something Taichi could not see. Taichi fidgeted, unsure whether to announce his arrival one more time. He knew Katashi did not like to be interrupted, even though he'd summoned his guard. After another deep breath, he decided to wait.

It was two full minutes before Katashi took a long, slow breath of his own. Finally, he acknowledged Taichi's presence. "Yes, Taichi, I sent for you." His grey eyes shone with tears as he turned to face Taichi.

Taichi was not expecting to see Katashi emotional—the man rarely displayed emotion of any kind, other than anger. More surprising still was the fact he'd been allowed to witness it. Taichi then relaxed when the faintest trace of a smile creased his boss's lips.

Katashi stepped forward and placed both his hands on Taichi's huge upper arms. He looked up and locked his gaze on Taichi's own. His moist, pale eyes were penetrating, and Taichi felt himself held in place by their power alone. Suddenly uncomfortable, he found himself unable to move even if he wanted to. It was as if he were being stared down by a wolf.

"You are a young man, Taichi. Yes, young, and very strong." The don squeezed his triceps with surprising strength, pulling Taichi in a little closer as he said, "Yet you have a lot to learn. Today, I will teach you a very important lesson."

Taichi's shoulders relaxed further, the relief running though him like warm saké. But his boss's fierce glare did not match his smooth words. Taichi wasn't quite sure what it was, but something in his boss's eyes unnerved him—such cold eyes. Calculating. Judging. Now, though, it seemed as if he were to be given some guidance, some valuable advice in order to better serve Katashi. It was just what Taichi had wanted to hear for a long time. Perhaps his career would finally progress.

Taichi heard footsteps. He turned to see Yoshi approaching. With Yoshi there, it meant one of the entrances was unguarded. Again, something made Taichi's stomach flutter. He wasn't afraid of anyone. But...

Katashi turned back to face the display of armour. "This magnificent samurai armour is a very important object in the history of my family," he said, his words clear and precise. "Do you know anything about it, Taichi?"

Taichi looked at the armour. He did not know. He was ignorant about the samurai, those outdated relics from a history he cared nothing for and that had zero impact on his life.

Is this a test? Is Katashi trying to trick me?

"I am sorry, Katashi-san. I know nothing about it."

Katashi nodded, his eyes on the samurai suit. "I know you do not. Let me enlighten you. This armour was once worn by my ancestor, the famous warrior, Takamochi Taira. Does that name sound familiar?"

"No, Katashi-san," replied Taichi quietly, beginning to feel stupid. "It does not."

"I knew that too. And what about this name: Fujiwara Minamoto?"

Taichi gulped at the mention of the name. His composure momentarily wavered, though he recovered quickly. With the slightest and unconscious raise of an eyebrow, Taichi decided that rather than fumble out some half-lies, he would again tell the truth. "So sorry, Katashi-san, I do not know this name either."

"Of course not," responded Katashi, his voice so calm and quiet that Taichi had to strain to hear. The don turned to him and smiled, and it was a smile that lacked any warmth. In fact, Taichi felt as if it emanated cruel apathy.

Taichi watched as the Yakuza don's eyes narrowed, and he said, calm and in complete control, "Let me tell you a story."

Chapter Thirty-Five

侍

Kane's initial—and very real—dread of being discovered had now been replaced by intrigue around the events unfolding quite literally before his eyes. Something sinister was taking place, he was certain of that now—and it was way beyond the mere theft of a samurai suit. Although he couldn't yet know what it was, he sensed in the tension floating round the room like static, and the chilling tone in the don's words to his youngest thug, Kane sensed it wasn't going to end well for Taichi.

Taichi's shoulders tensed and he felt and heard his pulse thrumming in his ears.

"A very long time ago," Katashi told him, "there was a violent war between two rival clans of samurai. One of those clans was the Taira. The Taira clan were my ancestors. This suit of armour here before us, unrivalled in its beauty and historical significance, belonged to Takamochi, one of the most famous of all samurai and founder of our the Taira clan. And yet, after living such a glorious and noble life, that life was ended in an inglorious and ignoble manner. Yes, Takamochi was defeated. But as any good Japanese man knows—as I am certain you also know—it is the right of a samurai to die with honour through the traditional and ritual act of seppuku."

Taichi listened, but at the same time he wondered why Katashi was telling him about some nonsense history story he cared nothing for. Something felt wrong about the whole situation, and his spine straightened, his back muscles clenching from nervous tension. Taichi never felt nervous, and he hated himself for it. Yet there it was, and he couldn't help it. The Yakuza boss continued.

"My revered ancestor would have taken to his knees, as was the custom. Next he would have carefully folded the traditional white kimono beneath his knees, then closed his eyes. He would have had his kaishakunin—his assistant—alongside him, ready to deliver the killing blow. No one can know what was going through Takamochi's mind in those last moments. However, we do know it was the practice of the time to recite a death poem, and we can assume Takamochi did that too. Unafraid, due to his proud clan and family heritage, he would have opened his eyes. He would have readied himself to die with honour, and with the care and precision befitting such an important ritual, then he would have positioned his short dagger before him, the sharp blade pointing towards his abdomen."

Katashi paused, inhaling deeply. Then he exhaled slowly and continued.

"My ancestor, Takamochi Taira, was about to thrust the blade into himself, restoring his honour, when his head was sliced off by one cowardly swing of a sword by the enemy's

The Samurai Code

leader. Thus, my revered ancestor died in shame, never able to regain his dignity due to that unforgivable act of disrespect commuted by the leader of the Minamoto clan."

The don paused, his gaze fixed on Taichi's, as if savouring the moment. Taichi didn't like the expression on Katashi's face as he said, "And do you know who the enemy was… Taichi Minamoto?"

Taichi's blood ran cold. He turned on his heels but was shocked to see Yoshi and Yosuke standing so close behind him. They stood with their legs apart—raised samurai swords shimmering with menace to their sides—ready to attack. Taichi fumbled inside his suit jacket for his revolver, but before he could reach it he felt the icy steel blade of a sword at his neck.

"Do not move," Yoshi hissed.

Taichi knew these men did not make idle threats. He closed his eyes. In a millisecond, he already knew what to expect.

"Remove your hand from your jacket, and put both hands behind your back," Yoshi instructed. "Slowly, gorilla, or I swing."

Taichi did as he was told. Katashi took a few calm steps until he stood in front of Taichi. Any humanity once visible in those eyes had departed. Instead, just two cold, grey orbs of hatred glared at him.

"So, Taichi Minamoto, now do you understand? It was your ancestor who betrayed the ancient rules of bushido, causing my ancestor to die an inglorious death. There was no dignity. It was the ultimate act of dishonour. The lowest form of betrayal. Your ancestor broke the samurai code."

"Kneel," demanded Yosuke.

Taichi resisted half a second too long. Yoshi pressed the sword into the muscled flesh of his neck, blood appearing immediately under the long blade's razor edge. He gritted his teeth and slowly dropped to his knees, the warm blood now seeping into his white shirt.

Yoshi clubbed the back of his head with the sword's hilt, and his mind and body shut down.

Chapter Thirty-Six

侍

Something pounded at Taichi's skull—at least that's how it felt.

His guts churned with nausea, but he didn't know why. He opened his eyes just a sliver. The pain almost made him puke. Pale light flickered around the edges of his vision, black and silver starbursts focusing his mind back into some sort of clarity. Then the flash of a memory followed by a bolt of fear worse than the pain.

Katashi's voice came from what felt only inches away. "Look at me."

Taichi opened his eyes then immediately recoiled, clamping them shut against the nightmarish vision silhouetted before him. Yosuke strode over and grabbed a clump of his hair, yanking his head backwards.

"You will look at Katashi-san."

Taichi slowly opened his eyes again, a cold comprehension settling over his body like a winter shroud. Standing before him was Katashi Goto, decked out in full samurai regalia. The don was covered from head to foot in the leather-and-iron armour suit he'd admired moments before. Taichi turned his eyes to the now empty stage. Things had taken a drastic turn for the worse.

Taichi was a tough man. He had been embarrassed by his ignorance. Next they had tried to shame him for an act of cowardice that took place many hundreds of years ago, and which had nothing to do with him. Yet he would not be shamed. He would not show them the fear they wanted to see. Instead, he fought hard to show them defiance.

Taichi was rattled, but he puffed out his chest and glared into Katashi's eyes, which glimmered from behind the gargoyle-esque warrior mask.

Kane could not believe what was unfolding before him. He'd sensed something nefarious was afoot, but this was way beyond his wildest speculations. To Kane's absolute horror, it looked as if they were actually setting up to sacrifice the big Yakuza bodyguard. He immediately thought of leaping from his hiding place to try and put a stop to the horrifying madness. But just as quickly as the notion came, he decided against it. If he did reveal himself now, he knew there would be not one but two corpses on the shrine's floor.

It was difficult to lie there and do nothing—that wasn't his nature. But to die trying to protect a vicious criminal who had signed up for the mafia life in full knowledge of its perils? Torment creased his forehead. Kane knew he was powerless against men with swords and who probably had guns too. He hated the feeling of helplessness that washed over him, but that's just what he was. Helpless.

From beneath the dais, Kane now had a clear view of Taichi's face. He saw the big man open his eyes, blood streaming from his neck wound. That in itself had been shocking. What he saw next was inexplicable.

Forced to his knees, a lethal samurai sword against his neck and facing a certain and imminent death, Taichi smiled, and an ancient Samurai proverb came unbidden into Kane's mind. He was't sure of the exact words, but it was something along the lines of:

The trail may be long,
the trials many and fraught with peril.
Pause to rest if you must,
but never turn from the fight.
Your next step could be a moment of victory...
Your next battle, the greatest of triumphs...

"It seems you are indeed a brave young man, Taichi Minamoto," Katashi muttered from beyond the mask. "Much braver than your cowardly ancestor. Of course, that is not much of a compliment, and the real test is yet to come. The test of true bravery. Are you ready?"

Taichi gritted his teeth. His breaths came through them in ragged spurts. He expected to die now. *But... how?*

Yosuke turned and grabbed a long leather pouch from a nearby shelf. As he held it out in front of Taichi, there was no mistaking what it contained. It held an O Tanto dagger, the samurai weapon of choice for committing ritual seppuku.

Taichi's eyes opened wide with the shocking realisation. His fears were right—they did expect him to kill himself by seppuku. His thoughts raced, desperate for some way out of this mess. He wanted to say something like, *You'll never get away with it—Yakuza men don't kill their own.* But he realised his situation was way beyond the realms of the Yakuza family. This was a private vendetta. And he was its victim.

Seppuku? There was no chance he would do that; no way he would disembowel himself to make up for the cowardice of an ancestor he had hardly even heard of. However...

If I go through the motions of the ritual, he thought, *trick them into believing I will do it, I could...*

Yes. It's my only chance.

Taichi relaxed his massive shoulders. His rigid spine loosened. His breathing slowed further as his eyes once more sought out Katashi's through the mask. The Yakuza boss returned the glare, his anticipation alight like a funeral pyre.

"Will you do it, boy? Will you die with dignity and regain your ancestor's forsaken honour?"

Taichi held the glare for several drawn-out moments, his dark eyes narrowed in focus. Without taking his eyes off Katashi's, he said to Yosuke, "Give me the O Tanto."

Katashi nodded slowly. Yosuke handed Taichi the leather package then stepped away. Taichi tried hard to compose himself, focusing his mind on the movements he would soon make. He was a big man, too big to outmanoeuvre Yoshi and Yosuke. He knew both were agile and skilled with weapons, more agile than himself, he reluctantly conceded. His only chance was to surprise them, so much so that he could snag his gun and put bullets in their fucking heads before they had time to react.

With slow and deliberate movements, Taichi opened the pouch and slid forth the gleaming O Tanto dagger from its sheath. It was an ancient yet beautiful object, and holding it in his hands seemed to instil in him some unlikely confidence. It was a killing weapon, but Taichi knew it would not be killing him this day. He would leap up, thrust it into Yoshi's face, then grab his gun and shoot that pig-fucker Yosuke before turning it on the old man.

Then we'll see how powerful this washed-up old relic Katashi Goto really is...

Taichi flipped the blade over, his gaze fixed on it. Then he flipped it back again, appraising it, as if one edge might despatch him to the afterlife quicker than the other. The room's silence closed in around him as the O Tanto's dark steel glimmered under the flickering lamplight. Taichi placed his two strong hands around its handle then gently placed the lethal tip of the blade against his taut abdomen. There he paused.

His chest rose and fell in long, slow inhales and exhales, his thoughts settling as he awaited the right moment. As Taichi knelt there, in that cold museum, in that archaic shrine, on that muddy, boring island, he allowed a wave of hatred to fill his heart. It entered through his ears and eyes, rendering him more focused than he had ever known. And yet, to his surprise, his hatred was not aimed at Katashi. Sure, some of it was reserved for those sons-of-dogs, Yoshi and Yosuke, men who lived only to serve, nothing more than a pair of sycophantic peasants. He wanted to kill them. Wanted to kill all of them.

Yet, most of his rage was channelled towards his own ancestor, Fujiwara Minamoto. It was his ancestor's cowardice that had resulted in him being shamed by weaker, lesser men than himself. Now, Taichi would use the wrath he felt for Fujiwara to give him the strength needed to claim an impossible victory from the jaws of his imminent defeat.

Taichi psyched himself up, his deeper, quickening breaths spraying spittle through his clenched teeth. His eyeballs bulged, and his knuckles turned white from the strength of his grip on the dagger. Muscles rippled beneath his shirt. Such was his blinding focus, he was not aware of any movement behind him, not did he see or hear Katashi step behind him and take the long sword from Yoshi.

Taichi roared. "Omae o korosu!" *I will kill you!*

His eyes stretched wide, his muscles flexing to explode upwards, when he spotted the dark blur growing on the ground beside him, the graceful arc of a shadow sword moving swiftly towards him along the floor. Even before he could flinch, he heard a whoosh and his head was sliced clean from his neck.

In the few seconds after his head thudded to the floor, his still beating heart pulsing his blood in great red arcs of death, Taichi's brain registered Katashi Goto standing over his headless body. Then his world turned black forever.

Chapter Thirty-Seven

侍

An eerie quiet settled over the Armour Room at the Itsukushima Shrine.

The only sounds were the spectral whisperings of wind that had penetrated deep into the ancient structure. Beams of lamplight danced and flickered on the floor and walls of the hall, their crazed movements appropriate to the scene Kane had just witnessed. The yellow light cast long, distorted shadows that seemed to writhe across the tatami mats like living things. Each subtle shift in the air sent the flames stuttering, making the darkness pulse rhythmically against Kane's dilated pupils.

Fucking hell! They just cut off his fucking head!

A coppery tang of blood filled his nostrils—metallic, and primal. The scent triggered something deep in his hindbrain, a instinctual repulsion that stood tall the hairs on his arms and neck. He thought he could taste it too, like a soda can on his tongue.

At the moment of impact—sword on neck, steel on flesh—Kane had flinched so hard that his shoulders shot up and he'd once again cracked his head against the underside of the stage. The impact sent a bolt of pain through his skull, stars dancing momentarily at the edges of his vision. He felt a warm trickle of blood from a fresh cut. With the Yakuza men all captivated by the violence they were administering, the solid thunk had somehow gone unheard. Kane peered out through the vent, nausea roiling in his guts. The wooden boards beneath him felt suddenly unstable, as if the world itself were tilting on its axis. He wretched so hard his eyes watered, yet he managed to refrain from throwing up, though acid rose up and burned his throat.

Breathe through your mouth, not your nose, he commanded himself, fighting the primal urge to gasp for air. Each pulse of his heart sent tremors through his body, the beat so loud in his ears he feared the men might hear it.

The decapitated head had fallen and rolled close, and Kane now lay eyeball-to-eyeball with the dead-eyed face of a murdered Yakuza man. The slain thug's expression was frozen in a moment of horrified surprise; mouth agape, wide-eyed.

It was the most horrific thing Kane had ever seen, shocking beyond all comprehension. The skin had already noticeably paled, the man's life force ebbing away as Kane watched on.

'Don't look away,' a voice in his head whispered. *'Remember every detail. You might need it later.'*

He carefully rolled onto his back, staring at the wood barricade just inches above him. He let his breathing slow and his shock come under control, focusing on the rough grain of the dark timbers. His hands shook, fingers tingling with adrenaline. He clutched the fabric of his shirt to prevent them shaking too much. The sturdy material, worn soft from at least a decade of use, anchored him to reality.

This isn't happening. This can't be happening, his mind protested, even as his senses confirmed the brutal truth. Cool air seeped through cracks in the building's aged structure, raising more goosebumps on his now sweat-dampened skin.

And yet, as he lay there, his mind already started processing it all. The initial shock was giving way to a curious detachment, a survival mechanism kicking in. Even when confronted with such horror, and he was indeed horrified—despite some of the barbarism he'd witnessed in recent years—the sentiment behind the act was something that captivated Kane. He felt he was witnessing history. The weight of centuries pressed down on him; how many other deaths had these ancient walls witnessed? He had garnered enough meaning from Katashi's words to at least understand his reasoning, that connection to tradition and custom, and total condemnation of Taichi's ancestor.

His pulse gradually slowed, the initial fight-or-flight response ebbing like a tide. The boards beneath him creaked slightly as he shifted his weight, almost as if the building itself whispered its warning.

Dying for truth and honour, maybe even killing for it. These were acts that Kane could not rule out in his own life. The question was, what exactly constituted honour? Could a violent criminal truly be trusted to be the judge of it? Was it subjective? The scent of blood seemed to intensify as he mulled those questions.

How swiftly humans rationalize violence, he thought bitterly. *Even me.*

And what now? This musing on morality had passed by in only a few seconds, which were a few seconds too long. His diabolical opinion of Katashi hadn't changed, and the incident had been a brutal reminder of the very real, very tangible threat Kane himself faced. His next move was crucial. His muscles tensed, ready for action though his mind hadn't yet decided what that action would be. He felt his pulse in his fingertips, his temples and in the gash on his head.

Fact; Katashi was still going to steal the suit of armour. Kane's mind's eye drifted to the ancient samurai armor the Yakuza don had put on—lacquered plates gleaming dully in the lamplight, the face mask a witness to the brutality of its wearer's act.

Fact; Kane still wanted to stop him, whether it was the mafia man's to claim or not. But would the Yakuza men also remove the body? Or would it be found by the museum's current steward, poor Mika, and become the focus of the international story way beyond the theft of a dusty old suit?

He imagined Mika's face upon discovering such horror in her sacred space. The thought made his stomach clench anew.

These men had proven how dangerous they were, the two henchmen and Katashi himself all cold-blooded, no doubt experienced killers. Kane had sensed the lack of hesitation, the practiced efficiency. The sound of the blade—a whisper followed by a wet thud—echoed in his memory, making him wince.

If I really want to die for honour, I guess now is my best chance, Kane thought.

The deep irony wasn't lost on him. Here, surrounded by artifacts of warriors who had lived and died by a code of honor, Bushido, he was contemplating his own moral stand.

There must be something I can do. There has to be.

Chapter Thirty-Eight

侍

With a little help, Katashi removed his samurai armour, one delicate, beautiful piece at a time. First off was the weighty helmet, followed by the bulky chest plate and armoured sleeves. It was heavy gear, but the mafia don was still in decent shape and handled it well. Despite its heft, it was many hundreds of years old and needed handling with care, lest it become damaged.

Next, he stepped out of the all-in-one trouser and boot sections. Finally, and with some reluctance, he removed the grotesque mask. He turned it around in his hands. He felt as if the gruesome face looked back at him. For a few seconds, he stared at it, as if trying to give or receive some message, some kind of acknowledgement from his ancestor or perhaps an even higher authority. At last, he nodded, and with a deep sigh Katashi took a seat on the stage. His heels rested inches from a metal grate in the wood panels.

For several minutes, Katashi studied the severed head on the ground in front of him. On his lap lay the sword, still dripping blood to add to the growing pool on the floor. The sword was significant. During the legendary Dan-no-ura battle of 1185, the emperor at that time, the juvenile Antoku, had drowned, apparently clutching a sword that myth suggested had been brought down from heaven by the very first Japanese emperor, Jinmu-tennō.

Although it was believed lost, the sword had in fact been retrieved from the waters of the Shimonoseki Strait off the southern tip of Honshū. Over generations, it eventually became one of Japan's greatest imperial treasures. Unlike the samurai suit, however, Katashi had procured the priceless artefact through various shady dealings, years ago after it was stolen from the Atsuta Shrine in Nagoya.

Seeing the dead eyes and the pools of blackish enemy blood gave Katashi no pleasure. It was a gruesome spectacle, and even he was surprised at the amount of blood spilled, and Katashi was a man who had experienced a lot of blood over the years. It was one of those things. How could you know what it would be like each time until you saw it with your own eyes? He almost smiled when he imagined Taichi himself looking back at his own headless body. Almost. But not quite.

Yet, Katashi Goto was satisfied. It was a ritualised act that had returned dignity to his fallen ancestor, removing the lifelong monkey of shame from his own back and transferring it onto the treacherous backs of the Minamoto clan.

Would he sleep better for it? No, because he slept just fine anyway. Would he die happier when his time came? That too was a *no*, because he had always embraced death. And, since he was going into the monastery to take his first steps along the path towards Buddhist enlightenment, Katashi understood death was just one part of the greater cycle of life anyway.

But, would it eradicate many hundreds of years of shame from the clan of Taira samurai? Yes. It would.

By slaying a descendant of the hated Minamoto, placed in his path just months before, one swing of a shining steel blade had achieved just that.

He could retire from mafia life now. Today's event wasn't directly linked with the Yakuza, though Katashi was wise enough to know the power he wielded as a Yakuza boss would deflect any repercussions within the criminal world. Taichi Minamoto may only have been a low-level mafia thug, but he undoubtedly had connections beyond the Yamaguchi syndicate, and they would almost certainly demand retribution for this act of supposed treachery.

Yet Katashi firmly believed any true samurai descendant would have agreed with his actions today; even descendants of the hated Minamoto clan. To go after someone as high up in the Yakuza hierarchy as Katashi Goto, a potential enemy would have to have good reason. Once the weight of history was taken into account, it would be difficult for anyone to argue that Katashi deserved punishment. Honour and tradition were layered through the Yakuza like stitches in samurai armour.

"So sorry, Katashi-san." It was Yoshi, who addressed his boss in a quiet, respectful tone. "We need to go."

Katashi looked up, shifting his gaze from the unseeing eyes of Taichi. He nodded.

"Yes, Yoshi, it is time to go. You bring the armour. Yosuke, you drag the body behind the platform and hide it. Maybe tomorrow someone will find a rotting corpse there. No matter. We will be gone."

"We can clean up the operation, Katashi-san," Yoshi insisted. "We have done it many times before, and we are very efficient."

"Do you think what we did here today was supposed to be a secret?" Katashi asked, the contempt in his voice echoing off the walls. "This act sends a message to bloodlines across Japan. It is a statement. A correction of history."

Katashi stood, pausing at the head of the slain foe. His eyes narrowed. "For my ancestors," he whispered. In a final moment of redemption, he spat at the severed head of Taichi Minamoto.

"Yosuke, hide the body just enough to buy us some time. The girl may come in here soon, and she will wonder if the blood is from an injury. Better for her to be standing here confused than screaming loud enough for the whole island to hear. Yoshi, now we go."

Without another look at the fallen enemy, Katashi Goto walked with assured strides out of the Armour Room for the last time.

Chapter Thirty-Nine

侍

"Bollocks," Kane muttered as he realised with clarity it was all over.

It had looked for a while as if he would actually get away with hiding under the stage. He'd successfully recorded the entire macabre spectacle on his phone's camera and had all the evidence he would need to present to the authorities. Now, however, the game was up. One of the henchmen was dragging the headless body behind the platform, and in less than thirty seconds he would discover Kane for sure.

Do I run? Lie still? Do I jump out and fight?

Kane was generally fearless, and would risk his own life without a second's thought if it meant saving the life of a friend or loved one, or one of the members of his expeditions. It was something he had proven often.

Yet, though he cared nothing for the butchered man with the lifeless eyes in his removed head just feet away, witnessing his grisly death had stirred up painful memories from Kane's past… triggered something locked away for a long time in his psyche... so much so that, without even realising it, his blood began to boil. His teeth ground together with such force that his jaw slipped and he bit hard into his bottom lip. He licked the blood away as his eyes locked on Yosuke.

Then Kane made his move.

He scrambled fast to the stage's rear opening and slammed his whole body upwards, his strong shoulders shifting the entire stage platform on its base. Amid the noise of the stage crashing back down he hustled out from the shadows so fast that he was on his feet before Yosuke knew what was happening. The look on the man's face was priceless—it was as if he'd seen a ghost.

The once silent ancient temple erupted in carnage as Kane charged Yosuke, crashing his lead shoulder into the thug's chest. The two big men tumbled over the corpse, arms and legs tangling as Minamoto blood smeared their exposed skin and clothes. Yosuke, huge yet agile, sprang to his feet with surprising dexterity. His initial confusion soon morphed into a cocky smirk, a sign of underestimating his opponent.

Excellent, *Kane thought, grinning inwardly.*

Kane knew Yosuke couldn't know he held a ninth dan black belt in taekwondo, technically a grand master of the Korean martial art. They circled each other slowly, as Kane's experienced eye appraised his new enemy. Kane had knowledge of many martial arts, and as he analysed Yosuke, the Yakuza man's stance betrayed his jujitsu training. Kane spotted it easily in the temple's dim light, which glinted off centuries' old porcelain vases and sent shadows dancing across the floor, walls and ceiling. Kane understood he had to finish this soon before Yosuke learned the full extent of his ability, and instead of fighting, he'd likely pull a gun and shoot him, like Indiana Jones with the Arab swordsman in Raiders of the Lost Ark.

As he sized up his foe, a random and untimely thought sprang unbidden into Kane's mind. He had always had a thing for phrenology—the shape and size of a person's skull versus their character and intelligence—though it had long since been debunked as a scientific theory. Dickens' Magwitch was a case in point. Written as an oafish, uneducated criminal, Dickens fans know well just how that perception turned out. Kane wasn't so sure. Looking at the massive head of Yosuke, with his wide, flat forehead crisscrossed with scars, a massive squared jaw, arched eyebrows and a face upon which even a smile appeared as a scowl, Kane grinned at the notion the Victorian theory of phrenology was alive and well. Yosuke looked exactly what he was; an overgrown, vicious, morally inept and dangerous thug.

With volatile speed, Kane launched into a roundhouse kick. His extended right foot impacted Yosuke's jaw, the thud reverberating throughout the space. He staggered, but the mafia thug somehow remained standing. Immediately transitioning into a second kick, Kane leapt again, but this time, Yosuke dipped his shoulder with a grunt, avoiding the strike by mere inches.

Yosuke countered swiftly, narrowing the distance before aiming a vicious left cross at Kane's face. Kane ducked beneath the devilish punch, hearing the whoosh of air above him, and as he rose again, he powered his elbow into the general region of Yosuke's heart. The goliath exhaled, winded… the blow had struck him right in the solar plexus.

Siezing his advantage, Kane let loose with a flurry of devastating strikes—a side kick to Yosuke's ribs, another to a shin, both of which wobbled the giant, followed by a sickening upper cut to his chin. Yosuke stumbled back into a massive vase and for Kane time seemed to stand still as the beautiful ancient artefact wobbled precariously too.

Straightening up quickly, Yosuke hefted the huge porcelain vase and propelled it towards Kane, who instinctively spun, his forearm block connecting with the no-doubt priceless vase mid-air, shattering it, jagged shards crashing down all around them.

"Kuso!" Yosuke bellowed, finally understanding Kane was a dangerous opponent. *Shit!*

Kane noticed the realisation, and sensed the Yakuza man's frustration as he adopted a lower stance, changing tactics. Yasuke beckoned Kane, opening his plam and gesturing Kane forwards with a flick of his fingers. Still wary of Yosuke's fighting skills, he kept his distance as they resumed circling, searching for a chink in the other's armour.

Yosuke suddenly lunged, attempting a grab at Kane's clothing, and though Kane dodged, Yosuke's huge hand snagged his forearm. Using Kane's own momentum against him, Yosuke launched into a perfect hip throw, which he managed to execute and Kane felt the world spin as he was thrown into the air.

Kane's almost three decades of fighting experience and training kicked in. He tucked and rolled as he hit the ancient floorboards, lessening the jarring impact, and he leapt back up, avoiding Yosuke's incoming stamp towards his skull.

Kane backed up, now on the defensive. His heel latched onto a raised board in the archaic wooden flooring and he tripped, and Yosuke was on him in a flash, forcing home his advantage and closing in for the kill. His massive arms wrapped around Kane, easily the smaller man, his biceps bulging, ready to crush him.

Kane flailed, expecting to hear his ribs crack under such huge pressure. He inhaled, then smashed forehead into Yosuke's nose; he heard and felt the cartilage crunch. The mafia man's grip slackened off slightly, and Kane snatched the opportunity, bringing his knee up and connecting with Yosuke's groin with debilitating accuracy.

The Yakuza man's eyes widened as he dropped to a knee, then he doubled over in obvious agony. Kane didn't hesitate. He swivelled, delivering a side kick to Yosuke's throat that sent him sprawling backward into a wooden stand holding a carved stone lantern. The stand collapsed and the lantern dropped to the floor, breaking into several large jagged shards and spilling oil across the deck.

Flames shot up, and Kane suddenly had a terrible premonition he was about to burn to death.

Chapter Forty

侍

Fortunately, it was soon obvious the ancient yet culturally important structure had been so well-cared for that the flames were contained to the immediate area.

There was smoke though, and through that smoke and shimmering light Kane spotted the lumbering Yosuke hauling himself to his feet, his face a mask of pain and rage as blood poured from his destroyed nose. With an unbridled roar of hatred, the Yakuza thug charged Kane like a bull.

Kane crouched and held his position until the last second, then ducked low and slammed into the shins of his assailant, who then proceeded to crash face-first into an unforgiving, solid wooden wall decorated with ancient scrolls. The collision shook dust and debris down from the ceiling.

Kane remained cautious, and knew better than to believe this fight was over. Cautiously, and with his guard up, he approached the downed mafia goon, whose hand shot out, grabbing a shard from the broken vase and flinging it into Kane's face.

Kane staggered, instinctively spinning away from the projectile, then felt rather than saw the huge fist coming towards his face. Yosuke had sprung up amid the smoke and chaos, and Kane ducked again, somehow dodging the second incoming blow, then he countered, his right fist connecting with what he hoped were Yosuke's lower, more fragile ribs. The giant roared in pain, indicating an accurate shot.

Kane backed away. The smoke was permeating swiftly now, choking the Armour Room with billowing black clouds. Kane saw Yosuke advancing, a mere silhouette in the clogging haze.

Jesus... this has to end now. Yosuke launched another punch, and Kane sidestepped. Yosuke seemed tired and slower than before. *Thank fuck for that!* Kane snagged the man's extended arm and, using the gangster's own momentum, he twisted hard, and let his own weight succumb to gravity, hauling Yosuke face-first into the floorboards with a nauseating crunch. Kane shifted quickly into an arm bar, harshly hyperextending the bastard's joint.

The man howled in agony, yet still he fought, so Kane increased the pressure to the verge of breaking. "Stop!" Kane shouted. "Tei-shi!"

But Yosuke was not done yet, Kane knew, as his left hand searched the floor for a weapon and found a shard of the broken vase and he swung it wildly, the jagged porcelain cutting deep into Kane's thigh.

Kane unclenched the arm bar, scrambling away. He saw the blood leaking from his sliced leg, but didn't feel any pain. *Thank God for adrenaline,* he mused, then Yosuke was up on his feet again, his weapon glinting in the lamp and firelight.

Both men were bleeding and battered as they faced up

again, surrounded by swirling smoke and the rubble of destroyed artefacts. Kane assessed the situation, and his foe, and knew what was coming.

3…

2…

Yosuke charged once more, and Kane waited as long as he dared, then, digging deep into the last vestiges of his skill and power, he threw himself into a spinning roundhouse and believed as he spun he had executed it to perfection. Upon impact, he was certain. His heel clattered into Yosuke's temple with an audible crack. He somehow remained standing for a beat before Kane saw the whites of the thug's eyes grow large as he finally collapsed unconscious to the ground just as an unearthly groan emanated from the despatched and forgotten head on the floor.

Gasping in surprise, Kane turned towards the source of the morbid sound. As if this shitshow wasn't crazy enough, what happened next was terrifying; the severed head actually wailed. Kane had heard of postmortem movements, something to do with muscles flexing during rigor mortis. Muscles also controlled the vocal cords, he guessed, causing the grisly sounds now emanating from the head. It was the weirdest thing he'd ever witnessed, and he found it totally unnerving. It was time to get the hell out of there.

Kane appraised the scene, breathing hard, bleeding from his leg and a couple of scuffs on his face, but relatively unscathed. The unconscious Yosuke lay amid the shards of stone and ceramics, the smoke starting to clear.

Kane didn't waste a second bundling the stricken mafia thug towards the stage. Unleashing two ropes positioned across the stage from their hooks, Kane quickly used them to tie his beaten foe's wrists and ankles together. With Yosuke restrained, Kane took a few moments to breathe

The Samurai Code

deep and compose himself, and then he left the Armour Room and walked as quietly as possible along the lamp-lit corridor towards the shrine's main exit. He kept his wits about him, expecting to be confronted by more Yakuza men any moment. Taut with anger and fuelled by adrenaline, he primed himself for whatever came his way.

Kane was nearing the exit when he thought he heard distant voices. He paused to listen. The corridor was gloomy, lit only by a series of dim lamps. Yet there was no doubting what he saw up ahead; the shadowy movements of two men.

Challenging them together was out of the question. Kane was fired up, but he wasn't stupid. He knew he had to somehow separate the other thug from his boss, lure him deeper into the shrine and attempt to overcome him, just as he had Yosuke.

He ducked into an alcove behind a giant terracotta vase, thinking on his feet.

"Hey," he shouted. "Hey, Katashi Goto. Saikin dō?" *What's up?*

The voices fell silent as they too paused. They had definitely heard him call out. Surely they would know it was him, too. Ideally the boss would despatch the henchman after him, and Kane hoped to surprise him enough to get in a debilitating shot before the thug could respond. He waited, heart now racing as he tucked himself in a little closer behind the artefact, when he noticed a beautifully stylised ying and yang design on the vase. Kane grimaced. *What I wouldn't do for a little peace right now.*

Seconds later, the sudden echo of heavy footfalls thudded his way and Kane's muscles tensed, readying for more brutal combat, wondering abstractedly if this time it would be life or death.

Chapter Forty-One

侍

The deteriorating weather had plunged the already dim corridors into near darkness, and the few lanterns did little to illuminate the sacred shrine. It was perfect for an ambush.

Like Katashi, Yoshi assumed it was the Englishman who had called out to them. It was not Yosuke, and it was... *It's obviously not Taichi.* The slightest hint of a lopsided grin slipped onto Yoshi's hardened face when he imagined the head on the floor speaking. He wasn't the humorous type, but the image tickled him.

The amusement was over in an instant, replaced by a surge of anxiety in his stomach. Though he appeared to be of little threat, Katashi had expressed concerns about the so-called tourist. Yoshi focused his mind.

Where the hell is Yosuke?

He strode on, his senses on high alert for any movement or sound. However, as he walked deeper back into the vast complex, he neither heard nor saw anything. The corridor came to a T-junction. Left headed to the western exit, and right he knew veered back towards the Armour Room they had just left. He decided on returning to the Armour Room —just in case. He turned right and took two steps. Something smashed hard into the back of his skull, snapping his head forward. It had emerged from the shadows, giving him no chance of protecting himself.

Katashi waited for his man at the exit. The Yakuza boss was not duly concerned. He knew it was the Englishman trying to cause trouble, and was confident Yoshi could handle the situation. Katashi thought it was a shame the man had to die. Without knowing anything about him, he nevertheless admired him, and wished some of his own men possessed such a big pair of balls. Mind you, he didn't want them too ballsy. He wasn't as young as he once was, and the last thing he needed now was a coup from within.

It was a little too early to go to the dock. Katashi's helicopter was still fifteen minutes away and there was no point waiting outside in the storm. The ritual he'd acted out in order to emancipate his family from shame had gone smoother than expected. He had reckoned upon Taichi resisting more than he had, to put up more of a fight. As it turned out, he had proven himself a coward, just like his treacherous bastard of an ancestor. It mattered little now.

The mafia don was a little surprised when he spotted the young woman still standing behind the ticket counter. *We Japanese are so dutiful,* he thought. *Maybe I should offer her a position in the firm?* He smiled. He was leaving that life behind, and in truth, he no longer gave a shit.

Katashi walked past the woman, who seemed to ignore him as he passed—*A wise choice, my dear... very wise*—and then he took a seat on an ornate bench by the exit and gazed out into the gloom that now hung over Miyajima like an ominous blanket. It was cold, and the mafia don hustled deeper into his suit jacket. The rain had finally stopped, *Thank fucking God,* he thought, but black clouds still scudded past as if to pave the way for another massive storm.

Katashi then thought of his pilot's words, and a sudden concern about his man's ability to bring the chopper in at all gnawed at his wits. Perhaps the concern was more about the pilot's willingness. Katashi had threatened the lives of his wife and kids, after all, and there was a chance he'd abandoned his job and rushed to be with them, perhaps even flee Kyoto altogether. Katashi could hardly blame him.

I'm getting soft in my old age, he mused with a sigh, and inhaled and held the breath for a long moment. Then he exhaled through his teeth. He did not want to be stuck on this Godforsaken island another night.

He had better fucking make it.

Unfortunately, Kane had failed to deliver a knockout blow. It would have floored most men, but he understood quickly Yoshi was not most men. Though he stumbled for a moment, he righted himself quickly and spun to face Kane before he could follow up with another assault.

The corridor was more confined than the Armour Room, and though Kane didn't yet know the man's skills, he sensed immediately he was a tough opponent, probably tougher even than Yosuke. He appeared slightly younger too, and if anything, a little bigger than the last opponent. Yoshi snarled like a Dobermann as if to illustrate the point.

Through the snarls, Kane saw the curl of a smile, as if the big man was relishing the victory to come. Kane knew that often, men like these clearly thrived on such moments.

Kane, in turn, thrived on the opportunity to wipe the smile from the face, just like he had with Yosuke.

"*Omae o korosu,*" the Yakuza man growled, echoing the threat his comrade had recently made. *I will kill you!*

Yoshi lunged—Kane knew it was really more of a feint to test his reactions. But with his tae-kwon-do training, Kane wasn't fooled. A few more testing lunges from Yoshi followed, then a couple from Kane. Both men were poised, focusing on the other's movements... prowling. Suddenly, the two launched at each other, colliding heavily, each desperate to get a solid grasp on the other man's clothes and execute a take-down.

Kane was a strong man. Yoshi was stronger. He'd managed to grapple his way to a grip on Kane's clothes, his huge hands tightening, vice-like as he dragged Kane to his knees. The collar of Kane's jacket tightened like a noose. The mafia thug soon had Kane gasping for breath. It was barely seconds before Kane's eyesight blurred under the immense pressure.

Fuck! he thought. *Is this how I die?*

He buckled, thrashing his arms and legs in wild arcs to create slack in Yoshi's grip, but it was futile against a man with biceps like anvils. He simply would not yield. Kane weakened by the second, his already worn out muscles tiring from the exertion and a lack of desperately needed oxygen. His vision began to fade at the edges, darkness creeping in. Kane searched his mind for options, but all he found was brain fog.

The faint hum of what sounded like helicopter rotors breezed down the corridor, and the dutiful Yoshi, whose main responsibility was to get Katashi on the chopper, was momentarily distracted. It was the glimmer of hope Kane needed. He slumped, letting his body fall limp as if unconscious. For a solitary moment, Yoshi relaxed his grip and let Kane fall to the floor. A nanosecond later, Kane freed one leg out in front of his body and launched it backwards into Yoshi's groin. The strike landed with such force that the man doubled over. The cry of agony that followed sounded more like a wounded hyena than a pet Doberman.

Carpe momento? Sieze the moment? Fuck it!

Kane took his chance. He leapt to his feet and shook away the oxygen-starved dizziness. He took two steps back and watched as Yoshi dropped to his knees, retching, still trying to come to terms with the blow. Kane looked the man up and down, searching for a weak spot. As Yoshi tipped his head back while trying to deal with the pain, Kane *carpe fucking momentoed* to administer some more.

Kane's knee struck that chin with such force the lower jaw crumpled like a tin can. Unconscious, Yoshi fell forward, his obliterated jaw taking the full weight of his body as it hit the deck with a sickening thud. A couple of teeth scattered across the floorboards like spilled rice. A pool of blood spread out around Yoshi's head, forming a glistening near-black puddle in the dim lamplight.

Kane's broad chest rose and fell as he stood over the slumped Yakuza enforcer. Fists clenched, his arms now at rest beside his body, his ears buzzed with the roar of his pulse and the rush of adrenaline. The gloomy corridor smelled of sweat and lamp oil, the lamplights glowing eerily on the fallen man's face.

Kane shook his head. It had happened so fast. One moment, Kane had left the other thug behind, trussed up hidden behind the stage. The next he was heading out of the shrine, half expecting to encounter this man but not so swiftly and so violently. As many had before him, the stricken mafia thug had clearly underestimated Kane, imagining the smaller, physically weaker... and non-Yakuza man... to offer nothing more than an easy victory. The fact he couldn't have known about Kane's two decades of taekwon-do training was not Kane's problem.

Now, as the thrill of the fight faded to match the low lights within the shrine, Kane felt it coming; the familiar, dark urges rising unbidden within him. He shook his head again but knew it wouldn't help. Instead, he focused on his breathing, as his master had taught him all those years ago. He allowed his gaze to settle on the man's exposed throat, where it lingered. He saw the man was breathing and didn't care, and for a terrifying moment, Kane fantasised about just how easy it would be to take this bastard's life. One carefully placed stomp from his boot was all it would take. He didn't know the man, not really, didn't know his history, but he had seen enough in the last hour to understand that he was indeed a cruel and violent Yakuza gangster more than capable of murder. *Who would miss him? It might save more lives. More innocent victims. One simple action and it would be over.* Kane felt his toes clench inside his boot and sensed his breaths quicken. He felt the muscles in his legs tighten. All he needed to to was decide to act. He closed his eyes and took a half pace forwards, then froze. He inhaled, held the air in his lungs for a long beat, then exhaled, opening his eyes as he stepped back again.

As unbidden as the dark urge that had risen, so too came his old master's words into his mind: "A true warrior knows the weight of his power. He uses it not to dominate, but to protect. To bring peace, not violence."

Kane inhaled a harsh breath, taking another step back. His fists unfurled, and he stretched his fingers as the surge of adrenalin ebbed slowly away.

That isn't me. I am not a killer.

He glanced at his strong hands. They were capable of destructive actions, he knew that. Tonight, they had been put to efficient use and no lines had been crossed. Kane was determined to keep it that way.

The Yakuza thug moaned from the floor, beginning to rouse. Kane had to get out of there before the man regained full consciousness. It alarmed him somewhat how the line he swore he would never cross had been as close as it ever had.

Kane forced himself to breathe, slow and steady, based on his master's instruction. Each inhale, a reminder of his humanity. Every breath out, letting go of the darkness that had threatened to emerge from deep within.

Kane glanced once more at the thug on the ground. The man's eyelids fluttered and he groaned again. *Good. Not dead,* came a small voice from the recesses of Kane's mind. *Let's keep it that way, shall we?*

Chapter Forty-Two

侍

Kane shook his head again, pushing his wandering thoughts aside, and refocused on whatever challenges lay ahead.

This bastard was out of service, at least for a while. His partner, too. Kane was sweating, despite the cold. The other one was dead. That only left Katashi Goto… the murderous Yakuza boss who thought himself a priest.

What a fucking joke, Kane thought. Though Katashi Goto was an older man, Kane guessed that didn't mean the danger was over. Not even close. Kane put Katashi at around sixty, yet he was fully aware that a man did not become a feared mafia boss without being ruthless, capable of brutality, possess an ability to instill fear… and he would probably have a gun. Unlike the others, the older don would probably use his gun as soon as possible rather than take the opportunity to test his hand-to-hand combat skills.

Kane neared the entrance. He hoped his assumption was right that Katashi had already made his way out of the area.

He was wrong. He turned into the final corridor that led

back past the ticket counter, and there was Katashi Goto. Kane stopped, automatically cautious. Their eyes locked.

Next Kane spotted the suit of ancient samurai armour, placed with obvious care against the wood-panelled walls, just inside the entrance and safely out of reach of the rain. Katashi, on the other hand, had chosen to stand just outside the exit, as if to show he was not troubled by the elements.

Then he saw Mika. "What the hell are you still doing here?" he hissed, devastated she was still here and thus likely in danger. "You have to go."

Mika seemed to set her gaze on him, as if to challenge him. "I should say the same to you. This is not your problem, Hiram," she stated, and then a little quieter, she added, "It is a Nakamura problem. My problem."

Kane glanced from Mika to Katashi, then back again. He saw from her firm expression she would not back down. *What the hell are the Nakamuras into?*

He looked back to Katashi... right now, a madman who probably had a gun was more urgent.

There was still twenty yards between them—about eight seconds, Kane thought as he considered charging. He didn't. He knew Katashi could pull out a gun and shoot him before he got there. He waited, inhaling deeply as he allowed his eyes to adjust further to the gloom, ever darkening as both the dusk and the storm conspired to usurp the day's light. And yet despite that darkness, and the distance, Kane saw Katashi smile. It was almost as if the mafia boss had been proven right about something. Maybe because he knew he was right to have worried about the curious tourist snooping around. Maybe because he realised the same tourist had taken down his two guards, and the smile was rueful admiration. The smile now warped into a challenging glare.

For a long moment, they stared at each other. It was Katashi who finally broke the stand-off, calling out from his position. "I am impressed, Mr...?"

Kane said nothing. He only glared back. A line from *Shogun* came to mind: *The first rule of survival in enemy waters: reveal nothing.*

It was uttered by the main protagonist John Blackthorne. Kane thought it very appropriate.

"Well, it appears that Yoshi and Yosuke were wrong to underestimate you," Katashi said, his voice calm and his English clear, despite the heavy accent. "They were wrong, but it seems as if I was right. In my experience, it is the least likely looking men who should be feared, not the obvious ones." Katashi paused, as if trying to gauge the man before him. "What is it you want?"

This time, Kane answered. "I know who you are. Katashi Goto. Yakuza boss… and a murderer. I know what you have done. I have evidence that you killed a man. I want you to leave that armour where it is, then sit down on the floor and allow me to make a citizen's arrest." Kane knew Katashi would do no such thing, but he wanted to make the don initiate violence, if such a thing had to take place. Otherwise, the old man could rely on his façade of 'honour' again.

Katashi raised an eyebrow. "Is that a threat? Are you threatening me with more violence if I do not do as you ask?" He laughed. It was a bitter laugh void of all mirth. As the wind stirred up the waves beyond the shrine, Kane tried to analyse what Goto might be thinking. It was no more possible than trying to control the tide in the bay.

Katashi had no family aside from the so-called mafia 'family'. His wife had died years before, and he had no children. There had been mistresses. None of them counted for anything. It was just him, and he had nothing to lose and no one to fear. Besides... *He is right, I am a Yakuza boss. I am also a descendent of the samurai. Katashi Goto takes orders from no one.*

I am going to take that suit, and nothing—or nobody—can or will stop me.

And yet, something about the Englishman suggested he remained a threat. Katashi did not think him a killer, and he doubted Yoshi and Yosuke were dead. But there was something about the fearless way the man stood there, displaying almost no emotion of any kind. It unnerved Katashi. He could not beat him in a fight, not at his age, that was certain.

His hand moved subtly to his jacket, feeling the gun inside against his chest.

No. Not yet.

He thought of Taichi. Cutting off the head of a man on his knees was one thing. Fighting a stronger, younger man hand-to-hand... well, that was different. He also knew that killing a foreigner was poles apart from expiring that lowlife bastard dog, Taichi. No one would miss the young Yakuza thug. The authorities might even consider it a gift, the removal of yet another dangerous criminal from the streets. But killing a tourist? That was something no amount of government connections or mafia power could protect Katashi from.

Once they caught him—and they would catch him—the mob boss would be sent down. Since Japan still retained capital punishment, he knew he would probably receive the death penalty. Because of his age, he would likely spend the rest of days on death row. He would not allow that to happen.

Katashi Goto hung his head. He knew what he had to do. Slowly, he stepped forward, carefully removing the gun from inside his jacket. Kane didn't move.

"Okay. You are right," Katashi said as he edged forward another few steps. He held the gun aloft, as if to show he wouldn't use it. "I am much too old for this nonsense. I have achieved what I came here to achieve. I am finally blessed to have worn my ancestor's samurai suit that I have revered for so long. It has filled me with immense pride. I have at last found some solace in the revenge of my ancestor's name. It is time for me to retire from this horrible game and take up my position at the monastery. I have made many mistakes. A lifetime of them. Too many. I will not make another mistake here today." Katashi lowered his head again and, in a voice so quiet Kane hardly heard, he said, "You have my word.

Kane listened, but he remained unmoved and far from convinced of Katashi's sincerity. The mafia boss edged forward a little more, one short, slow, shuffling step at a time. There were now just ten yards between them. To Kane, the closer Katashi got, somehow the older he seemed. His shoulders were hunched, and he moved with the gait of a man sick and tired of it all…

Then, with a speed belying his years, the mafia don darted past Kane. He flew behind the ticket counter and grabbed Mika by the arm, dragging her into the corridor. To his surprise, Mika seemed not to struggle, almost as if she had expected it and allowed it to happen. *What the f…?*

Kane watched on with horror as Katashi rammed his gun into her temple.

Chapter Forty-Three

侍

Mika!

Kane felt the heat rise up his chest and neck as his face contorted with rage and anger. *How could I be so naïve? So damn stupid!* He took two instinctive steps towards Katashi, then thought better of it and held his ground, certain now the old man would shoot her dead if threatened at all.

"Okay," said Katashi. "Okay, very good. You are very wise to stop there." He fell silent for a moment, as if thinking about what to do next. He looked from Kane to the girl, who was now squirming in his clutches, then back at Kane. "This is what will happen. You will stay there. I will take this girl and my suit of armour. We will go out to the dock. There I will board my helicopter. Then I will fly to my home in Kyoto. A week later, I will travel to the monastery, where I will live out the rest of my days in peace. If you do not try to follow me, I will leave the girl on the dock. She will not be harmed. On that, you have my word. Believe it or not, I am a man of honour."

Katashi's face remained impassive, but his words did

nothing to convince Kane. He remembered once again that the honour of a criminal is barely honour at all.

Katashi continued, calmness personified. To Kane that was just further evidence of the cold, cruel monster he was capable of being. "However, if you do follow me, I will take off in the helicopter with the girl. Once we are high enough, I will throw her from the open door, and she will fall very far and suffer a horrible death. On that, you also have my word."

Mika suddenly bucked and thrashed against Katashi's grip, hearing how her life was now undoubtedly in his hands. Kane flinched, but daren't risk any sudden interventions. Katashi's wiry arms clearly remained strong, and he soon convinced Mika to be still and quiet when he unceremoniously forced the barrel of his gun hard into her mouth. Kane assumed she must be terrified, but in her eyes he saw only defiance and something like disdain, as if she were not afraid at all.

Kane inhaled, his fists clenched at his sides, knuckles white under the strain. Katashi was just an ageing gangster who happened to have risen pretty high… physically, he was an average specimen. Yet in those small, liver-spotted hands he still held all the power.

What now?

Why didn't she just get the hell out of here when she could? At least to call the cops…

As much as Kane hated it, he'd been outwitted by the old Yakuza man. All he could do now was stand back, stay alert and prepped for action, and see how things played out.

He eyeballed the mafia man for a long moment, then broke his gaze and made eye contact with Mika. Katashi had her in a crushing headlock, though her eyes were fixed on Kane.

"Okay," Kane called out. "You win. I will not follow you. I give you my word, Katashi-san, but please, do not harm the girl. She is innocent. One murder is enough for today."

"How are my men?" the mob boss enquired, one eyebrow arched.

"Sleeping," replied Kane, no trace of humour in his voice.

Katashi smiled. "Sleeping, you say? Well, best we let sleeping dogs lie, eh?" He then nodded, as if he didn't especially care if they were alive or actually dead. "Stay there. I promise she will not be harmed."

There were a lot of permutations for Kane to work through in his head during what amounted to around three seconds. If Katashi only wanted the suit and his freedom, it was possible he would leave Mika safely at the dock as he had said. Additionally, the events of the day had shown how far Katashi would go for honour. If Kane refused to listen to him, Mika could be dead in a moment.

In the end, Katashi made Kane's mind up for him. The old man began walking calmly in the direction of the dock, passing Kane as he went, gaze fixed on him. He had removed the gun from her mouth but was still digging it into Mika's skin, like a child tormenting a puppy. Mika's gaze remained connected with Kane's. The steadfast resilience he saw in her was the polar opposite of Katashi's smirking expression. The hint of respect Kane had sensed earlier had vanished, replaced now by smug contempt. And Kane was just standing there, passive, thinking and regretting. Watching her being taken. He was doing nothing. *Who have I become?*

Time seemed to slow as the two people—villain and victim—moved past Kane, close enough, he mused, to smell his shame. His thinking phase hadn't gone well. Now, he was done with it. Passive no more.

He felt himself moving. Change of plan. His stiff, straightened palm smashed into flesh and bone. He had connected perfectly with the inside of Katashi's wrist, forcing his fingers to open. Mika glanced at Kane and then was running before the gun clattered to the ground. As Katashi growled with anger and probably some embarrassment, Mika darted out of the shrine's exit and Kane watched as she sprinted across the street and was soon into the back alleys behind the nearest row of shops and restaurants.

Relieved, Kane turned his gaze back to the mafia don and then paused, wishing he hadn't seen what he thought he saw.

Two large, silhouetted figures were trotting across the street after Mika in the low light. *Yoshi and Yosuke? Fuck!* Once again, Kane cursed his idiocy. He should have secured them tighter. Should've have eliminated them from the game. *Should I have eliminated them completely?*

They had both obviously recovered enough to put Mika's life in danger again. It was all happening so fast, and he turned in time to see Katashi reaching for the weapon on the ground, and Kane reacted swiftly, and kicked it hard, sending it spinning into the near-submerged street. Suspecting Katashi wouldn't lower himself—either physically or metaphorically—to scrabbling around in the mud and puddles, Kane didn't even bother to look at him or deal with the don at all. Instead, he left him standing there with his precious suit of armour, and bolted into the street and after Mika and her would be murderers.

Chapter Forty-Four

侍

He assumed Mika knew the area well, and would be able to find an escape route and shake off the two men trailing her. *Shit, does she even know they're following?* Kane knew that if she wasn't aware of her tail, the fuckers would catch up with her quickly. Kane had to proceed with caution. He had kicked the shit out of both of these thugs. They wouldn't give him a second chance. If they knew he was following, they would shoot him until he was dead. Thus, for now he followed as quietly as he could, ducking behind trees whenever they slowed even for a stride or two, any hint to suggest they might spin around and look behind.

Stopping briefly behind the trunk of a gnarly maple tree, the scent of damp, rich soil filled his nostrils as he drew in deep breaths. The smell reminded him of his happy treks and how much he wanted to be out among nature during a long future, anywhere in the world, exploring instead of fighting. He pushed the thought aside and moved.

He heard footsteps squelching on sodden leaves, but he

could no longer see the two Yakuza men. A flash of red in the gloom caught his eye, perhaps fifty yards ahead. Mika's jacket. He followed her now, wary of where the thugs had gone. The small town was behind him, back down the hill towards the shrine and the dark waters of the bay beyond. Now there was nothing around except trees—swaying with significant force as the wind continued to gust with greater intensity. It meant that for Mika, any hiding place would barely be a hiding place at all. She might be able to stay out of sight for a few seconds, but she would have to move on, and keep moving.

As Kane kept moving too, long legs powering him upwards, he spotted something between the trunks. A small, square wooden structure half-covered with dirt and leaves.

No, Mika, bad idea.

He knew the squat building might look tempting as a hiding place but would ultimately leave her cornered. His instincts told him that she would be tempted to take cover, and he moved towards the structure too. As he approached, he saw it was a tool shed; it appeared so flimsy, Kane thought it had been lucky to survive the recent storms.

As he had predicted, he saw a red jacket adjacent to the shed. Mika pulled open the door and stepped inside, then yanked the door closed, and Kane heard the sliding of a bolt.

Mika's sense of safety must have lasted less than five seconds. Yoshi stepped out from the misty shadows and put his boot through the wooden door, breaking it loose and sending it crashing into the shed. Kane was still several yards away, but he heard Mika gasp.

He could also hear the two men speaking.

"No. No gun," one told the other. "Too messy. Too much evidence. The throat."

Mika had clearly seen too much to be allowed to just walk away. She had become too involved. Regardless of whether the authorities cared about a dead criminal lying on the ancient floor of the shrine, they would not stand by and do nothing after a young woman reported having a gun held to her head and being threatened with kidnap. Kane knew that if these men strangled her, they could have her buried in minutes. As far as they were concerned, she might never be found.

Also, Kane understood that if he stepped inside the building, he could be shot dead out of pure panic on the part of the criminals... or out of revenge for rearranging their faces. Kane grinned inwardly. He realised it wasn't at all funny, and approached slowly, looking for options. He circled around the left side of the shed. A few old-looking, rusty tools were hanging on the outside.

Kane stepped lightly up to the wooden structure, crouching low as he reached the wall. He plucked a hatchet from its hook and glanced at it. It was weather-worn, but it would have to do.

Just needs a little extra brute force, Kane mused.

His senses were heightened, and every word of Japanese he had ever picked up from books, films or brief periods of study was ready and waiting in his mind to help him figure out what the bastards were saying. He also understood what Mika was saying. She was addressing one of the men as "older brother," an attempt to pacify and show respect to him, to what Kane hoped might elicit a show of mercy in return. *Or perhaps she's just buying time... for me?*

"Strangle her," one of them stated. "Don't be afraid. She might even like it."

The other grumbled a response... Kane thought it must be difficult with a smashed jaw.

Kane's whole body tensed up with anticipation and anger. He had to wait for the right moment. As Mika took a step backwards, a futile attempt to distance herself from the attacker, Kane saw her dark hair resting against the thin window. She raised her shoulders as she hunched up defensively, like prey spotting an airborne predator.

Kane then saw a hand, its fingers curled and stiff, creeping towards her throat. He thrust up the window just as one of the fucker's fingertips met Mika's skin. Kane grabbed the forearm for leverage and dragged the hatchet through skin and flesh. Yosuke—he realised—howled as Kane reached in with his other hand and lodged it under Mika's armpit. Gritting his teeth, he pulled her quickly through the window. He continued to hold her arm as he began to run, helping her get her balance until she could run on her own. They sprinted away from the cabin, not back down the hill, their feet pounding the wet ground as they dodged trunks and jumped over roots. When they were a hundred yards away, Kane gestured to the biggest trunk he could see, and they crouched on their haunches while gorging on oxygen.

"Where should we go?" Kane asked after catching his breath. "You know the island. Where would be safe?"

"Safety is not a priority," Mika replied calmly, breathing nowhere near as heavily as Kane.

"It isn't?"

"No. The armour is the priority. It is priceless. At least, it is to me."

"Forget it, Mika," Kane stated in disbelief. "You'll get yourself killed."

Mika fixed her gaze on Kane's now. Kane believed she was around twenty, but there seemed to be decades of wisdom and experience in those eyes. There definitely didn't seem to be any fear. *Who the hell is this woman?*

"That is a price I am willing to pay."

Kane shook his head. "That's very noble, but I don't understand. If what you're saying is true… I don't doubt you by the way… then why did you run away from the shrine… and leave the armour?"

"That was a necessary decision. He had a gun, and I can't help anyone if I'm dead. Besides, it gave me time, and now I have a plan."

Kane's head shook almost of its own volition. "Which is?"

"Render those two animals redundant, and then go back, deal with Goto, and recover the armour."

"You know who he is?"

Mika nodded slowly, a spark of fire in her eyes. "Yes. Sadly, I do. We all do."

Kane nodded back, and thought maybe he was beginning to understand. "Well, I'm sorry I interrupted your plans!"

Mika's lips curled into a smile. She soon regained her earnestness. "What does honour mean where you come from, Hiram?"

"It means make sure you buy a round in the pub."

"I'm sure you are trying to be funny, but this is serious," she said, indeed sounding serious but retaining a glimmer of amusement in her eyes.

"I'm just trying to kill time and hope those thugs get off the island before you do something stupid."

"I have no doubt there are times when you want to honour your ancestors?"

"Yes, and I find it's a lot easier when I'm alive. I'm sure

they wouldn't want me to be the most honourable corpse in the woods."

"Then I will do it alone."

Mika sprang up like one of the native deer and before Kane could even try and stop her, she was off down the hill and out of sight behind a dense copse of trees.

Chapter Forty-Five

侍

"Who the hell are these Nakamuras?" Kane muttered to himself as he too pushed up and moved, giving chase to the person he had believed he was coming into the hills to rescue. Mika was almost back down at sea level by the time he caught up with her. She reached the shrine beside the bay just as the Yakuza thugs did the same thing, albeit from a different direction.

Kane spotted Katashi, and saw see the anger on his face even from distance as the boss watched his men emerge from behind the end shop in a row of stores. As soon as Yosuke had stopped in front him, Katashi reached inside his man's jacket and pulled out his pistol. He pointed it right at the centre of Yosuke's forehead as the man froze.

"Where is the girl?" Katashi spat, the contempt in his voice carrying to Kane despite the roar of the ever-growing wind.

"I am here," Mika announced.

Katashi slowly rotated his arm, moving the pistol away from his man's head and towards Mika's. Impressing Kane yet again with her stoicism, she continued, regardless of the imminent threat of being shot. "Give the suit of armour to me. It does not belong to you."

Kane expected to see a smirk blossom on Katashi's face as the young woman told the Yakuza boss with a gun how to proceed. The smirk did not come. Katashi was wet and windswept. He looked thoroughly pissed off, and ready to kill. It was fleeting, but Kane could not believe he had to consider stepping into the line of fire to save a person he had thought he'd had to saved once that day already. This time, he was sure Katashi would shoot.

After all, Japanese prisons and Buddhist monasteries are not so different. Total silence, lots of sweeping up and plenty of time to think.

Despite the murderous look on Katashi's face, Kane found himself taking a step forward. This situation would not end without loss of life. He could just feel it. He took another step.

From out of nowhere, an animalistic roar of unbridled rage froze him in his tracks. In the five seconds of chaos that followed, Katashi had been sent sprawling to the floor, the gun spiralling through the air until it crashed against the wooden wall of the shrine.

From what was now total darkness, the owner of the restaurant, Daijiro Nakamura, had emerged and attacked Katashi. He had arrived at such speed and with such force that Katashi couldn't react, and his head had smashed into the ground with a sickening thud. His two supposed protectors just looked down at him as if they were unmoved by his injuries. Their apathy left Kane wondering if they somehow thought this was a blessing in disguise.

Daijiro, the new player in this most unlikely of dramas, locked eyes with Kane. Then, with a cursory glance at the prone Katashi, he turned his attention to his sister.

"Mika? Are you hurt? Mika?"

Mika had stumbled back against the wall, wide-eyed in shock at Daijiro's sudden entrance. "I am... yes, I'm okay."

Kane was also shocked, shaking his head at the latest development. Finally, he took a couple of steps towards the pair, at the same time glancing at Yoshi and Yosuke, who still seemed at a loss as to what to do next.

Too late, Kane heard the vicious crack of a gunshot and watched on with horror as Daijiro clutched at his stomach. Mika screamed as her brother looked down at his hands, the steady flow of blood pulsing black as oil through his fingers. Daijiro's knees buckled, and he foundered, falling against the wall next to Mika, slowly slipping to the floor.

Kane turned on his heels as another gunshot reverberated; it took another three seconds to realise he'd been hit.

A third bullet smashed into the wall above him, missing his head by an inch and splitting the ancient wooden panels like an axe through kindling. Instincts threw him to the floor, his eyes fixed on the onrushing Yakuza gunmen. Kane had been lucky—the first bullet had merely grazed his shoulder. He found the strength to drag himself just inside the shrine.

Yoshi and Yosuke charged towards Kane from the shadows, their feet slapping on stone. Kane braced himself but was surprised when they bypassed him and ran directly to Daijiro, who had already been neutralised. Yoshi grabbed Daijiro round the neck and dragged him without mercy away from Katashi and flung him against a wall, his groans of agony ignored. Mika yelled in protest and moved to attack Yosuke, but she was too slow and a giant hand clamped her jaws shut as Yosuke hoisted her over his shoulder like a sack of rice. Yoshi trotted over and quickly retrieved plastic cable ties from his pocket and bound

Mika's wrists together, pulling the ties tight. Mika grunted as they cut into her skin. Yoshi grinned and pulled them a little tighter.

With Daijiro and Kane down, Yoshi then helped his boss to his feet. The old man stood there, his expression unreadable. With a slow, tired movement, Katashi raised a hand to his forehead. He pulled it away and glanced at it. It was smeared in blood. His eyes narrowed, creasing his brow in harsh lines as he surveyed the scene around him.

Daijiro was completely still as he lay slumped against the wall, blood staining his ivory kitchen clothes. Even in the darkness, Kane was horrified by the pale tone to Daijiro's skin. He'd seen that colour before. Though the poor guy still drew breath, his skin was the colour of a dead man's. Katashi glanced at Kane, an odd look in his eyes.

Kane winced and clutched his shoulder. The pain was now incredible, but his own gaze was firm.

What's that look in the mafia don's eyes? he wondered, and didn't think it was anger. *Is it sympathy?*

"I did not want this," said Katashi quietly. "I only wanted to leave this island in peace. Take my heirloom and leave Miyajima. These kids…" He waved an arm, first at Daijiro then at Mika. Both were now silent. "These kids did not need to get hurt. But you… you had to get involved. It was not your business. Now, their blood is on your hands. This time, I am taking the girl. Do you know why? Because I told you that if you respected me, she would be safe. But you did not."

"Then why not kill me right now?" Kane asked, unsure why he'd said that to a cold-blooded murderer.

"Because I want you to live with the shame of watching me walk away with this person you thought you could protect."

"Katashi-san," said Yosuke quietly, his jaw issues making it barely more than a mumble. The pain was obvious. "Let me eliminate this mosquito. He knows too much, and he—"

"He what, Yoshi? This mosquito just beat you up. He beat you both like whimpering dogs," he added, glancing at Yosuke. "Now that dog can not even bark," he grumbled, gaze settling on Yoshi's, who looked away, the shame of his broken jaw acute. Katashi shook his head, not even trying to disguise the disdain he had for his two most-trusted lieutenants.

Yosuke lowered his head. Softly, he said, "Katashi-san, we need to—"

"Enough!" hissed the mob boss, cutting his man off instantly. Katashi stepped towards Kane. "I do not know who you are, and I do not care. I admit, I admire your courage. But be warned... you have had your last chance. We will leave now. I *know* you will not follow."

Yoshi carried Mika towards Kane. Kane noticed Mika was not struggling. *What's she up to?* The thug's gun was pressed hard into her temple. Her eyes were wide, but Kane was sure she was not afraid. It was helpless rage. There was no doubting the implication. Kane clenched his teeth, exhaling through them. The urge to attack was almost overwhelming. But it was clear the thugs were right on the edge, their nerves shredded, and it was too risky. One more move, and she would be dead in seconds. Probably himself too. He remained still.

Then the Yakuza men and Mika were gone.

Chapter Forty-Six

侍

Kane slammed a fist against the wooden floor, immediately regretting it for the horrific jolt of pain it caused in his damaged shoulder. Nauseous, he took a long deep breath, then several more until the pain passed.

A small part of him hoped Katashi would leave Mika unharmed, once the old man had regained his composure. But the don was clearly unhinged, and how could Kane trust a killer? The bottom line was, he couldn't. On top of that, he didn't trust the thugs either. Kane had witnessed their momentary pause when Katachi had been felled, even if the don himself hadn't noticed it. It was strange. Then again, these were criminal bastards who obeyed only their own moral compass, which Kane believed was wayward at best.

Thus, he thought it possible they would go against their boss and take matters into their own hands, which meant they would simply eliminate Mika. They had much to lose if they were caught, and although falling foul of the mob chief was a bad idea, going to prison for his weaknesses wasn't an option either. Their situation was different to that of their boss. He was in the twilight of his mafia career, while theirs were likely just dawning. Their loyalties, Kane guessed, were not born from the same traditions as the samurai descendent. Mika had seen their faces, and she had witnessed one of them shoot her brother, Daijiro. There was just no way Kane could trust Yosuke or Yoshi. He felt sure that if it came down to a choice between their futures or Mika's, then she was as good as dead. His decision not to act rashly had only bought her time. Nothing more.

Kane pulled himself up to stand straight and tall, then he moved over to Daijiro. The restaurant manager's eyelids fluttered. Kane again noticed that his skin was deathly pale, as a single trickle of blood escaped the corner of his mouth. He had lost too much blood, pints of it, Kane guessed. He believed with some certainty that if Daijiro didn't get to a hospital soon, he would die.

But what about Mika? Kane found himself forced to make a simple choice about who's life to try and save, and who was most likely to be savable.

He closed his eyes and thought back to that earth-shattering day when he was a teenager. He had made a grave mistake that day, and until very recently, he'd had to live with it every day since. He wouldn't make the same mistake again. Kane looked down at Daijiro then placed a hand on his forehead. It felt cold. Daijiro looked up at Kane, pain evident in his eyes. There was also anger there, and frustration.

"I will be back for you. Stay awake." Kane didn't know if Daijiro understood anything that was going on. "No sleep, okay?"

"Okay," Daijiro whispered, trying to raise a smile. Kane pulled out the man's phone from his pocket and dialled 119, the number for ambulance service in Japan. He placed it into Daijiro's hand then turned to leave. He had no choice. Kane span on his heels and went after Mika.

The storm beyond the temple walls now rampaged at full force, the wind howling about Itsukushima Shrine in wild gusts strong enough to cause a power failure across the entire island. Just as Kane set off, every single one of the shrine's interior electric lamps died instantaneously. The soft glow of the real flaming lanterns—still somehow alight despite the wind rushing through the corridors of the shrine—offered the feintest of glows from within. The outside lights suddenly went out too, plunging the whole area into near complete darkness.

The totality of that darkness was profound. One one good thing about it was that if Kane couldn't see, then neither could the Yakuza thugs. He snatched his mobile phone from his pocket to use its torch. "For fuck's sake, what next?" Kane growled. The screen was smashed and service was dead. His first concern was the lost video evidence of the theft and the ritual murder he'd recorded, but that thought quickly paled into insignificance in comparison to Mika's life.

He edged his way out of the exit, surprised to step down into almost a foot of water. The storm surge was raising the sea level with frightening speed. He scooted around the western edge of the shrine towards the dock, using the railings to guide him along the submerged decking. By day it was a beautiful spot, with its view out over the O-Torii Gateway an iconic symbol of Japan, just as it had been for a millennium. Now, Kane hoped it wouldn't be forever associated with murder, chaos, death and destruction.

From every angle, the rain pelted him in vicious squalls. The wind had become a screeching tempest, and he had to pause every few seconds to catch his breath and check his progress. Struggling to keep his footing, Kane felt certain the wind was now as powerful as it had been that night in Hofu, when the ryokan roof was flipped off like a tiddlywink. Being struck by lethal, invisible projectiles was now a very real possibility.

Kane believed that no one could fly a helicopter in those conditions. Not safely. It gave him hope that the group might not depart at all. Just then, the sound of what must have been chopper blades drifted his way.

"Are you kidding me?" he said out loud into the dark, such was his disbelief. He pressed on in short, careful steps, any hint of moonlight rendered useless by the thick, scudding storm clouds. He expected an ambush at any moment, under the cover of the new darkness.

Just a second later, the mafia men became the least of his worries. A monster storm surge battered the coast, collapsing some of the shrine's structural pylons. The entire deck shifted to one side, spilling Kane into the inky waters of the bay. He grappled against the anarchic power of the current and tried desperately to cling to something solid. After a few seconds of violent struggle, he managed to clasp his right hand around a solid piece of wood and pull himself up the now sloping walkway to the opposite edge, which angled out of the sea like a half-sunken boat. Kane couldn't see more than a few yards, but the crashing and creaking of ancient timber nearby left him in no doubt as to its origin. In his heart, he knew that a portion of Itsukushima Shrine itself had collapsed into the bay.

Chapter Forty-Seven

侍

Kane pulled himself up the destroyed walkway and onto dirty ground. He had to focus on Mika.

The storm winds howled like a pack of haunted wolves as Kane pushed his body hard up against the ancient wooden support pillars of Itsukushima Shrine, trying desperately to find some shelter and protection against the elements. Another massive gust ripped around the shrine and he covered his head with his arms. Somewhere in the distance he heard a massive crack—likely one of the old pine trees at last succumbing to Mother Nature's wrath after withstanding her fury for perhaps centuries. The sound brought back memories of the floods, and he shut his eyes tight against the past and focused on the now.

Thunder rattled the wooden structure, and he opened his eyes in time to see lightning carve open the sky, and for a few seconds the shrine's vermillion-painted pillars burned bright as blood.

Mika!

He should have moved faster. Kane knew he should

have reacted quicker and gone after her before the bastards dragged her to the helicopter. More deafening thunder followed, quaking the very foundations of the sacred building.

The rain felt like bullets, a relentless barrage of ice-like needles penetrating his inadequate clothes straight to his bones.

Dammit! He knew he'd been too cautious, too worried for Mika's safety, ultimately and ironically putting her in more danger.

He scrambled to his feet and another violent gust almost swept him off balance, and he stumbled, his shoulder crashing against one of the wooden pillars as the entire structure seemed to groan under the strain. Kane had often thought his end was imminent. He'd been close to death before. Too many times. Most recently, deep beneath a pyramid in Mexico and at the mercy of a madman. Somehow, he'd escaped with his life, but he again wondered now if this was how it would end—if, after everything he'd been through, everything he'd survived, he would die here today, his body pulverised beneath the rubble of such a holy and ancient place, unable to help Mika while those bastards did whatever they...

No. I must move. Now!

The wolves' howls rose to a fever pitch as the ferocity of the wind whipped the rain sideways, and he tasted salt and knew the waters of the bay were churning beneath the tempest.

Another massive crash made him flinch. He peered through the darkness and sheets of rain to the source of the sound and though he could barely make it out, a flash of lightning illuminated the scene and he realised with horror that one portion of the tiled roof of the sacred O Torii Gate had collapsed into the broiling seawater. The massive structure was suffering as monster waves crashed against its base. Amid the strobe-like lightning flashes, Kane watched it appear, then vanish, then reappear, and each time he expected it to be gone completely. One second there; the next, swallowed by darkness. The sacred floating gateway had stood for centuries, withstanding wars, natural disasters and even time itself. For Kane, things seemed different. Somehow, it all felt like the end of things.

He turned back to the shrine structure and forced himself to breathe, taking a moment to count the seconds between lightning and thunder like his grandfather had taught him what felt like a thousand years ago. The storm seemed to be gathering itself for something bigger. Something apocalyptic.

The wind direction changed again, and suddenly he was being assaulted by more than just rain; branches, trash, chunks of wood and tiles from the roofs of nearby structures.

Another ungodly typhoon gust knocked him off his feet and he lay there helpless for a second, a small part of him wondering if he should just close his eyes and let the storm take him, but just then he recalled an old Japanese proverb, and he almost laughed at the timing of it all and yelled the words into the void, "'Fate whispers to the warrior, 'You can not withstand the storm,' and the warrior whispers back, 'I am the storm!'"

He put the perils of the storm out of his mind, concentrating his efforts on going after Katashi and his men. He had no choice. Even if they allowed her to live, what fate might she suffer at their hands? Death could even be preferrable for her.

After battling the ferocious elements and negotiating the

shifting jetty in sheer dark, Kane found he was closing in on the small dock. He saw the helicopter lights blink like a lighthouse in the darkness. When the dock was designed a thousand years ago, helicopter landings weren't part of the plan. It would be another five centuries before Leonardo Da Vinci first imagined that men could fly.

And yet, by some small miracle, the end section of the dock remained intact. It had been built stronger in order to take the relentless impact of heavy seas over decades and centuries. The small chopper perched precariously at its end a hundred yards away. Hammered by constant typhoon winds, it looked set to topple over at any moment. Kane realised with some admiration the level of skill it must have taken to even land the thing in such conditions.

The helicopter's bright headlamp was now the only thing emitting light anywhere in sight, perhaps on the entire island. As long as he approached the bastards from outside the reach of the beam, Kane thought he might just make it to the dock without being seen. Then he spotted the men.

A mere fifty yards ahead of him, Yosuke ushered the injured Katashi towards the chopper. Despite his injuries, Katashi clung onto the heavy samurai suit like a baby clutching a comfort blanket. A few yards back from them, Yoshi was forcing Mika along like a stubborn goat. Again, Kane's anger piqued, and he hustled his progress, careful not to break a leg while attempting to stay out of the light.

The rain thundered down, a deluge borne on a gale that apparently couldn't decide which direction to gust from, so instead it gusted from them all. "Anything else you wanna throw at me?" Kane shouted into the maelstrom, taking his anger out on Mother Nature as she had done with him on numerous occasions, nearly to the point of his mortality. It would have been the perfect time to question his own decisions, but Kane chose not to. He was trying to save a life he believed would soon be extinguished.

He was close enough to the group to hear the shouts of the Yakuza thugs.

"Keep moving, Katashi-san," barked Yosuke with little apparent respect for heirarchy.

Kane saw that they were just yards from the helicopter now. Mika struggled with everything she had, kicking out and scratching at Yoshi, landing more shots than might have been expected considering her condition. Physically, she was no match for a man built like an ox. But she fought and fought, knowing her very life depended on it.

As he closed in, Kane saw it all.

Thirty seconds until they board... I have to do something. I have to do it now...

Putting all his fragile eggs into one lethal basket, Kane sacrificed his anonymity and hurried forward, standing directly in the chopper's powerful beam. He was certain he'd soon be seen and shot at, but he surged on anyway, the gnarly wind and pummelling rain just more foes to face down. Driven on by Mika's survival insteincs, Kane closed to within twenty yards. Another mighty storm swell surged his way. The wave swept him off his feet and dumped him on his back. By the time he'd struggled to his feet, Katashi, his thugs and Mika were aboard the chopper.

The helicopter door remained open as the craft hovered just above the ground, and Kane watched as Yoshi's head whipped around, his eyes searching the surroundings. Kane was caught in the beam, and he was sure the pilot must have seen him and trained the powerful spotlight on his figure.

The gunshot was loud even amidst the roar of the storm.

With the wind and the movement of the chopper, it was surely more luck than judgment, but the bullet found its mark. Kane was hit, his left pinky finger obliterated above the first knuckle. His roar of agony was louder than the gunshot. He couldn't help but look at the damage done to his body, but he then forced himself to look away.

He powered on and closed to within a dozen yards of the helicopter. Yoshi planted his feet onto the chopper's landing skids as it eased further off the ground, his gun still pointed directly at Kane as he closed the last few steps.

Yoshi fired again. The wind was buffeting the craft with such large gusts that it tipped over a little just as he pulled the trigger. The bullet was close enough for Kane to hear its whistle. He was now barely six feet away and so close that he was an easy target.

As Yoshi grimaced and squeezed the trigger, Mika at last freed a leg and kicked out hard at his elbow. The bullet flew harmlessly into the blackness. Yoshi bellowed with fury—intelligible words weren't especially forthcoming with only half a functioning jaw—then turned, and kicked her in her temple with sickening accuracy. She fell back, silenced.

With his energy all but sapped to nothing, Kane was propelled only by his anger at seeing that act of violence. He launched himself at the chopper's skids as it lifted clear of the dock. He was now dangling beneath the helicopter, out of sight of the people on board. The wind buffeted his body, and the carbon fibre skids were slippery with rainwater. Worse still, the hand with the injured finger was almost too painful to use. Beneath him, the black sea raged.

Chapter Forty-Eight

侍

The rhythmic drone of the helicopter blades pulsing through the air above Hiroshima Bay was second in volume to the roar of the tempest blowing through the open doors of the chopper. Mika's slim wrists burned from the zip ties cutting into them, but she ignored the pain and focused instead on the massive thug standing across from her, staring at her. The Yakuza man's shoulders were twice the width of her own. She knew she couldn't beat in him a battle of strength. She didn't think she'd need to. Between him and the other huge bastard in a suit, they filled nearly half the passenger compartment.

A quick glance through the open side door, Mika spotted the distant glow of Hiroshima city and the nearer lights of the shrine sparkling on the churning dark water far below. The ferocious gusts of wind whipped Mika's long hair around her face. With her hands bound, she couldn't do much about it as her analytical mind worked out distances, angles and possibilities.

The Samurai Code

She thought the smaller one's name was Yoshi. *Gorilla. Ha.* She was half his size. *Sometimes,* she mused, *size did not matter.*

Yoshi noticed Mika now staring back at him, and he smirked. "You should have kept running away," he yelled, his deep voice almost lost beneath the noise of the engine and the wind. He shook his head and grinned. "Now we can have some fun... mile high club?"

Mika knew exactly what that meant. She would rather die than allow that monster anywhere near her body. She abstractedly imagined her body washing up on a rocky island somewhere in the bay, if it was ever found at all. *Well, you big ugly bastard, rather yours than mine.*

Mika knew Yoshi had made one critical error—he'd bound her wrists in front of her body instead of behind. Mika knew that simple mistake would cost him terribly.

The chopper suddenly banked, and instinctively Mika let herself sway with the motion, her balance on her seat faltering, as if she were dizzy. She had been acting more submissively than she'd have preferred to since they had snagged her, as if the fight had left her. It was very far from the truth. *Let them think I'm just a weak woman, afraid of scumbags...*

"Please," she muttered, letting her voice tremble. "I will... I will do whatever you want when we land. Just... please don't hurt me."

Yoshi stepped towards her, his bulk now looming over her. "It is much too late for that, little one. I always do what I wa—"

In one slick motion, Mika edged forward on the seat, leaned back and drove both her feet hard towards his head. One caught him in the throat and the other crashed into his already smashed jaw. Yoshi's head snapped back and Mika was already moving. In a blur of movement, Mika brought her tied hands up and over his thick neck as he stumbled backward, and she twisted her body, using the bastard's own bulk against him as she yanked the zip ties tight against his windpipe.

Yoshi flailed, but Mika had her legs wrapped tight around his torso, clamped to his back like a spider. Her muscles burned as Yoshi spun and he slammed Mika's back into the wall of the helicopter. Up front, the pilot yelled something Mika couldn't make out.

Through her pain, she continued squeezing her arms and legs around Yoshi, but her strength was waning. She glanced left and saw the other huge bastard—*Yosuke?*—watching on passively, with something like a smirk curling his lips. Evidently, he wasn't interested in helping his Yakuza colleague.

Momentarily distracted Mika winced as an elbow dug into her ribs and she gasped, somehow managing to hold on. She could see Yoshi's cheeks turning red, and felt his movements grow more desperate as he tried to free himself from her grip. The helicopter suddenly dropped and she felt her stomach lurch, but Yoshi lurched too... right towards the open door.

The other man reacted and grabbed Yoshi around the waist and pulled them both away from the door and away from certain death, then Mika released her grip, letting the momentum of Yosuke's pull carry Yoshi forward as she slammed both feet into his lower back and shoved. Yoshi stumbled, just as the chopper banked again, and he barreled towards the gaping door, saving himself at the last moment by grabbing the door frame with one hand.

The helicopter tilted hard back the other way and Mika

tumbled across the floor as Katashi fell from his seat and for just a moment they were face to face, eyeballing each other. Before she could spit in his face... or headbutt the bastard... the shifting chopper sent the old man rolling away and she rose to her feet, her shoulder slamming into the opposite side as Yoshi turned to face her, murder in his eyes.

"You little fucking bitch," he growled, clutching his neck.

Mika scanned around the cabin for something to help. She knew she had only a few seconds before Yoshi recovered enough to attack her. No longer with the element of surprise in her favour, she knew she couldn't win. She spotted a metal bracket on the wall above a now reseated Katashi. Risking the don stabbing or shooting her, she lunged for the bracket and yanked, ignoring the agony of the cable ties cutting further into her skin.

Mika pulled and glanced over her shoulder and saw Yoshi charge... just as the bracket came loose. She dropped and ducked, dodging his wild attempt to grab her, and swung the bracket up into the fleshy part behind his knee. Yoshi roared, and staggered against a wall.

Still Yosuke let it play out... staring at Mika as she stared back at him. He was clearly enjoying what he was witnessing. *Why doesn't he just kill me?* Mika mused, but then a hand clutched her ankle and pulled hard. Mika went down and her chin smashed against the rigid edge of a seat as Yoshi dragged her across the cabin floor. She kicked wildly, her free leg clattering into his injured knee; Yoshi lost his grip for half a second.

It was all Mika needed, and she twisted and freed her ankle from his clutches and threw herself towards the cockpit, ducking below Yoshi's swing. She reached for the pilot's headset and yanked it free with her bound hands, and the pilot screamed in surprise and then terror as Mika then reached for the cyclic steering stick. Before she could grab it she felt herself being hauled backwards by two powerful hands and shoved into a seat. When she looked up, it was the other bastard, Yosuke, glowering down at her and pointing a gun into her face.

Chapter Forty-Nine

侍

Mika wasn't afraid of these bastards. At least, that's what she told herself.

They were nothing but overgrown meatheads with *unko* for brains. Still, they did have guns. That was an inconvenience. If she did not choose her actions carefully, she knew she would be dead before she could fulfil her duty.

A long time ago, the Nakamura family had inherited a sacred mission. That duty was disguised behind the curatorship of the Itsukushima Shrine museum. The role of curator was a front, though they each took their respective duties very seriously.

The real role—their sacred task—was of a more ancient origin. Right now, it had fallen upon Mika to uphold their oath.

She knew what she had to do. Getting it done would prove more difficult. It was risky, of course. She would probably die either way. But the priority now was not her life. The samurai suit had to survive. It could not fall into the wrong hands. That was the priority. The Nakamura family knew their lives were secondary to the artefact. They always would be.

Mika wasn't exactly sure what the men would do to her. Yet, she knew she could live with physical pain more easily than the emotional pain of letting her family and her ancestors down.

What happened next was the very last thing she had expected. The old man, Katashi Goto, who was now sitting opposite her in the rear of the helicopter, had his unfastened seatbelt hanging loose at his side. He appeared to be content with how things had gone so far, unconcerned by the mayhem he had caused, and that which Mika had caused since. The two henchmen stood rigid, focused, eyes darting around the cabin… clearly on edge, and apparently waiting for orders from Katashi. Nobody was speaking. It seemed to Mika as if there was some unknown tension in the air towards Katashi, though Katashi seemed unaware of it.

The chopper twisted and dipped in the storm. The pilot was struggling to hold the craft steady as they ascended further from the island. No one—*except the pilot, hopefully,* Mika thought—seemed too concerned by what Mika believed was a very real chance of crashing. Her stomach churned under the duress of the inconsistent rise into the dark sky.

Suddenly, the two thugs nodded at each other without speaking. Yosuke, the slightly older one, grabbed Goto by the scruff of his suit jacket and hauled him to his feet.

"What is this?" Katashi demanded. "Yosuke? What the fuck are you—"

Yoshi caught him on the chin with such a sharp jab that Katashi didn't finish his sentence. Except, he didn't fall. Yosuke held him upright. Next, he thrust the don towards the open door. Yosuke then grabbed his gun and shoved it into the mafia boss's back.

"Any last words, old man?" Yosuke asked, smirking. "You have less than ten seconds to live, so we don't have time for your usual rambling diarrhea."

Katashi didn't speak. He closed his eyes for a moment, then took a deep breath, as if coming to terms with the sudden betrayal. He opened his eyes again and exhaled. He nodded so subtly it was as if it were only for himself, but it did not go unnoticed by Mika.

"No," he said quietly. He angled his neck to look at the girl he had forced into this situation. His eyes softened a fraction. "No words."

There was a moment of silence, and Mika wondered if the two bodyguards were already regretting their actions.

"Do what you think you need to do, Yosuke," Katashi said calmly. "It matters little. You will never amount to anything. Neither of you. If you had the strength of character, you would have done this many years ago. You would have acted, as men, years ago, as I did with Daiko Okana, when I was younger than you are now. Yet, you did not. Because you could not. You were not capable. You couldn't even beat this little woman," he added, flicking his head Mika's way. "I pity you. I pity both of you. You are weak. You are mere thugs. You are nothing."

Katashi faced the open door straight on and looked out into the void. The wild wind whipped his white ponytail around his face, leaving his expression unknown to the others in the chopper.

"I am ready," he whispered, waiting for the act that would prove Yosuke's resolve. It did not come. He grinned a little wider. "See. You are not capable, Yosuke. Maybe you should hand the gun to Yoshi. Maybe he is more of a man than you?"

"Do it," Yoshi yelled, the result more a sound than actual words. "Shoot him!"

Yosuke faltered. It was clearly proving more difficult to kill his boss than he had thought it would be. He glanced at Yoshi, who stared back at him, willing him to get on with it.

Yoshi was about to grab the gun, but Katashi Goto turned towards him and said, "A man's fate is a man's fate, and life is but an illusion. I am wise, you son of a pig. Wise men prepare for treachery." Then he started laughing, just as Yosuke pulled the trigger and shot him in the back. Visibly trembling, he shoved Katashi out the door.

"Why didn't you shoot him in the head?" Yoshi yelled, or at least tried to.

"I... I couldn't bring myself to..."

"You pushed him out of a fucking helicopter... what are you talking about?!"

Yosuke clasped his hand around his own forehead like a claw as if trying to control his brain, which must have been twisting and spiralling like the helicopter.

Mika froze. Seeing such violence up close was shocking, no matter how determined she was to be unafraid. But the act had given her a moment to think. When the mob boss had glanced at her, she had sensed what might have been a hint of sympathy in his eyes. It meant nothing to her. This was his fault. They had turned on him because he was a bastard. They would kill her next, with the don out of the picture, of that she was certain.

She waited until Yosuke sat down again and remained still while he finally gloated with Yoshi about killing the don. The excited, childlike expression on his face disgusted Mika. Then, moving with a speed fuelled by hatred and adrenaline, and of course, duty, she ducked past Yoshi, grabbed the samurai suit and launched it out of the open door.

"Noooo!" Yosuke yelled.

He grabbed wildly at Mika. She was fast, and she was done with being grabbed by these men today. She fended him off with stiff open palms, and he couldn't grab her tight. She squirmed away before arcing a vicious elbow into his cheek, then another to the eye, and he stumbled back. She swivelled and slammed a right foot hard into Yoshi's sternum, momentarily disabling him. At that moment, she was glad her grandfather had insisted she practice her martial arts skills in the gym.

She stepped to the doorway and was about to jump, knowing it was her best chance of survival. As she bent her knees, Yosuke grabbed her ankle, his momentum taking him sliding onto the floor. Mika lifted her other foot and stamped down on his face, hard and uncompromising. He yelled and released his grip. Then Yoshi surprised her, grappling at her arms, but she turned on him and headbutted him square on the bridge of his nose. Blood erupted, and he again staggered back, his face full of shock at the attack she had attempted.

Yosuke was on his feet now, and he clasped Mika's forearm. He dragged her to the doorway and held his gun to her head.

"One bullet left for you, bitch," he growled.

Mika grinned as she tumbled out of the doorway.

Chapter Fifty

侍

Mika's arms flailed in the air. She had planned to jump, yet her exit from the chopper had been accelerated by external force. But her eyes were open. Even in this perilous situation, she found herself wondering why she was not dead. Had she not been shot in the head?

Then she felt the pressure around her ankle. She was no longer falling. As a strong grip clasped her leg, she grasped the arm, heaved herself upright and found herself staring at… *Hiram Kane?*

She screamed over the noise, "What the hell are you—"

Kane ignored her and cut her off. "We're going to drop," he yelled into her ear. "Cross your legs at the ankles. Keep them tight until we hit the water. Under the surface, spread your limbs out to stop sinking. Got it?" Mika nodded. "Good. Go!"

Dozens of feet fell away in milliseconds. The water impact felt like being hit by a speeding truck. Thoughts of spreading her limbs out to maintain the best form crashed out of Mika's mind immediately. She was sinking. She had long been preparing for these moments—for the the biggest moment of her life—but she had not anticipated it would involve deep, dark and dangerous water. The black sea was like a monster swallowing her whole. She could not breathe, and she didn't know if she was drowning or panicking. Either way, one would soon lead to the other.

She tried desperately to flap her arms and project herself towards what she hoped was the surface, but she was just tumbling in the engulfing, cloying darkness. Trying again to push up, she realised her right hand would not move. She was sure it was trapped in seaweed or rope. Another tug did nothing to release it.

Then she was gliding through the water. Now, she thought it was a rope around her wrist that was pulling her to shore. As she glided more smoothly and the water became only slightly less churned up, she saw Kane's boots and realised that the object around her wrist was a hand. The same firm grip that had halted her fall in the air. She forced her head above the gnarly surface and gasped for breath. Only fifty yards away the safety of the shore awaited.

The waves fought against them, pushing and pulling like a living thing determined to keep its prey. Salt burned her eyes and throat as another surge crashed over her head. Kane's grip tightened, anchoring her against the current's relentless pull.

"Kick!" he shouted, his voice barely audible above the roar of the water and the distant thrum of the helicopter's retreating rotors.

She complied, her legs working frantically beneath her. Each stroke sent pain shooting through her injured ankle— a souvenir from their hasty departure. The cold had numbed it somewhat, but not enough.

Through the spray and foam, she glimpsed land. *If we can just reach the shore...*

A sudden undertow yanked at her legs, threatening to drag her under again. Kane jerked her forward, his powerful strokes cutting through the resistance. His face was a mask of determination, jaw clenched against the effort.

"Almost there," he grunted. "Don't stop now."

The beach seemed impossibly far away still, but she could make out details now—the rocky outcropping to the left, the steep embankment rising behind the narrow strip of sand, the distant silhouetted masses of the surrounding hills. Safe haven, if only they could reach it.

Her lungs burned with each labored breath. The adrenaline that had carried her through the fall and impact was fading, replaced by bone-deep exhaustion.

Her foot scraped against something solid—the seabed. They were reaching shallower water. Kane shifted his grip to her upper arm, half-dragging her now as the water level dropped to their waists, then their knees.

Strong hands clutched hers, pulling her the final few yards onto land. She collapsed onto the gravelly shore, coughing up seawater as her body trembled uncontrollably.

Kane and Mika lay on their backs on the stony beach, drawing in the wonderous oxygen as the storm still swirled around them and battered their bodies, swathes of stinging, salty water burning their skin and stinging their eyes. Finally, Kane yelled above the din of the wind, "Are you okay?"

"I... yes, I think so. Thank you!" She struggled onto an elbow and turned to face him. "And you? Are you okay?"

"Yes, I am, somehow... and you're welcome." Kane shook his head. "And you're also lucky, Mika. Very lucky.

You could've been killed. Those men... I thought you were—"

"But I wasn't killed. You saved me. Yes, I am lucky."

Kane closed his eyes and exhaled, shivering from the cold. "That's the last time I ever go in the sea. I'm totally over water. I'm done with it!"

Chapter Fifty-One

侍

"You fucking idiot," Yoshi grunted, almost snarling. "How did you let that little girl overcome you?"

Yosuke glared at his cousin. "She messed you up too. She busted your nose. Anyway, she is dead now. Goto is dead. That means there is no evidence of us being there on the island. You know the police are with us. And our man turned off all the security cameras at the shrine. That means the only people who knew we were there were Goto. Dead. And the girl. Dead. The—"

"How do you know she is dead?" Yoshi interrupted. "She jumped before we could shoot her."

"She tumbled under the chopper; she had no control at all. She probably hit the water headfirst. The prick from the restaurant will not survive. That only leaves the Englishman. We will send someone to deal with him before he can leave the island."

"What about him?" Yoshi said, pointing at the pilot. "He knows too."

The Samurai Code

Yosuke leaned in closer, keeping his voice low. "He is not a problem. I will deal with him once we have landed."

Yoshi nodded, but not with conviction. "What about the armour?"

"Fuck the samurai suit. That was only money. The power we will get now old man Goto is gone will be worth a hell of a lot more. And do not worry, cousin, there will be more money. There will always be money for the Yakuza. Especially for the new dons." Yosuke grinned.

Yoshi finally grinned back. "You are right. We will finally get the power, the respect and the recognition we deserve... and the money."

The cousins embraced. Up front in the cockpit, however, there were no smiles to be seen.

"I knew it," Kuru barked. "It is too dangerous. We are not going to make it."

"Quit your fucking whining," Yosuke spat back over his shoulder. "You sound like that little girl, Taichi... and you know what happened to him." He laughed. "At least you do not have that fucker's giant fat head weighing this helicopter down. Or the don, or the girl. See, we have done you a favour. So fucking get on with it."

"Anyway, we are the dons now, Kuru," Yoshi added. "It would be wise for you to remember that."

"If... if we do not make it through the storm we will all be dead," the pilot replied.

Yosuke leaned forward, putting his head close to Kuru's, blood dripping from his battered face. "You will land this chopper," he mumbled, "or you will be taking a high dive, just like that bitch and Goto."

"If you kill me... we all die."

Yosuke did not need to be told that. He also did not need to be mocked by a pilot. "You remember the concrete foundations, Kuru? One more comment like that, and I will be paying your wife a visit. Except, unlike Katashi Goto, I am not a used up old man with a worm for a dick."

Yosuke suddenly leaned past Kuru's other shoulder and snatched the photograph pinned to the chopper's dashboard. It was a photo of Kuru's wife and children. "Yes, she is very beautiful. I think I would like to visit her. I think she would like it too. I think I will spend some quality time getting to know your wife before I bury her and your two children alive beneath a million tons of fresh concrete."

As Kane's breathing returned to normal, he noticed that the precious air was dry. "Has the damn storm finally stopped?" he asked Mika, but with his face towards the heavens, it was as if he were asking the gods.

At that very moment, the island's backup generators kicked in. The whole bay around the shrine was suddenly bathed in the dazzling glow of dozens of blinding floodlights. It snapped Kane from his abstracted thoughts. He glanced out over the water's raging, silvery surface and froze.

Movement? Yes... there.

Amongst the dips and troughs of the choppy surface, something moved. Kane was sure it was a person, thrashing in the water.

On instinct alone, and forgetting his very recent declaration about never again going in the sea, Kane sprang into action. He sprinted for the water's edge and dove in, ignoring once again the trepidation for dark water he'd endured since almost drowning as an eight-year-old. His strong legs surged him up over the high swells and out of the deep troughs, towards...

Katashi?

Under normal circumstances, Kane knew the bay was shallow so close to the shore, perhaps only three feet. No one could survive a three-hundred-foot fall into three feet of water. But these were far from normal circumstances, and Kane guessed the depth beneath the storm surge could be nearer twelve feet, maybe even fifteen. Maybe the old man had even drifted closer to shore from farther out. If he was alive when he fell, there was a chance he could have survived the fall.

Tough old bastard.

What Kane cared about, though, was justice, and, as unlikely as it had seemed seconds ago, he now saw a glimmer of a chance to help serve it up to Katashi.

Kane finally reached the Yakuza man, aided by a feisty current. He gripped Katashi, facing no resistance and ensuring that their eyes did not meet. A few powerful kicks later and he hauled Katashi's limp form onto the rocky beach.

Kuru swallowed hard and refocused on his windscreen, glaring into the maelstrom beyond the glass and praying he could somehow land the chopper before being slammed to the ground in a monster fireball. Even if they survived the inevitable crash, they would be burned alive.

He didn't know Yoshi or Yosuke well. He had heard about them on the Yakuza grapevine and knew what depravity they were capable of. Rape and murder were an almost weekly occurrence for the two cousins, at least that was the word on the street. They were worse, even, than Katashi Goto was supposed to be, and that was saying something. So the more he thought about it, the more he came to believe that Yosuke would do what he said to his wife and kids even if he got them safely back on the ground in Kyoto. One way or another, in that moment he did not think he would see his wife and children again.

Which meant there was only one choice left for Kuru. He would take the destiny of his life and that of his family into his own hands. He waited until they had moved back into the rear of the helicopter again and heard them talking. Then he pulled his mobile phone out and sent a brief message to his wife. It was simple:

I love you. Tell the boys I love them too. I am sorry.

And then Kuru angled the chopper down so sharply that Yoshi and Yosuke fell from their seats and slammed to the floor, screaming and shouting as the craft sped directly towards the face of a large cliff on a small island in Hiroshima Bay.

Kuru was accelerating as hard as the engine would go. With just a few seconds left before impact, he leapt from his seat and turned to face the crazed men behind him, revelling at the fear in their eyes.

"No one hurts my family," he yelled. "No one!"

Kuru had saved his family from an appalling fate, and he was sure he had saved the lives of the criminals' many future victims. His own life was the price. The two thugs had pleading looks in their eyes, as if they deserved mercy. Like children begging their father not to hurt them. In that moment, Kuru knew that he was stronger than they had ever been.

An instant later, it was all over.

Chapter Fifty-Two

侍

After Kane returned to the shore with Katashi, he immediately realised Mika wasn't doing so well. Her eyes were closed, her breathing shallow. He quickly rolled her onto her side, and she vomited out seawater in heaving spurts for several seconds. She then fell onto her back, her body completely spent from the desperate struggle to survive in the volatile water. Kane cast his eyes over her prone form, looking for blood. He soon spotted a bullet wound in her trapezius muscle, just above her collarbone. He was no expert, but the bullet seemed to have made a clean exit, which he hoped was good news.

It was Kane's guess that he had pulled her out of the chopper at the moment the shooter fired, the bullet having whizzed past her head as she tumbled out. Mika would need serious medical attention, but she would likely survive the nightmare.

Shock surged through Kane as Daijiro suddenly appeared, wobbling on legs weakened from a dangerous loss of blood. He staggered close to Mika, almost fell down next to her, and embraced his younger sibling. His eyes found Kane's.

"My... my sister," he said. "Ari—" Daijiro winced, his pain palpable. "Arigatō."

Kane nodded. A half-smile was the best he could offer. He wanted to tell Daijiro he shouldn't have moved, tell him that he should have stayed where he was in the sanctuary of the shrine and called an ambulance, instead of searching for his sister. But he knew that if the roles were reversed, he would have done the same. Daijiro didn't look good. He looked as if he had only minutes to live.

The shrine!

Kane had almost forgotten that the whole front edge of Itsukushima Shrine had collapsed into the bay. Daijiro was lucky to have gotten out of there alive. Yet, if help did not arrive soon, his luck would mean nothing. Knowing his phone was destroyed and likely those of everyone else involved too, Kane searched his surroundings for a solution. With the storm beginning to subside, a crowd had gathered along the top edge of the beach, watching the prone and injured people with morbid fascination. Yet, unlike at the river a few days earlier, nobody was rushing to help. Kane suspected that Katashi was widely recognised, and people were putting their own safety first. Surely one of them had at least called an ambulance. He searched his exhausted brain for the Japanese word, but he could not find it.

Instead, he called out in English, "Ambulance!"

"Okay!" came a shout from the edge of the beach. Kane felt relief on hearing possibly the most universally understood word in the world. A minute later, he heard sirens in the distance.

Kane turned his attention to Katashi. He hustled over to the don's inert body then hauled him against one of the last intact jetty posts. He appraised the mafia man and saw the bullet wound in his lower chest. He'd been shot in the back from point-blank range, and the bullet had left his body through a gnarly exit wound in his chest, from which his lifeblood seeped in a steady flow. Kane believed that, like Daijiro, the Yakuza boss was not long for this world.

A surge of pain reminded Kane of his own destroyed finger. It was just one more reason to see Katashi receive justice. Looking down at the man, slumped against the post, Kane knew he needed a hospital soon to have even the slimmest chance of surviving.

Katashi grumbled something Kane couldn't make out. His eyelids twitched, then slowly parted. He squinted against the blaze of the floodlights, and his eyes widened when he saw Kane looking down at him. Very subtly, he nodded, recognition settling in his eyes. Kane thought he looked calm, despite what would surely prove to be a fatal injury. Kane stepped back from the don.

"It is good... it is good that you are the last man I will see before I die." The criminal's voice came out thin and raspy, so quiet that Kane had to lean in closer to hear.

"Why?" Kane asked, baffled to hear those words from a man whose plans he had tried his very best to ruin. "Why didn't you kill me? You had the perfect chance. You have to know I will turn you in to the police."

Katashi tried hard to shake his head but failed. A low wheeze escaped his lips, turning an ominous shade of blue from the cold. "N-no. I do not think you will." Katashi almost smiled, almost laughed, until a spasm of choking clenched his throat. Droplets of blood sputtered from his lips. The blood-filled chokes of a man close to death.

Recovering slightly, Katashi managed to say, "There is no time."

Going to hospital—surviving—would mean certain prison for the notorious Yakuza man. Perhaps even death row. Kane now understood Katashi had chosen not to fight that last fight. Yet the man was a murderer. In part, he was also responsible for the attempted murders of Mika and Daijiro—and of Kane himself. That wasn't Kane's main concern right now. Though he didn't pull the trigger, Yoshi and Yosuke were Katashi's men. Regarding the slaughtered Taichi, it was Katashi who had swung the killing blade. He simply had to face justice. Kane moved to Katashi's side, ready to haul him to his feet.

"Wait," muttered the mafia don, wheezing again. "Stop. You are... a man of honour. I want you to know I... I have honour too—"

"I watched you cut off a man's head," spat Kane. "How can that be honourable? You murdered him!"

Katashi winced, clutching his chest. He closed his eyes. "It is true," he said, the words coming between wracking breaths. "I did kill a man today. And yet... it is murder only in your foreign eyes. You are not Japanese. In my world, and in the world of my ancestors, an act of vengeance is... it is an acceptable act." Katashi's eyes opened briefly, then screwed tightly shut again. The man was clearly in agony. He continued with obvious difficulty.

"The shame of... of what Taichi's ancestor did, it has shadowed my family for hundreds of years. Believe me when I..." His voice faltered, and Kane thought he might pass out. After a few laboured breaths, he continued. "... believe me when I tell you how that shameful act has shadowed the Minamoto clan too. I believe they, and any true samurai clan, would... would have sanctioned what I did today. It is bushido. It is the samurai code. Not murder, whatever you think." Katashi wheezed again, weakening by the second. "There is only one... there is only one judge of the honour of a samurai; himself. The decisions we make and the actions that follow... they are the true reflection of who we really are. We cannot hide from ourselves. We... we cannot hide from who we are."

Kane was well read on the culture and philosophies of the samurai. As little as a century and a half ago, Katashi's argument might have been valid. But the days of the samurai had long finished, and there could be no moral justification for what Kane had witnessed today. It had been cold-blooded, pre-meditated murder, plain and simple. If the mafia boss thought he could justify his sickening act based upon some ancient code, Kane knew he was wrong. That was Katashi's world. It was not the world of Hiram Kane, and he would never be a part of it.

Katashi managed to find a few more words. "I can see by the look in your eyes that you... you struggle to accept my words. I understand, Mr—?"

"You don't need to know my name."

The last few minutes had seen a significant lull in the storm. Kane needed to move fast—he had to ensure Katashi received his justice. He leant over the don in order to haul the Yakuza man to his feet.

Then he heard another voice.

Chapter Fifty-Three

侍

Kane's eyes widened.

Another old man was standing there, a man older even than Katashi. This new man was short and lean and had a shock of white hair cropped close to his scalp. Despite his diminutive stature, the man had a certain presence about him, and in his small, shining eyes Kane sensed great strength and wisdom and no shortage of authority. Somehow, he thought he knew who it was.

"I am Nori Nakamura."

On hearing the name, Mika looked over. "Sofu?"

She tried to stand, but her grandfather rushed over and crouched beside her, easing her back down.

"My granddaughter," he said as he appraised her wounds. A subtle nod followed. Then, apparently satisfied, the old man turned his eyes on his grandson, Daijiro. The young man was not moving, and his eyes were closed. His chest rose and fell in the tiniest of swells. Yet Nori remained unerringly calm. He stood up.

"My little ones," he said, "help is coming. Do not worry.

Now, you are safe." He placed a palm on each of their cheeks. Mika closed her eyes to rest. Daijiro did not respond.

Nori Nakamura turned back to Kane. "Thank you for helping my family, Mr. Kane."

"I'm not sure how much I've helped," Kane replied. "They are very badly injured. We need to get them to a hospital."

"A few more minutes, Mr. Kane. The paramedics are coming. They are imminent. We cannot move the children —we need to wait for the ambulance. Listen."

Kane listened. The increasing volume of sirens told him help was approaching soon. He wasn't at all convinced Daijiro would make it that long.

Nori turned his head to look at the stricken Yakuza boss. "Who is that man?" he asked, though Kane sensed he already knew.

Kane gave Nori Nakamura a hasty run-down of the events of the last few hours. Nori listened with intent, his eyes fixed on Katashi with intensifying rage. When Kane had finished explaining, a strange expression took over Nori's face.

Nakamura approached the mafia boss with short yet confident strides and knelt down beside him. "Can you hear me, Katashi Goto?"

Katashi did not respond for a while. Nori Nakamura gently slapped his cheek.

"Katashi Goto." This time it was a statement.

Katashi's eyes opened and his pupils dilated in obvious shock, as if he'd seen a ghost. He closed them again and nodded just once. After a few seconds, he opened them again and looked into Nakamura's eyes with something like disdain.

"It is quite a story you have told," Nori said. "However, it is unfortunate for you that I know a different tale. My duty here is to protect the artefacts in the Itsukushima Shrine. It has always been that way. Sadly, it seems as if many of those artefacts are now lost to Mother Nature, including much of the shrine itself. The shrine will be rebuilt, restored to its former glory. The legacy of the artefacts will live on. However, reputations cannot be rebuilt. And I know something about your reputation, Katashi Minamoto."

"What?" Kane blurted. "His name is Minamoto?"

"Yes, Mr. Kane," Nori answered, his gaze never leaving Katashi. "For many decades he has gone by the name of Goto to hide from his inglorious past. But this… this *man*… he has been living a lie. Many Yakuza men are descendants of the samurai. That means the name of Minamoto is infamous among them, synonymous with betrayal and dishonour. This man—this *Goto*—was ambitious. He wanted to ascend the Yakuza hierarchy to satisfy his selfish lust for wealth and power. He also knew it was impossible with the name Minamoto, so he changed it. You see, not only am I director of antiquities and the curator here on Miyajima, but…" Nakamura paused. He looked around at Daijiro and Mika, pride evident in the radiance of his eyes, then continued. "Well, I am also what you might call an expert on the ways of the samurai. There is perhaps one more thing you might like to know, Mr. Kane."

Kane's mind twisted and turned at this new revelation, while out of the corner of his eye he saw the red and blue flashes of fast-approaching ambulance lights.

"So, you're telling me Katashi Goto is actually a descendent of the warrior he was claiming to take revenge upon? And that he killed his own kin, cut off his head, just to feed the lie?" Kane was incredulous and looked at Katashi Goto —*or Minamoto, whatever the hell his name is*—with a whole new level of loathing.

"Yes, that is what I am saying. Katashi was Minamoto, and he was ashamed to be Minamoto. By slaying yet another member of that clan, he believes he has removed that shame. I do not understand it any more than you do. A diseased mind, like the criminal mind always is."

Kane just nodded, words failing him amidst the madness.

"And that other thing I mentioned?" added Nakamura. "Would you like to know what it was?"

Kane nodded again

"You met my son, Naki, in Hofu. Now you have met my grandson, Daijiro, and my granddaughter, Mika. And now you have met me, Nori Nakamura." Nori faced Kane. "Mr. Kane, we are the last descendants of the noble clan of Taira samurai. The suit of armour this man stole belonged to us. It has been under the watch of my family at the Itsukushima Shrine Museum for the last thirty years. It is one of Japan's most important national treasures. We have known about Katashi's desire for the armour for many years. We hoped that perhaps he had given up. But it seems we were wrong—I was wrong."

Kane and Nori Nakamura now turned to face a beaten and exposed Katashi Minamoto. At least, they thought he was beaten. The mafia man now stood before them, a tight, blue-lipped smile on his pallid face. To see him standing there was itself surprising, but what they saw in his right hand was much more shocking. The O Tanto dagger had been cleaned of blood by the waters of the bay.

"Honour is an overused word, Nakamura," he said

quietly, "and your words are cheap. Life is too short not to have what we want. Would you not agree?"

"You have lived a selfish life, seeking *only* what you want. If I do not agree, then I would condemn your whole life. And I must tell you that I do not agree."

"It does not matter what happens to me now," said Katashi. "I have worn that suit of armour, and if I die—and die I most surely will—it will be the death of a fulfilled man. I felt as if I had been transported back to the great battle to begin again. Now, it is time to demonstrate how I really feel about you." Katashi pointed the dagger towards Kane's chest. "People should not stand in the way of destiny," he said.

He drew back his arm and flicked his wrist, sending the knife slicing through the air.

Chapter Fifty-Four

侍

Kane heard a horrified scream. He wondered for a second if it was his own, caused by the knife entering his flesh. Then he saw Nori Nakamura on the floor beside him, a wound in his chest and blood already spreading across his cotton shirt like the black stain of death itself.

"No! No!" Kane yelled.

It had all happened so fast. Katashi raised the weapon, and Kane felt sure he was about to die, certain the dagger had been pointed in his direction. Then it clicked.

With the reflexes of someone half a century younger, Nori Nakamura had flung himself in front of Kane and taken the hit. Mika's scream was raw and wild; the scream of someone whose heart was broken. In desperation, the old curator grabbed the handle with two hands and yanked the blade out of his body and flung it aside. Kane knew that would only make the bleeding worse, and in seconds he had stopped moving and went still. Dead.

Nori Nakamura's final act in a long life of service was to sacrifice himself to save Kane. Beneath the enormous weight of that knowledge, Kane slumped to his knees, his head buried in his hands. He was so distraught, that he didn't see Katashi approach. He only felt the blade against his windpipe, already drawing a trickle of blood from beneath the skin.

"Why must people always interfere? Why is that? The old man is dead, and yet he has achieved nothing. I am afraid he was right, though. I am who he said I was. But what does it matter? He is dead, I am dying, and I will still kill you anyway. Before that, I will educate you on the meaning of the word 'honour.' Honour is to let each man make his own choices."

Kane's jaw twitched. His jowls flexed. His eyes narrowed as rage flooded through him like an avalanche. A man had just saved his life, dying in the process. Katashi was right. It had achieved precisely nothing.

So this is how it finally ends, he thought.

He experienced no images of his life flashing before his eyes, not like in the movies. Kane was almost disappointed. He closed his eyes. He'd enjoyed a good life up until now. He'd travelled the world, and been on fantastic, life-changing adventures. He had some brilliant loyal friends and had worked with and studied under so many inspiring people and professors. There had been loves and losses, the greatest love of which had been his kid brother. But after eleven-year-old Danny went missing in mysterious circumstances, it had become Kane's greatest loss until, thirty years later, he had turned up out of the blue a few months ago. There was of course his supportive family. And there was Alexandria Ridley, his soul mate. It was Danny's smiling face he saw now, seconds before his death.

"Goodbye," said Katashi. He slowly rotated the blade to ensure it was at the perfect angle for slicing open Kane's throat. The lengthy blade glinted in the first ray of sunlight after the storm, shining like a mirror.

"Before you kill me, Minamoto," Kane said, "I must tell you something. You have lived a life obsessed with honour, so please do me the honour of listening to my final words."

Kane could see Katashi's face reflecting in the blade that extended beyond his jaw. The man looked irritated but allowed Kane his final wish.

"Speak," he hissed impatiently.

"There is one thing more important than honour." Kane paused as he took another glance at the blade.

"And what is that?" Katashi growled.

Mika smashed Katashi's head so hard with the rock that he slumped to the ground immediately, losing consciousness before his skull bounced off the floor. He did not move; not even a twitch. Kane opened his eyes. Mika just stood there before him, her face expressionless, nothing to indicate any emotion at all. She had just watched her grandfather murdered in cold blood. Her brother was likely going to die.

Kane stood up as the enormity of it all became too much for Mika. Her legs buckled. Kane caught her under the armpits just before she fell. He looked at her with admiration. He had saved her life, and now she had returned the favour, helped by the reflection in the blade that told Kane he should buy time while she approached Katashi from behind.

He eased her over to where Daijiro still leaned, his back resting against the post, unmoving, just as the paramedics arrived and set to work on the Nakamura siblings.

Kane heard a low groan. He turned to face the fallen mafia boss lying on the ground. Kane wasn't taking any chances. The sea was significantly calmer now, and a length of rope had drifted onto the half-submerged dock. Kane grabbed it and used it to bind Katashi's hands behind his back. He dragged him into a sitting position, and looked once more into the hard, cold eyes of the Yakuza man. He saw no fear there, despite the fact he would be put to death or at least spend the rest of his life in isolation on death row. Kane searched that worn out face for any trace of emotion and found nothing. Katashi's own men had betrayed him, and for a lifetime of greed, violence and corruption, he would pay the ultimate price.

"So, what is the answer?" Katashi croaked. "You... you did not tell me."

"What is more important than honour?" Kane narrowed his eyes. "I am."

The corners of Katashi's mouth dropped as he realised he had been tricked, the supposedly noble conversation nothing more than a ruse to buy time. As police arrived to carry the Yakuza boss away, Kane added, "Maybe you can serve your time with dignity to honour your many victims. Oh yeah... and you wanted my name. My name is Hiram Kane."

Chapter Fifty-Five

侍

Katashi let out a long, rattling sigh—his last breaths as a free man. Seconds later, he was laid on a stretcher, being given a shot of something Kane could only guess at. He was then wheeled away to face a long overdue comeuppance.

After several deep breaths, Kane turned to check on Daijiro and Mika Nakamura. Mika had been given a heavy sedative and was now lying back on a stretcher, her eyes open but unseeing.

"How is she?" he asked the attending paramedic. "Will she be okay?"

"Yes," the paramedic replied, though he didn't smile. "I think she will. But I am not sure about..." The paramedic shifted uncomfortably, and he turned back to Mika.

Kane knew why the medic looked so concerned. Daijiro's wounds were much worse. Kane knelt down beside him, next to the second paramedic. He didn't need to ask. He could see for himself. The paramedic looked at him, sympathy in his eyes. "So sorry," was all the man said.

Kane stood up and stepped away, gazing out across

Hiroshima Bay. So much death and suffering, all because of one man's selfish flaws and complete disregard for other people and their lives. The waters of the bay were churned up and dirty, a sight far removed from the blue sheen that had greeted him to Miyajima.

Today may be the last time I ever set foot in the water, Kane thought, flashes of his childhood near-drowning, the horrors of Hofu and the plunge from the chopper all flashing through his mind. He shuddered, not helped by the wind on his still-wet clothes.

"Sir?"

"All so damn pointless," he said absently, his mind still whirling over all that had happened.

"Mr. Kane?"

Kane turned. It was the paramedic tending to Mika.

"I think she wants to speak with you," the man said in English. Kane knelt down next to Mika.

She had tears in her eyes. Kane assumed she had picked up what was being said around her and knew about her brother's terrible condition and the likelihood he wouldn't make it. And yet, despite that, she looked as if she wanted to tell Kane something important. Kane crouched down a little closer. With great effort, Mika leaned forward and placed her hands on his forearms. "Go… go and find it."

Mika was weak and clearly disoriented. Her eyelids fluttered and it looked as if she might pass out. She didn't have much energy to continue the conversation, but there was something Kane wanted to say to her first.

"Mika. I am so sorry about your brother. And your grandfather. If I hadn't dragged Katashi out of the sea, your grandfather would still be alive. I thought the man should face justice, but…"

"You did… the right thing," Mika replied, her voice

weak and wheezy. "And so did they. Daijiro and my grandfather... they... fulfilled their duty..." Mika winced as a wave of pain overcame her. She inhaled, and said, with obvious effort, "They protected something more important than themselves. They have... they have lived a fuller life than someone who lived to one hundred but did not protect their heritage. But... I need you to finish their work. Go find the..."

The paramedic gently laid her back down on the stretcher. He threw Kane a look that said it was time to stop troubling her. Yet Mika's eyes fluttered open again and settled on Kane's. "Go," she whispered. Then the sedative overcame her, and she slipped away into sleep.

Kane stood and stepped away. He walked to the water's edge and hung his legs over the edge of the dock. As he sat there, one of the paramedics approached and insisted they take him to hospital. Kane declined. "Though I'll take some antiseptic and a bandage for this if you have it?" he said, holding up his truncated pinkie. The medic looked at him as if he were crazy—Kane mused that they definitely had a point—but nevertheless obliged Kane and treated him on the spot. The paramedics also insisted that Kane needed to get his grazed shoulder cleaned up, but he shrugged them off and told them it could wait. He had something more important on his mind.

Wincing, Kane lifted his bandaged hand and considered his missing pinky finger. *It could have been worse,* he knew. *Could've been much worse.*

Despite himself, the wry smile was back as he looked out across the vast expanse of Hiroshima Bay. The smile faded as soon as it had come. He would have to go back into the water.

Kane trudged up the beach to where stores were finally beginning to open up after the storm. He knew that souvenir stores in Japan all sold ice cold beer, and seeing as such a store was the first one he saw, he stepped inside and looked for the fridge. As he had hoped, there was a fridge of shining silver Asahi cans. A gift for his dry mouth and tired body.

Finding a semi-dry note in his decades-old leather wallet, he paid for and downed the can right there in the shop. The elderly shopkeeper looked impressed and confused at the same time, but not nearly as confused as he looked when Kane tried to speak Japanese.

"Sukyūbadaibingushoppu wa dokodesu ka?"

The guy squinted at Kane, then looked down at the empty beer can in his hand, as if he couldn't tell if Kane was speaking the local language or slurring drunken English. Kane made one more attempt at asking where the scuba diving shop was. He was sure there must be one in a coastal community popular with tourists. This time, he spoke more slowly.

"Su kyūba daibing ushoppu, wa dokodesu ka?"

The shopkeeper's eyes lit up, a smile taking over his face. "Scuba diving!" he declared.

"Yes!"

"I will show you!"

The two men headed out of the shop, and the shopkeeper pointed down the street. "Two hundred yards, right side," he said. Kane thanked him then made his way in the direction of the scuba diving place. As he walked, the sun pushed away the clouds and cast its warmth on his shoulders. It felt amazing, but it was merely drying him out just in time to get wet again.

Thirty minutes later, he stood along the waterline, his

toes curling in the sand. The sea felt just like a foe standing in front of him, ready to fight. He had to take it on. Kane thought of one of his favourite movies, grinned, and muttered, "Gonna need a bigger pair of cahones," and without allowing himself to think any longer, he ran three steps and plunged in.

The water close to the shore was murky with barely any visibility, a reminder of horrible experiences both old and recent. Kane kicked his legs and pushed on. He swam hard, each stroke like pushing away trauma.

As the sea became deeper, it also became clearer. He saw swaying sea plants and colourful fish, their scales gilded by sunlight that pierced the surface. Yet as pretty as it was, he was looking for something else. Something that would make the sacrifices made by Daijiro and Nori meaningful.

He swam for more than an hour, mentally admonishing himself for feelings of fatigue. Instead, he reminded himself how lucky he was to be alive, swimming and breathing. Every glimpse of brown or silver made his stomach tighten, but every hope turned out to be false. After another hour, and more than twenty-four hours since he had slept, pushing away feelings of exhaustion became more difficult. He thought about heading for the shore and returning tomorrow. But would the suit have washed farther out to sea by then? *Today could be my only chance.*

He thought about how difficult it would be to tell Mika that he had not been successful. He also thought about how little Sayaka wanted to grow up to be a museum curator, caring for artefacts like the one he was now searching for. He suddenly felt himself sinking and realised his eyes had closed right there in the water, sleeping as if he were in a bathtub. There was a limit to how much longer he could keep going.

Another deceitful flash of brown tricked him into thinking he had glimpsed the suit. He ignored it and pushed on. Then he stopped. There was something about the rounded shape. Like the shoulders of an ancient warrior. He flicked his ankles and turned back. As he swam closer, energy came surging back to him. The sturdy suit was intact, having survived yet another trial in its long history. He clenched his fist and punched through the water in celebration.

Kane scooped it up just like he had with people caught in the Hofu flood. He turned and headed for the shore. Sediment had settled, and the water glistened like crystal. Or maybe like the gin and tonic with ice he knew awaited him somewhere along the beach.

Epilogue

A Week Later

Hiram Kane cuffed a dribble of his favourite Cusqueña beer from his chin and exhaled.

Following the surreal events of Miyajima, Kane got stuck into a few days' rest at his newish flat overlooking the lively Plaza De Armas in Cuzco, Peru. Since most of his expedition business was centred around the heart of the Peruvian Andean mountains, a year earlier he'd purchased himself a small place to live. He had always felt at home in the ancient Incan capital, a beautiful city that paired Spanish colonial architecture with the colourful art and traditional culture of the native Quechuan people. Besides, it was about time he put down some roots, and his beloved Cuzco was the perfect place to start.

He had planned to invest some time in refurbishing the property after he returned from Japan, as the flat was in dire need of some maintenance and a blast of decorating. Right now though, all he needed was some serious rest. And another beer.

It was late afternoon in Cuzco. Kane grabbed a third beer from the fridge then took a seat on his balcony and tried to put the traumatic memories of Japan behind him. If not behind him, at least give them some kind of context. Before his flight departed Hiroshima's international airport, Kane had called the city hospital. He had spoken to his friend Naki, who informed him that his daughter Mika was recovering well from her ordeal. She had cried with joy when Naki informed her the suit of armour had been found, and that it was barely any worse for wear from its plummet from the helicopter and its short stint in Hiroshima Bay. "They made things to last in those days," Naki had said. Mika had apparently smiled a little wider when Naki told her it had been Kane who'd recovered it.

The conversation turned sombre when they discussed Daijiro and Naki's father, Nori. They had both died heroes; one shot while trying to protect his sister, the other killed while trying to protect a stranger. Kane's emotions swelled when he thought about what both men had done, especially the clan patriarch, Nori Nakamura. Nori had known Kane only a few minutes when he'd sacrificed his own life to protect him, and a tear tumbled down Kane's cheek at the total waste of life brought about because of one man's lies and deceit.

Katashi Goto. Katashi Minamoto. Whatever the truth of his story, all that had transpired in Miyajima recently was his fault. Lots of blood had been spilled, and every drop of it was on his hands.

Naki expressed to Kane the deep gratitude of the Nakamura family. Though in his immediate family there remained only Naki himself and his daughter, Mika—Naki's wife had died several years earlier in the line of duty—he knew that little Sayaka would grow up to continue the family's quest. Naki also passed on a message his niece had wanted to give to Kane: "Sometimes, I am not sure if the samurai suit is good or evil. But what is important is whether the future will be good or evil. Museums are a place of learning, not violence. Mr. Kane, you have given me a future of learning. And I will always remember that whether power is good or evil depends on who wields it."

Taking a sip of the crisp ale, Kane smiled and shook his head at the young girl's wisdom, and that of the whole family.

Naki had also assured Kane that what he had done had been vitally important to the family, and that his selfless acts would never be forgotten. He also added that the extended family, the modern Nakamura clan, would forever hold the Kane name in great esteem.

Right now, the armour was safely installed in a secure facility in Hiroshima whilst the damaged shrine underwent a long program of extensive repairs. Kane thought about the comparison. Just as the Nakamura family would one day heal from its trauma, the shrine would one day be rebuilt. Although they had both been damaged, some parts of which were lost forever, both would ultimately live on for many more years and hopefully generations to come.

Kane guessed that, before Sayaka, Mika would become curator of the Itsukushima Shrine museum in place of her slain grandfather. As soon as she was fully recovered from her ordeal, she would be following in the long tradition of a member of the Nakamura clan being the museum's curator, a tradition that had been upheld for a dozen generations.

Kane also now knew what else that detail entailed. They were not there simply to organise the exhibits and keep things in order. Theirs was a much more crucial role, known only to those within their family. Within their clan. Kane knew the shrine would be in good hands. The very best hands. The hands of the samurai.

His thoughts turned to the Yakuza men. Kane shook his head when he recalled a Japan Times newspaper article he'd read while waiting at the airport. A helicopter had apparently crashed after being struck by lightning in the storm, the chopper plummeting thousands of feet into a mountainside on another island in Hiroshima Bay. The three unnamed dead men on board were all believed to have links with the Yamaguchi branch of the Yakuza mafia.

Among the criminals, only Katashi Goto had survived the events on Miyajima. The irony was that he was probably the only one who didn't want to. Katashi was currently locked away in a maximum security prison in Kyoto, awaiting trial for a list of crimes spanning more than four decades, including extortion, tax evasion, torture, prostitution, murder and now, of course, attempted theft. Even a Yakuza boss only gets away with his crimes if he toes the line and keeps the authorities off his back. Katashi had pushed his position, and his luck, too far. His previous crimes would no longer be ignored.

The prison was tantalisingly close to both Katashi's home and the mountain retreat where he was planning on spending his twilight years in Buddhist meditation. Early reports suggested Katashi would receive the death penalty, but the truth was he would likely spend his last years rotting on death row. Kane imagined Katashi as a tormented soul who only wished he was dead. There was no smug satisfaction for Kane, only a sense of justice.

In contrast to Katashi's actions, Kane had witnessed a series of amazing acts of bravery and examples of what true honour really was. He'd learned some humans lacked it, while others, like the Nakamura family, had more courage and honour than he'd ever believed possible.

Kane had unwittingly received a glimpse into a world he would never fully understand, a world of ancient samurai traditions and centuries' old codes of honour. But what had become apparent to Kane was that even if they claimed the illustrious heritage, some men lived by those rules of bushido, the samurai code, and others lived beyond them.

As he cracked open another icy Cusqueña on his modest balcony, Kane knew it wouldn't be long until he was once more out in the wilds of the Andes, leading another group of tourists among the ancient Inca ruins while regaling them with mysterious tales of lost treasure and fabled cities reclaimed centuries ago by an unsympathetic jungle.

He could still do all that.

He *would* still do all that—despite missing half a finger.

It was what he lived for. It seemed, in fact, it's simply what he was born to do.

That was, if he didn't accept the random yet exciting job offer he had recently received. He hadn't given it a lot of thought due to recent events. *Perhaps now's the time,* he mused, grabbing the ancient Inca sun disk he kept on a leather strap around his neck, and which had hung there for more than two decades. It was his favourite thing he owned, and when he was anxious or unsure of something, he imagined it guiding him in some profound way. It hadn't always worked, of course, but he grabbed it often nonetheless.

Kane didn't know much. That's what he'd tell you. Yet,

while he'd already lived through enough adventures to last most people several lifetimes, the one thing Hiram Kane did know for sure was that his greatest adventure was always just around the corner.

Next in The Hiram Kane Archaeological Thriller Series

vinci-books.com/curses-kings

A retired explorer. A priceless artefact. A mission that could change everything.

Hiram Kane, haunted by his past, takes on a job to return an iconic artefact for the British Museum. But as he navigates ancient Egyptian tombs, a mysterious organisation with ruthless plans emerges. With global consequences hanging in the balance, Kane must confront his demons and make a life-altering decision. Will he succumb to the weight of his past, or forge a new path?

Turn the page for a free preview…

Of Curses and Kings: Prologue

London, 2005

Eight men, all dressed in black, moved with stealth into the concrete stairwell of Richmond House, southwest London. The leading man was only recognisable by his eyes, which darted left and right in a well-practiced pattern of survival learned during long shady assignments overseas. With a flick of the wrist, he signalled his men forward.

The men climbed the stairs, their Heckler & Koch MP5-SF Parabellum machine pistols scanning for any movement in the shadows. The stairwell stank of piss and weed. Used vials of crack crunched beneath their tactical duty boots. This occurred often enough to turn an unprepared stomach. These men were wound so tight and were so well-prepared they didn't even notice.

They moved up to the first landing. A bulkhead light bathed the bare concrete in a blue glow, designed to thwart the resident junkies in their attempts to find veins. To anyone else, it might have seemed ethereal.

The Samurai Code

The men swept the area and headed in silence for the next set of stairs. The last man glanced down over the concrete bannister. Although the city around them seemed quiet, he knew three more tactical units—with enough firepower to bring down a small town—waited half a mile away. They would be watching the whole thing now via the cameras fitted to their Kevlar helmets, and by the drone which hovered two-hundred feet above this hell hole.

The walls surrounding the men bore the names of local gangs. Various words had been scrawled and sprayed on top of each other in a palimpsest of graffiti, as though the battles for space on the once-bare walls were the ultimate expression of their power.

The first man reached the top of the staircase and stopped. He held up his hand and the men behind him paused.

Somewhere nearby, a door slammed. A raised voice echoed through the stark corridors. A baby cried. No footsteps came their way. The men moved on, taking the next staircase with quick steps.

As they reached the third floor, the men turned right towards flat 301. Each of them had memorised the building's layout. To its occupants it was just a high-rise housing estate in southwest London. Yet these men now considered themselves behind enemy lines, and each knew how fast things could change in the theatre of war.

Life and death balanced on a knife edge.

Of Curses and Kings: Chapter One

The Kane Estate, England

Present Day

Hiram Kane was in a coma.

At least, to any observer it would've seemed like that. Kane lay on his front, his face wedged into the sun lounger. An unfortunate dribble of saliva dampened his chin. He wasn't aware of it; but if he had been, he wouldn't have cared. It spoke of the tranquility he felt, the safety of his surroundings... the distance he currently enjoyed from things and people that could kill him and wanted to.

He had hardly moved in hours—days? It was exactly what he needed. June this year was especially warm, and he was taking a hard-earned break from... Well, from everything. His body needed it, that was for sure. He still felt the aches and pains from a month ago, still wore the scars, and relished the opportunity for stillness. More than his physical need for rest, his mind needed to recuperate. To recover.

Kane had just returned from a trip to Japan, where a series of traumatising experiences had left him with deep mental scars. In a calculated effort not to end up on any more crazy adventures any time soon, he holed up at his grandparents' house in the English countryside, just on the border between rural Norfolk and Suffolk.

It was the perfect place to find some kind of normality again after the tribulations of the last couple of months, and indeed, of the last several years. With the early summer sun beating down, and a beautiful outdoor pool to laze around, it was the proverbial heaven on Earth. So, a little dribbling right now was just fine with Hiram Kane.

Kane stirred at the sound of a splash in the nearby pool. He rolled over and propped himself on an elbow, just in time to see Alexandria Ridley surface at the far end of the pool. She turned, then powered through the water, one graceful stroke after another. Her strong arms cut through the surface with practised ease.

For a long while Kane had loved Alex Ridley. They had shared many moments together over the last twenty years since they'd met. Such was their affection for one another, most people who met them assumed they were a couple. Yet, for reasons known only to her, Ridley had always held back from making a firm commitment to him, despite his best efforts.

Ridley finally slipped out of the pool after a swift ten lengths, and let the water drip from her lithe body as she walked over towards Kane.

"Hello, handsome. How was the nap? No doubt you were dreaming of me," she teased.

"No doubt," Kane replied. "Who wouldn't? You're a

gorgeous woman, Alexandria Ridley." He grinned. Ridley grinned back.

"You should cut back on the compliments… might just give this girl a complex."

"Get you a drink?"

"Wine. Thanks."

"Be right back." Kane stood from his sun bed, his athletic frame browning nicely after several days slouched in the sun. His body was more or less recovered, and his mind was close to healing too. He glanced at the stump where a finger had once been before it was shot off by a Yakuza gangster. The memories would always remain, bearing testament to a good man that had died in Japan recently. But Kane had made an important decision in the last couple of weeks, probably the most important of his life. Now it was made, there was no point sitting around feeling sorry for himself any more. Life was short; Kane knew that better than most.

It was time to move on.

On bare feet he trotted to the nearby annex where a large fridge chilled a generous stash of beer, wine and champagne. He scooped up his phone from the table. One missed call. He recognised the number. He'd been expecting this call, though not until next week. It didn't matter. When he called back, the conversation would change everything.

That could wait. Taking a drink to Ridley could not.

"M'lady," he said as he approached the love of his life. "One icy glass of sauv blanc."

"Why, thank you," she purred, taking the glass and savouring the crisp first sip. After a second, she sighed with pleasure. "That is so good, thanks."

"And you're so welcome." He had to tell her. "So… I

had a missed call." He gazed at Ridley now, waiting for her reaction.

"From who I think it was?" Kane nodded. "Are you going to call back? It's important, right?"

Kane didn't answer for many seconds as his eyes drifted from Ridley to the huge stand of oak trees bordering the property. He remained silent too, as if waiting for the right words to come. Finally, he turned his gaze back to Ridley. "Yes, it's important, though it can wait until tomorrow. But..."

"But, what?"

"Well... I know we've already made the decision. But..."

"But what, Hiram? It's an amazing opportunity, and just what you need. What *we* need." She reached out and took his hand in hers. "You're the perfect person for the job, I know that."

Kane nodded, the hint of a smile curling his lips. "You're right," he said. "So, we'd better pack our bags. We're going to Egypt."

Of Curses and Kings: Chapter Two

Egypt

Present Day

Abbe Abidi placed down his cup of mint tea and leaned back in his chair. He gazed out across the railing of his balcony and squinted against the dazzling orange sun as it dropped closer to the horizon. He scratched at his aquiline nose and glanced at the small glass of tea.

Who the hell am I kidding?

He ducked back inside, poured himself a large scotch and downed it in one gulp. Then he poured another and returned to the balcony.

His fancy apartment in the upmarket area off El-Gaish Road in western Alexandria overlooked popular Abo Haif Sidi Bisher Beach, where the passive waters of the Mediterranean lapped at its shore. The soothing sound of those gentle waves was often the soundtrack Abbe fell asleep to at night. Well, that, and the constant accompaniment of beeping car horns and angry, shouting drivers on what was one of Egypt's busiest roads four storeys below his terrace. Half the reason he went to work so early every morning and left so late most evenings was to avoid the heavy traffic. Besides, it wasn't as if the director of the Alexandria International Museum had anything better to do than be at work anyway.

Except drink. These days he always drank.

Abbe gazed back out at the sinking sun and thought, as usual, of his beloved wife. Fatima had died a couple of years ago. Cancer. Way too young. His children had flown the nest too, both studying abroad and, sadly, not following in the academic footsteps as he'd hoped they would. Abbe's daughter was studying science in Philadelphia and his son, his pride and joy, was following his own passion for media in Berlin. Neither of them had said more than a dozen words to their father in many months. Still, Abbe was proud of them both and was glad they'd taken more after their mother than him. *At least they're seeing the world,* he mused... *more than can be said for me these days.*

After studying antiquities for the best part of four decades, Abbe knew that without Fatima and his kids around, he was turning into an antiquity himself.

Abbe heard an aggressive knock at the apartment door. He finished the scotch in two gulps and stood up. He wasn't expecting company. No one ever came to see him anymore. He made his way to the door and, in the hallway mirror, he glimpsed his bland clothes hanging looser on his already slender frame.

He took a deep breath and opened the door. The bright hallway was empty.

Strange. Abbe scowled and looked around. *Is someone*

playing tricks with me? Then he glanced down at the floor and saw an unmarked envelope on the doormat.

Abbe bent down, his back protesting with sharp pangs of burgeoning age, and retrieved the envelope. He turned, closed the door behind him, then tipped the contents of the envelope into his hand.

He recoiled violently as the contents fluttered to the floor. A wave of dizziness threatened to overwhelm him, and he dropped to his knees. His eyes bulged wide with horror and all colour drained from his cheeks.

Now scattered on the floor around him lay several incognito pictures of his children taken from a distance. In the centre, a piece of paper lay folded in half. With shaking hands, Abbe picked it up. It read:

You will help us!
Conference call tonight.
9 pm.

Of Curses and Kings: Chapter Three

London

2005

The leader reached the door of flat 301 and paused. This building was designed so that each flat opened onto an exposed walkway, no doubt to give the occupants some semblance of outside space. The leader glanced around. Operationally, that made things difficult, as the men were visible from the ground or the surrounding towers. He looked over the concrete wall. The yard, fifteen metres below, was empty. He signalled to the men, who arranged themselves in the pre-planned formation: two at each end of the balcony, two behind nearby pillars, and one beside him. They were now invisible.

He examined the door. The light blue paint flaked off in large curls. Someone had attempted to wash off a patch of graffiti. The words were still legible: *Fuck off Pakis*.

He laid his hand against the wood and pushed. The door moved a fraction before the locking mechanism bit. The whole thing was flimsy and would open with nothing more than a shoulder barge.

"Looks weak," he whispered to the man beside him. Normally, they didn't speak before a raid. There was no need to be quiet here. Heavy music blasted from the flat next door. The glass windows rattled in their frames.

They'd planned to blast the door with small explosive charges; looking at it now, it wouldn't be necessary. He glanced left and right down the passageway. Windows of the flat to the right were dark.

The second-in-command nodded and prepared to barge the door with his shoulder. The leader beckoned for two men to join them.

"On my count," he whispered once the men were in formation. "Now!"

Grab your copy...
vinci-books.com/curses-kings

About the Author

Englishman Steven Moore grew up by the seaside, thus his first true joy was the great outdoors. His innate love of travel and a degree in anthropology, archaeology, and art history, help inform his fiction writing. Steven also loves painting, photography, and both playing and watching sport.

The travel bug bit the now perpetual nomad early, and to date Steven has lived and worked on five continents, and visited almost seventy countries. Steven combines an age-old writing adage; Write what you know, with his own mantra; Write where you know, and sets most of his novels in places in which he has either lived or spent an extended period of time.

When not on the road, Steven divides his time between Norwich, UK, and San Miguel de Allende, Mexico, which he shares with his rescue cats Ernest Hemingway and F Scott Fitzgerald (Ernie and Fitz), and his rescue puppy, Charles Dickens. Oh yes, and his beautiful travel writer wife, Leslie.

A lifelong love of food, wine, and beer, have demanded a new-found love of yoga and hiking in order to fend off the imminent arrival of middle age.

Acknowledgments

I don't know of any author who can finish a book of any kind without a lot of help and support, and I'm certainly no different. The assistance I've received for this novel and all my books has been both necessary and invaluable.

So, a quick shout out to these lovely folks—I couldn't have done it without you.

To Ken Preston and John Hopton, your structural advice was well received and appreciated.

My gratitude to Anja Peerdeman, Michael Rhew and Tim Birmingham, my crucial BETA readers. Any remaining mistakes are my own. Thanks, guys.

I also want to thank the incredible team at Vinci Books for believing in me and supporting me on my journey. I appreciate you all.

And as always, to the one and only Leslie, my unstintingly supportive wife, I say thank you.

May you always be you!

Thank you! Arigatō! ありがとう!

Steven